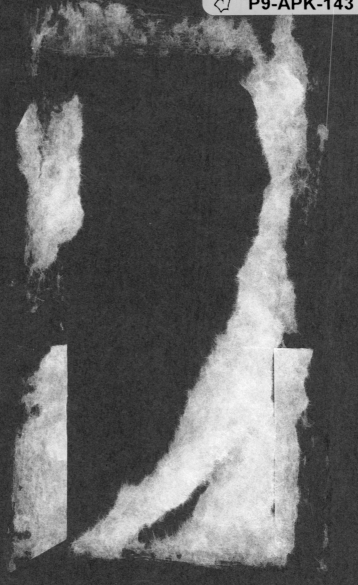

Things That Go Bump in the Night

Things That Go Bump in the Night

A collection of original stories
Edited by Jane Yolen and Martin H. Greenberg

Harper & Row, Publishers

Library of Congress Cataloging-in-Publication Data

Things that go bump in the night : a collection of original stories /
edited by Jane Yolen & Martin H. Greenberg.
    p.   cm.
    Summary: A collection of original stories about the noises,
dreams, and shadows of the night that frighten and beguile the
imagination.
    ISBN 0-06-026802-6 : $. — ISBN 0-06-026803-4 (lib. bdg.) : $
    1. Horror tales, American.   2. Fantastic fiction, American.
[1. Horror stories.   2. Fantasy.   3. Short stories.]   I. Yolen,
Jane.   II. Greenberg, Martin Harry.
PZ5.T318   1989   88-34065
[Fic]—dc19   CIP
                                                              AC

For M. Jean Greenlaw
who keeps a clean house,
a full bookcase,
an open mind and heart,
and a dog who goes bump in the night.

Table of Contents

Things That Go Bump in the Night

Introduction

From ghoulies and ghosties
and long-legged beasties,
and things that go bump in the night,
good Lord, deliver us.

So goes the old prayer. And if there really were ghoulies and ghosties and other nasties going bump in the night, we wouldn't need to write stories in order to scare ourselves, would we? We'd just stay up all night with the lights blazing brightly, laughing hysterically or shivering with fright.

I remember staying up all night one time when I was fourteen because outside my bedroom something was clicking and scrabbling. By midnight, I was convinced it was some kind of slavering monster. But by the time it was light and I had the courage to open my door, I found a poor click beetle on the polished wood floor. My imagination had supplied the long-legged beastie. *That's* what imaginations are really good at.

That's what storytellers are really good at, too. Since there aren't cannibalistic leaves, or monsters in the woods, or giant snakes that become larger with every turn through a store, or critters that haunt the long dark hallways of Victorian farmhouses, it is up to fantasy writers to invent them for us and present them in the guise of stories that will make us shake with loathing—or with laughter.

After all, the worst of our nightmares are within. Buddy Morris discovers this when he goes on a diet, and Martin discovers this when he goes on elevators. Midori Snyder's young heroine finds this out when she lies in bed terribly ill. And Pamela Dean's trio of sisters understands this when the three of them can best a young devil only by first besting their own worst tendencies.

We invest inanimate objects such as leaves, chairs, earrings, belt buckles, quilts with power. Or we personify our fears—death, embarrassment, loneliness. Or we make jokes out of those things that frighten us, as in the television play "We'll Do Lunch." In other words, we *need* ghosties and ghoulies and things bumping in the night to remind ourselves of the daylight, as well as of honor and courage, laughter—and life itself.

So here are eighteen stories that take place at night—or in the even darker night of the soul. It is a time when shadows seem everywhere, when daylight is too far away, when the sounds we hear are magnified. Sometimes those sounds are transmogrified into fearsome images, the gibberings of nightmares. Sometimes they are simply odd, or unexplainable. Sometimes they are tender, touching—even amusing. But they are never *quite* what they seem. Each of these stories is by a master story-teller whose goal is to remind us that by setting down our fears in print, we can read, enjoy, and have a *cathartic* (that is, purifying and purgative) experience.

Only don't read through this book in one night's sitting, because though a few of the stories will make you laugh or sigh or nod your head wisely, there are enough that will have you bunching up the covers as a wall between you and the thing that is marching on its long legs down the long dark hall in your direction.

J.Y.

The Elevator

by William Sleator

It was an old building with an old elevator—a very small elevator, with a maximum capacity of three people. Martin, a thin twelve-year-old, felt nervous in it from the first day he and his father moved into the apartment. Of course he was always uncomfortable in elevators, afraid that they would fall, but there was something especially unpleasant about this one. Perhaps its baleful atmosphere was due to the light from the single fluorescent ceiling strip, bleak and dim on the dirty brown walls. Perhaps the problem was the door, which never stayed open quite long enough, and slammed shut with such ominous, clanging finality. Perhaps it was the way the mechanism shuddered in a kind of exhaustion each time it left a floor, as though it might never reach the next one. Maybe it was simply the dimensions of the contraption that bothered him, so small that it felt uncomfortably crowded even when there was only one other person in it.

Coming home from school the day after they moved in, Martin tried the stairs. But they were almost as bad, windowless, shadowy, with several dark landings where the light bulbs had burned out. His footsteps echoed behind him like slaps on the cement, as though there was another person climbing, getting closer. By the time he reached the seventeenth floor, which seemed to take forever, he was winded and gasping.

His father, who worked at home, wanted to know why he was so out of breath. "But why didn't you take the elevator?" he asked, frowning at Martin when he explained about the stairs. Not only are you skinny and weak and bad at sports, his expression seemed to say, but you're also a coward. After that, Martin forced himself to take the elevator. He would have to get used to it, he told himself, just the way he got used to being bullied at school, and always picked last when they chose teams. The elevator was an undeniable fact of life.

He didn't get used to it. He remained tense in the trembling little box, his eyes fixed on the numbers over the door that blinked on and off so haltingly, as if at any moment they might simply give up. Sometimes he forced himself to look away from them, to the Emergency Stop button, or the red Alarm button. What would happen if he pushed one of them? Would a bell ring? Would the elevator stop between floors? And if it did, how would they get him out?

That was what he hated about being alone on the thing—the fear of being trapped there for hours by himself. But it wasn't much better when there were other passengers. He felt too close to any other rider, too intimate. And he was always very conscious of the effort people made *not* to look at one another, staring fixedly at nothing. Being short, in this one situation, was an advantage, since his face was below the eye level of adults, and after a brief glance they ignored him.

Until the morning the elevator stopped at the fourteenth floor, and the fat lady got on. She wore a threadbare green coat that ballooned around her; her ankles bulged above dirty sneakers. As she waddled into the elevator, Martin was sure he felt it sink under her weight. She was so big that she filled the cubicle; her coat brushed against him, and he had to squeeze into the corner to make room for her—there certainly wouldn't have been room for another passenger. The door slammed quickly behind her. And then, unlike everyone else, she did not stand facing the door. She stood with her back to the door, wheezing, staring directly at Martin.

For a moment he met her gaze. Her features seemed very small, squashed together by the loose, fleshy mounds of her cheeks. She had no chin, only a great swollen mass of neck, barely contained by the collar of her coat. Her sparse red hair was pinned back by a plastic barrette. And her blue eyes, though tiny, were sharp and penetrating, boring into Martin's face.

Abruptly he looked away from her to the numbers over the door. She didn't turn around. Was she still looking at him? His eyes slipped back to hers, then quickly away. She *was* still watching him. He wanted to close his eyes; he wanted to turn around and stare into the corner, but how could he? The elevator creaked down to twelve, down to eleven. Martin looked at his watch; he looked at the numbers again. They weren't even down to nine yet. And then, against his will, his eyes slipped back to her face. She was still watching him. Her nose tilted up; there was a large space between her nostrils and her upper lip, giving her a piggish look. He looked away again, clenching his teeth, fighting the impulse to squeeze his eyes shut against her.

She had to be crazy. Why else would she stare at him this way? What was she going to do next?

She did nothing. She only watched him, breathing audibly, until the elevator reached the first floor at last. Martin would have rushed past her to get out, but there was no room. He could only wait as she turned—reluctantly, it seemed to him—and moved so slowly out into the lobby. And then he ran. He didn't care what she thought. He ran past her, outside into the fresh air, and he ran almost all the way to school. He had never felt such relief in his life.

He thought about her all day. Did she live in the building? He had never seen her before, and the building wasn't very big—only four apartments on each floor. It seemed likely that she didn't live there, and had only been visiting somebody.

But if she were only visiting somebody, why was she leaving the building at seven thirty in the morning? People didn't make visits at that time of day. Did that mean she *did* live in the building? If so, it was likely—it was a certainty—that sometime he would be riding with her on the elevator again.

He was apprehensive as he approached the building after school. In the lobby, he considered the stairs. But that was ridiculous. Why should he be afraid of an old lady? If he *was* afraid of her, if he let it control him, then he was worse than all the names they called him at school. He pressed the button; he stepped into the empty elevator. He stared at the lights, urging the elevator on. It stopped on three.

At least it's not fourteen, he told himself; the person she was visiting lives on fourteen. He watched the door slide open—revealing a green coat, a piggish face, blue eyes already fixed on him as though she knew he'd be there.

It wasn't possible. It was like a nightmare. But there she was, massively real. "Going up!" he said, his voice a humiliating squeak.

She nodded, her flesh quivering, and stepped on. The door slammed. He watched her pudgy hand move toward the buttons. She pressed, not fourteen, but eighteen, the top floor, one floor above his own. The elevator trembled and began its ascent. The fat lady watched him.

He knew she had gotten on at fourteen this morning. So why was she on three, going up to eighteen now? The only floors *he* ever went to were seventeen and one. What was she doing? Had she been waiting for him? Was she riding with him on purpose?

But that was crazy. Maybe she had a lot of friends in the building. Or else she was a cleaning lady who worked in different apartments. That had to be it. He felt her eyes on him as he stared at the numbers slowly blinking on and off—slower than usual, it seemed to him. Maybe the elevator was having trouble because of how heavy she was. It was supposed to carry three adults, but it was old. What if it got stuck between floors? What if it fell?

They were on five now. It occurred to him to press seven, get off there, and walk the rest of the way. And he would have done it, if he could have reached the buttons. But there was no room to get past her without squeezing against her, and he could not bear the thought of any physical contact with her. He concentrated on being in his room. He would be home soon, only another minute or so. He could stand anything for a minute, even this crazy lady watching him.

Unless the elevator got stuck between floors. Then what would he do? He tried to push the thought away, but it kept coming back. He looked at her. She was still staring at him, no expression at all on her squashed little features.

When the elevator stopped on his floor, she barely moved out of the way. He had to inch past her, rubbing against her horrible scratchy coat, terrified the door would close before he made it through. She quickly turned and watched him as the door slammed shut. And he thought, *Now she knows I live on seventeen.*

"Did you ever notice a strange fat lady on the elevator?" he asked his father that evening.

"Can't say as I have," he said, not looking away from the television.

He knew he was probably making a mistake, but he had to tell somebody. "Well, she was on the elevator with me twice today. And the funny thing was, she just kept staring at me, she never stopped looking at me for a minute. You think . . . you know of anybody who has a weird cleaning lady or anything?"

"What are you so worked up about now?" his father said, turning impatiently away from the television.

"I'm not worked up. It was just funny the way she kept staring at me. You know how people never look at each other in the elevator. Well, she just kept looking at me."

"What am I going to do with you, Martin?" his father said. He sighed and shook his head. "Honestly, now you're afraid of some poor old lady."

"I'm not afraid."

"You're afraid," said his father, with total assurance. "When are you going to grow up and act like a man? Are you going to be timid all your life?"

He managed not to cry until he got to his room— but his father probably knew he was crying anyway. He slept very little.

And in the morning, when the elevator door opened, the fat lady was waiting for him.

She was expecting him. She knew he lived on seventeen. He stood there, unable to move, and then backed away. And as he did so, her expression changed. She smiled as the door slammed.

He ran for the stairs. Luckily, the unlit flight on

which he fell was between sixteen and fifteen. He only had to drag himself up one and a half flights with the terrible pain in his leg. His father was silent on the way to the hospital, disappointed and annoyed at him for being such a coward and a fool.

It was a simple fracture. He didn't need a wheel-chair, only a cast and crutches. But he was con-demned to the elevator now. Was that why the fat lady had smiled? Had she known it would happen this way?

At least his father was with him on the elevator on the way back from the hospital. There was no room for the fat lady to get on. And even if she did, his father would see her, he would realize how peculiar she was, and then maybe he would understand. And once they got home, he could stay in the apartment for a few days—the doctor had said he should use the leg as little as possible. A week, maybe—a whole week without going on the elevator. Riding up with his father, leaning on his crutches, he looked around the little cubicle and felt a kind of triumph. He had beaten the elevator, and the fat lady, for the time being. And the end of the week was very far away.

"Oh, I almost forgot," his father reached out his hand and pressed nine.

"What are you doing? You're not getting off, are you?" he asked him, trying not to sound panicky.

"I promised Terry Ullman I'd drop in on her," his father said, looking at his watch as he stepped off.

"Let me go with you. I want to visit her, too," Martin pleaded, struggling forward on his crutches.

But the door was already closing. "Afraid to be on the elevator alone?" his father said, with a look of total scorn. "Grow up, Martin." The door slammed shut.

Martin hobbled to the buttons and pressed nine, but it didn't do any good. The elevator stopped at ten, where the fat lady was waiting for him. She moved in quickly; he was too slow, too unsteady on his crutches to work his way past her in time. The door sealed them in; the elevator started up.

"Hello, Martin," she said, and laughed, and pushed the Stop button.

The Baby-Sitter

Hilary hated baby-sitting at the Mitchells' house, though she loved the Mitchell twins. The house was one of those old, creaky Victorian horrors, with a dozen rooms and two sets of stairs. One set led from the front hall and one, which the servants had used back in the 1890s, led up from the kitchen.

There was a long, dark hallway upstairs, and the twins slept at the end of it. Each time Hilary checked on them, she felt as if there were things watching her from behind the closed doors of the other rooms or from the walls. She couldn't say what exactly, just *things*.

"Do this," Adam Mitchell had said to her the first time she'd taken them up to bed. He touched one door with his right hand, the next with his left, spun around twice on his right leg, then kissed his fingers one after another. He repeated this ritual three times down the hall to the room he shared with his brother, Andrew.

> *"Once a night,*
> *And you're all right,"*

he sang in a Munchkin voice.

Andrew did the same.

Hilary laughed at their antics. They looked so cute, like a pair of six-year-old wizards or pale Michael Jackson clones, she couldn't decide which.

"You do it, Hilary," they urged.

"There's no music, guys," she said. "And I don't dance without music."

"It's not dancing, Hilly," Adam said. "It's magic."

"It keeps *Them* away," Andrew added. "We don't like *Them*. Grandma showed us how. This was her house first. And her grandmother's before her. If you do it, *They* won't bother you."

"Well, don't worry about *Them*," Hilary had said. "Or anything else. That's what I'm hired for, to make sure nothing bad happens to you while your mom and dad are out."

But her promises hadn't satisfied them, and in the end, to keep them happy, she banged on each door and spun around on her right leg, and kissed her fingers, too. It was a lot of fun, actually. She had taught it to her best friend, Brenda, the next day in school, and pretty soon half the kids in the ninth grade had picked it up. They called it the Mitchell March, but secretly Hilary called it the Spell.

The first night's baby-sitting, after they had danced the Spell all the way down the long hall, Hilary had tucked the boys into their beds and pulled up a rocking chair between. Then she told them stories for almost an hour until first Adam and then Andrew fell asleep. In one night she'd become their favorite baby-sitter.

She had told them baby stories that time—"The Three Bears" and "Three Billy Goats Gruff" and "Three Little Pigs," all with sound effects and a different voice for each character. After that, she relied on TV plots and the books she'd read in school for her material. Luckily she was a great reader. The twins hated to ever hear a story a second time. Except for "The Golden Arm," the jump story that she'd learned on a camping trip when she was nine. Adam and Andrew asked for *that* one every time.

When she had asked them why, Adam had replied solemnly, his green eyes wide, "Because it scares *Them*."

After she smoothed the covers over the sleeping boys, Hilary always drew in a deep breath before heading down the long uncarpeted hall. It didn't matter which stairs she headed for, there was always a strange echo as she walked along; each footstep articulating with precision, and then a slight tap-tapping afterward. She never failed to turn around after the first few steps. She never saw anything behind her.

The Mitchells called her at least three times a month, and though she always hesitated accepting, she always went. Part of it was she really loved the twins. They were bright, polite, and funny in equal measure. And they were not shy about telling her how much they liked her. But there was something

else, too. Hilary was a stubborn girl. You couldn't
tell from the set of her jaw; she had a sweet, rounded
jaw. And her nose was too snubbed to be taken
seriously. But when she thought someone was treating her badly or trying to threaten her, she always
dug in and made a fuss.

Like the time the school principal had tried to ban
miniskirts and had sent Brenda home for wearing
one. Hilary had changed into her junior varsity cheering uniform and walked into Mr. Golden's office.

"Do you like our uniforms, sir?" she had said,
quietly.

"Of course, Hilary," Mr. Golden had answered,
being too sure of himself to know a trap when he
was walking into it.

"Well, we represent the school in these uniforms,
don't we?" she had asked.

"And you do a wonderful job, too," he said.

Snap. The sound of the closing trap. "Well, they
are shorter than any miniskirt," she said. "And when
we do cartwheels, our bloomers show! Brenda never
does cartwheels." She'd smiled then, but there was
a deep challenge in her eyes.

Mr. Golden rescinded the ban the next day.

So Hilary didn't like the idea that any *Them,* real
or imagined, would make her afraid to sit with her
favorite six-year-olds. She always said yes to Mrs.
Mitchell in the end.

It was the night before Halloween, a Sunday, the
moon hanging ripely over the Mitchells' front yard,

that Hilary went to sit for the twins. Dressed as a wolf in a sheep's clothing, Mr. Mitchell let her in.

"I said they could stay up and watch the Disney special," he said. "It's two hours, and well past their bedtime. But we are making an exception tonight. I hope you don't mind." His sheep ears bobbed.

She had no homework and had just finished reading Shirley Jackson's *The Haunting of Hill House*, which was scary enough for her to prefer having the extra company.

"No problem, Mr. Mitchell," she said.

Mrs. Mitchell came of the kitchen carrying a pumpkin pie. Her costume was a traditional witch's. A black stringy wig covered her blond hair. She had blackened one of her teeth. The twins trailed behind her, each eating a cookie.

"Now, no more cookies," Mrs. Mitchell said, more to Hilary than to the boys.

Hilary winked at them. Adam grinned, but Andrew, intent on trying to step on the long black hem of his mother's skirt, missed the wink.

"Good-bye," Hilary called, shutting the door behind the Mitchells. She had a glimpse of the moon, which reminded her of the Jackson book, and made a face at it. Then she turned to the twins. "Now, what about those cookies?" she asked.

They raced to the kitchen and each had one of the fresh-baked chocolate-chip cookies, the kind with the real runny chocolate.

"Crumbs don't count," Hilary said. She scraped around the dish for the crumbs, and having counted what remained—there were thirteen—she shooed the boys back into the living room. They turned on the TV and settled down to watch the show, sharing the handful of crumbs slowly through the opening credits.

Adam lasted through the first hour, but was fast asleep in Hilary's lap before the second. Andrew stayed awake until nearly the end, but his eyes kept closing through the commercials. At the final ad for vitamins, he fell asleep for good.

Hilary sighed. She would have to carry them upstairs to bed. Since she wanted to watch *Friday the Thirteenth, Part II*—or at least she thought she wanted to watch it—she needed to get them upstairs. It wouldn't do for either one to wake up and be scared by the show. And if she woke them, they'd want to know the end of the Disney movie and hear at least one other story. She would miss her show. So she hoisted Adam in her arms and went up the stairs.

He nuzzled against her shoulder and looked so vulnerable and sweet as she walked down the creaky hall, she smiled. Playfully, she touched the doors in the proper order, turning around heavily on one leg. She couldn't quite reach her fingers until she dumped him on his bed. After covering him with his quilt, she kissed his forehead and then, with a grin, kissed each of her fingers in turn, whispering, "So there" to the walls when she was done.

She ran down the stairs for Andrew and carried him up as well. He opened his eyes just before they reached the top step.

"Don't forget," he whispered. To placate him, she

touched the doors, turned, and kissed her fingers one at a time.

He smiled sleepily and murmured, "All right. All right now."

He was fast asleep when she put him under the covers. She straightened up, watched them both for a moment more, listened to their quiet breathing, and went out of the room.

As she went down the stairs, the hollow tap-tapping echo behind her had a furtive sound. She turned quickly, but saw nothing. Still, she was happy to be downstairs again.

The first half hour of the show was scary enough. Hilary sat feet tucked under a blanket, arms wrapped around her legs. She liked scary stuff usually. She had seen *Alien* and *Aliens* and even *Jaws* without blanching, and had finished a giant box of popcorn with Brenda at *The Night of the Living Dead.* But somehow, watching a scary movie alone in the Mitchells' spooky house was too much. Remembering the popcorn, she thought that eating might help. There were still those thirteen chocolate-chip cookies left. Mrs. Mitchell meant the boys weren't supposed to eat them. Hilary knew she hadn't meant the baby-sitter to starve.

During the commercials, she threw off the blanket and padded into the kitchen. Mrs. Mitchell had just had new linoleum put on the floor. With a little run, Hilary slid halfway across in her socks.

The plate of cookies was sitting on the counter, next to the stove. Hilary looked at it strangely. There were no longer thirteen cookies. She counted quickly. Seven—no, eight. Someone had eaten five.

"Those twins!" she said aloud. But she knew it couldn't have been them. They never disobeyed, and their mother had said specifically that they could have no more. Besides, they had never left the sofa once the movie had started. And the only time she had left either one of them alone had been when she had taken Adam upstairs, leaving Andrew asleep . . . she stopped. Andrew hadn't been asleep. Not entirely. Still, she couldn't imagine Andrew polishing off five chocolate-chip cookies in the time it had taken her to tuck Adam into bed.

"Now . . ." she said to herself, "if it had been Dana Jankowitz!" She'd baby-sat Dana for almost a year before they moved away, and *that* kid was capable of anything.

Still puzzled, she went over to the plate of cookies, and as she got close, she stepped into something cold and wet. She looked down. There was a puddle on the floor, soaking into her right sock. An icy-cold puddle. Hilary looked out the kitchen window. It was raining.

Someone was in the house.

She didn't want to believe it, but there was no other explanation. Her whole body felt cold, and she could feel her heart stuttering in her chest. She thought about the twins sleeping upstairs; how she had told them she was hired to make sure nothing bad happened to them. But what if something bad happened to *her*? She shuddered and looked across the room. The telephone was hanging by the refrigerator. She could try and phone for help, or she could run outside and get to the nearest house. The Mitchells lived down a long driveway, and it was about a quarter mile to the next home. And dark. And wet. And she didn't know how many someones were in the house. Or outside. And maybe it was all her imagination.

But—and if her jaw trembled just the slightest she didn't think anyone could fault her—what if the someones wanted to hurt the twins. She was the only one home to protect them.

As silently as possible, she slid open the knife drawer and took out a long, sharp carving knife. Then slowly she opened the door to the back stairs . . .

. . . and the man hiding there leaped at her. His face was hidden behind a gorilla mask. He was at least six feet tall, wearing blue jeans and a green shirt. She was so frightened, she dropped the knife and ran through the dining room, into the living room, and up the front stairs.

Calling, "Girly, girly, girly, come here," the man ran after her.

Hilary took the steps two at a time, shot around the corner, and ran down the hall. If only she could get to the twins' room, she thought, she could lock and barricade the door by pushing the beds and dressers in front of it. And then she'd wake up the twins and they'd go through the trapdoor in the closet up to the attic. They'd be safe there.

But the man was pounding behind her, laughing oddly and calling out.

Hilary heard the chittering only after she passed

the third door. And the man's screaming as she got to the twins' room. She didn't take time to look behind her, but slid into the room, slammed the door, rammed the bolt home, and slipped the desk chair under the doorknob. She didn't bother waking the twins or moving anything else in front of the door. The man's high screams had subsided to a low, horrifying moan. Then at last they stopped altogether. After all, he hadn't taken time to touch the doors or turn on his leg or kiss his fingers one at a time. He hadn't known the warding spell. *Once a night and you're* . . .

She waited a long time before opening the door and peeking out. When she did, all she could see was a crumpled gorilla mask, a piece out of a green shirt, and a dark stain on the floor that was rapidly disappearing, as if someone—or something—were licking it up.

Hilary closed the door quietly. She took a deep breath and lay down on top of the covers by Andrew's side. Next time she came to baby-sit, she wouldn't tell the "Golden Arm" story. Not next time or ever. After all, she owed *Them* a favor.

Things That Go Grump in the Night

by Elisabeth Waters

Julian Evans let himself in through the back door, collapsed in a chair at the kitchen table, and dropped his school books on the chair next to him. After fifteen years of living with two highly successful, *busy* professionals for parents, he knew better than to put anything on the kitchen table unless he had just personally wiped the table off. (He still remembered vividly the look on his fifth-grade teacher's face when he returned his report card with his mother's signature on the front and orange marmalade on the back.) Feeling thoroughly discouraged, he surveyed the mess around him. It made him feel tired just to look at it. He had skipped lunch, too, but the sight of his mother's kitchen was enough to take away his appetite, regardless of how hungry he'd been before walking in the door. Sighing, he started cleaning things up.

He had the kitchen about halfway cleaned up when he heard his mother's car in the driveway. A few seconds later she breezed in, dropped an armload of papers and magazines on the newly cleared table, and bent to kiss his cheek. "Hi, sweetheart.

Did you have a nice day?" Without pause she continued, "Mine was so hectic—and your father and I are going out tonight." She pulled out the hairpins that held her long blond hair in a prim bun and dropped them on the table, shaking her hair loose as she did so. "I did tell you that, didn't I?" She picked up the teakettle, shook it, took it to the sink to fill it, and put it on the burner.

"I think so," Julian said, "and, anyway, it's on the calendar—dinner with the Witkes and theater."

"Good." She rummaged around for several minutes, apparently looking for the tea canister, which was on a shelf across the room. The kettle started screaming just as she found it. She grabbed a mug out of the cupboard, made herself a cup of tea, brought it and a bag of cookies to the table, and buried her nose in a magazine.

Julian silently got up, turned off the burner, picked up the teabag from the stove, where she had dropped it, put it in the garbage, put the lid on the canister, and closed the cupboards that the mug and the cookies had come from. Then he flopped back into his chair, took a handful of cookies, and began munching moodily on them. His mother, engrossed in her magazine, ignored him. He wondered idly if he were a changeling; he certainly didn't seem to have much in common with his parents. It wasn't just that they were so sloppy and he was neat, but he didn't even look like them. Well, he did have blond hair, like his mother, but his father was dark haired and both his parents were tall, while Julian was only five foot six. Oh, well, maybe he'd grow some more—assuming they really were his parents.

A few minutes later his father arrived home, set his briefcase and coat on top of Julian's books, and dropped the day's mail on top of the pile already on the table. "You can certainly tell Christmas is coming," he remarked, indicating the two-inch pile of catalogs that comprised most of the mail. "How did we get on so many mailing lists, anyway?"

"Because I buy from them," his wife replied. "Where else can you do your shopping between three and four in the morning?"

"How much more stuff do we need—or, for that matter, how much more can we fit in this house?"

She ignored him. "Julian dear, do you have any ideas about what you'd like for Christmas?"

Julian, grimly surveying the chaos around him, replied promptly, "A brownie."

His mother looked confused. "One brownie? I think we've got a box of brownie mix around here somewhere—" She looked around vaguely.

"No, Mother," Julian said impatiently. "Not that kind of brownie—the kind that comes in at night and cleans up the place."

His father burst out laughing. "Son, if you can find a brownie willing to work in this mess, you can have it!"

His mother looked hurt. "I know I'm not the world's best housekeeper, Julian, but surely there are more important things in life." She grabbed her tote bag and rummaged in it. "That reminds me; I brought you a present." She produced a box from the local bakery. "Chocolate éclairs, your favorite."

"Thanks, Mom," Julian said. After all, what else could he say?

Half an hour later they were gone, but certainly not forgotten—the trail of coats, shoes, socks, and papers led from the back door to their bedroom, and the bathroom floor was hidden beneath a soggy mass of clothes and towels.

Julian made himself a TV dinner—after all, he had to eat *something*; a guy couldn't live on chocolate éclairs alone. Then he opened the box of éclairs and thought hard. Was it brownies you left food out for, or was that only for Santa Claus? Well, it couldn't hurt. Good thing she'd brought him éclairs and not brownies; that would be sort of cannibalistic. He seemed to remember something in the old stories about leaving out a bowl of milk, but that seemed rather insulting to anything in human shape. He compromised by using the widest, lowest glass he could find, and set the glass of milk and an éclair on a cleared spot at the edge of the table. Then he went upstairs to watch television.

He started hearing noises about fifteen minutes later, when he muted the sound during the commercials. He stayed where he was, thinking that if it *were* a brownie it probably wouldn't want to be disturbed, and a burglar wouldn't be able to find anything in the mess anyway. But about five minutes later he heard a series of loud bumps that certainly weren't coming from the television, followed by a slamming sound, a loud crash, and an unintelligible curse.

He ran for the head of the stairs and froze. At the bottom was a little brown man. It wasn't just that he was dressed in brown, although he was—he was brown all over, skin, hair, and eyes, including the part of the eyes that would have been white on a human. He had a pair of stockings tangled around his ankles, and he was lying amid the fragments of Mrs. Evans' favorite lamp, which had stood on a table at the foot of the stairs.

Julian, forgetting his manners, gave voice to his first reaction. "Oh, no, Mom's gonna kill me!" Then, realizing that this was a very inconsiderate thing to say when the brownie might be seriously injured, he pulled himself together and started down the stairs. "I'm sorry. Are you hurt?"

The brownie held up a commanding hand. "Just a minute, boy." Julian obediently stopped, and watched in surprise as the fragments of the lamp pulled themselves back together, returned to the table, and turned back on. "All right," the brownie continued, "now that you won't cut yourself, come untangle me! What the devil is this thing, anyway?"

"Panty hose," said Julian. "Haven't you ever seen them before?"

"Don't get smart with me, boy," snapped the brownie. "How could I have? They must be some newfangled invention."

"Well, they've been around as long as I can remember, but then I'm not all that old." Julian finished untangling the brownie's legs and held out a hand. "I'm Julian Evans, I'm fifteen, and I'm very happy to meet you."

"I'm sure you are," the brownie said, looking around pointedly. "I'm called Aiken, and I'm 486 years old. What was that thing with the milk?"

"A chocolate éclair," said Julian. "I hope you liked it."

"It will do," said Aiken. "It will do. The important thing for a brownie is to have work to do; the food and milk you leave are just a token of your agreement with the terms. Well, I'd best be about my work— you can go back to whatever you were doing. Pay no mind to the noise." He gathered an armload of clothes and stomped off in the direction of the laundry room. Julian, praying that a brownie's training covered automatic washers and what not to put in them, returned to his television program.

That was Friday night. Saturday morning the house was spotless, and Julian's parents were impressed by his diligence. Of course, it was a wreck again when they went out Saturday night, and when it was spotless Sunday morning, they asked Julian how he was feeling. Julian said, "Just fine," and buried his nose in the comics, ignoring worried whispers about "obsessive-compulsive behavior."

He was in his room after dinner when Aiken showed up. "Aren't your parents going out tonight?"

"No, sometimes they do stay home. Can't you work with them here?"

Aiken seemed fascinated by the section of shag carpeting he was stirring with his toe. "Well, it's harder." He looked up at Julian. "They can't see me, of course, but—"

"They can hear you?" Julian asked.

"I'm afraid so. And if they tell me to leave—even if they say that old prayer about ghosties and so forth—"

"Things that go bump in the night?"

"Yes, that one. If they say that—even as a joke— if they say the words, then I have to go and never return." Aiken looked glum. "And there's not all that much demand for brownies these days. So many of us have absolutely nothing to do." He sighed.

Julian chewed thoughtfully on his lower lip. "Don't worry, Aiken; I'll think of something. Can you manage if they're in the den with the television on?"

Aiken nodded. "It might work. Turn it on *loud*."

Julian promptly went downstairs, grabbed his parents, and demanded that they come keep him company while he watched TV. "It's okay if you bring your work," he pleaded; "I just want you with me."

This, of course, promptly got both his parents upstairs, determined to keep an eye on him. Julian assured them that no, they hadn't been leaving him alone too much, and everything was fine with him, really; he just wanted their company, as long as they were home anyway. He settled down to watch a fairly noisy movie, congratulating himself on the success of his plan. But even the noisiest movie has its quiet moments, and during those the noises from down-stairs were, unfortunately, quite audible.

"What was that?" Mr. Evans asked after a series of particularly loud thuds.

Mrs. Evans frowned. "It sounds like an unbalanced load in the washing machine. Julian, are you doing laundry?"

"What? Oh, yes! I'll go check on it. Be right back—you stay here." Julian dashed downstairs and found Aiken. "Can't you be quieter?"

"How silently can *you* do housework?" Aiken shot back. "I'm doing the best I can!"

"Okay, okay!" Julian sighed. *Are all brownies this noisy?* he wondered. *No wonder so many of them are out of work.* "I'll turn up the volume a bit." He went back to his parents and the movie. There was, of course, no way his parents were going to sit in a room with a TV loud enough to drown out the dish-washer being loaded immediately below them. Julian tried desperately to ignore the clank of dishes and prayed, to no avail, that his parents wouldn't notice the noise.

"What's that?" said Mrs. Evans.

"I didn't hear anything," Julian said firmly.

There was a loud crash, as if a platter had slipped and broken on the floor.

"And I suppose you didn't hear that, either," said his father. "Don't give me that, Julian, I saw you jump!" He stood up, got his rifle out of the closet, and headed for the door. "I'm going to find out what that is. You stay here."

"No!" Julian shouted, horrified. "Dad, put your

rifle down!" He ran down the stairs after his father, ignoring his mother's calling after him.

The three of them arrived in the kitchen within seconds of each other. "Freeze!" Mr. Evans yelled. Julian was in time to see Aiken jump and drop a plate, but all his mother saw over his shoulder was the pieces of the plate reassembling and taking their place in the dishwasher.

Aiken glared at Julian and silently mouthed, "Get them out of here." Then he went back to loading the dishwasher. Mrs. Evans fainted.

While his father carried his mother to the nearest couch, Julian grabbed the rifle, ran upstairs, and hid it under the mattress in the guest room. Then he returned with a glass of water. "Here, Dad, give her this."

His father took the water and looked concernedly at Julian. "Son, I think we'd better have a talk."

"Sure, Dad," Julian said. *What choice do I have?* "But can it wait till tomorrow? I'm really tired." He faked a yawn.

Mr. Evans silently watched his boots put themselves away in the hall closet. "All right, Julian, tomorrow. But then I want to know what this is all about."

Julian exchanged helpless looks with Aiken and trudged up to bed.

When Julian got to his room after dinner Monday night, he found Aiken sitting on the desk, with the mending piled up next to him. Aiken, looking up from the sock he was darning, asked anxiously, "Are you going to send me away?"

Julian shook his head and flopped onto his bed, now neatly made. "Nope."

Aiken's expression brightened considerably. "Wonderful! What did you tell them?"

"I told them the truth," Julian said. "And I reminded Dad that he *said* I could have a brownie if I could find one—and you know what?" he asked indignantly. "Not only do they not believe me; they think I'm a poltergeist!"

"A poltergeist!" Aiken's indignation at least equaled Julian's. "Why those—They're daft! Have they ever seen a house that a poltergeist's been in?" He was almost screaming with rage, and Julian wondered what his parents were making of this—they must be able to hear it, even if they weren't listening outside his door.

"No, I'm sure they haven't," Julian said hastily, "and neither have I, but I'll bet it looks a lot like the bathroom after they've dressed to go out for the evening."

Aiken looked startled for a minute, then fell over laughing. When he could speak again, he said, "It does, indeed it does." Then he stopped laughing and lowered his voice to a near whisper. "They're not going to bring in a priest and do an exorcism or anything like that, are they?"

"No," said Julian gloomily, "they're sending me to a psychiatrist. There go my Saturday mornings. I don't know what they're so upset about—they're getting the house cleaned and the laundry done! Why do they have to understand it all? Why can't they just be happy with the results?"

"I'm sorry," Aiken said after a moment. Then he added hesitantly, "Do you want me to leave?"

"No!" Julian said quickly. "Don't you *dare* leave me stuck with having to see a shrink *and* doing the housework on top of it! Besides," he added, "even if you did leave, they already think I'm crazy and I'd still have to see the shrink. You're the only good thing that's happened to me this year—you've *got* to stay."

"Gladly." It was the first time Julian had seen Aiken smile.

Dr. Leith turned out to be pretty decent, not at all what Julian had expected a psychiatrist to be. He'd expected somebody old and grim and serious, but Dr. Leith was middle-aged, with medium-brown hair only half turned gray, and a few extra pounds around her hips, which the loose slacks she wore didn't hide. She was comfortable-looking; in fact, she looked like Julian's idea of what a mother ought to look like. When he told her this, she just smiled and said that she'd started out as a pediatrician and raised four children, so perhaps she'd led a less sheltered existence than most psychiatrists. "Does that bother you?" she asked.

"Just *being* here bothers me," Julian said. "I'm not crazy, I don't need a shrink, and there are lots of other things I'd rather be doing on Saturday mornings."

"I'm sure there are," she agreed. "Do you know why your parents wanted you to see me?"

"No," he said with mock innocence. "Why?"

"Think about it," she said. "What was happening in your life when they asked you to come see me?"

"*Told* me to, you mean," he muttered. She seemed okay, and she wasn't giving him a hard time about being a smart aleck, but he wasn't going to tell anyone else about Aiken. Telling his parents had been quite enough. If he told her, she might think he really was crazy and lock him up somewhere, and he didn't want that. He looked around the room, seeking something safe to talk about. "You have a lot of toys here," he remarked.

"Yes, a lot of my work is with young children."

"Tidy young children, it looks like," Julian said. The room was amazingly neat, especially considering all the stuff in it.

Dr. Leith laughed. "That's because you're my first appointment today. What you see is the way the cleaning service leaves it, not the way it looks after a few hours of being played with."

"Cleaning service?" Julian asked. "Do you mean that somebody comes in at night and cleans up?"

"Yes, exactly," Dr. Leith said. "Many office buildings contract with a cleaning service to come in at night and clean."

"When there's nobody here to be bothered by the noise," Julian said slowly. In his mind he could hear Aiken sighing, *So many of us have absolutely nothing to do.* He thought furiously for a minute and then asked, "How does one start a cleaning service?"

"Well, you have to be at least eighteen to start your own business," she began.

"That's okay," Julian said cheerfully. *After all, what do three years matter to people who live for centuries?*

When he arrived home for lunch, both of his parents were waiting for him. "How did it go, dear?" his mother asked, almost before he was through the door.

"Fine," Julian said briefly.

"You seem pretty cheerful," his father observed. "Do you like Dr. Leith?"

"Yeah, she's okay."

"But do you think she'll be able to help you?" his mother asked anxiously.

"Mother," Julian said with a smile, "you have no idea how much she's helped me already."

The Door

by Leigh Ann Hussey

"Give that back!"

The paper passed from hand to hand of the laughing men while Evan tried vainly to retrieve it. In the dim light of the safety lamps, his poem fluttered like a white bird beating against cage bars.

"Going to win the chair at the eisteddfod, are you, boyo?" mocked one man, passing it over Evan's head to another.

"Fancies himself a poet, does he?" laughed the man who'd received it. "Listen to this, boys—"

"Don't you, you devil!" Evan shouted, stumbling over the men's boots.

The man opened his mouth and took a deep breath to read, then suddenly doubled over coughing. There was an awkward silence, and Evan snatched the paper, running out of the light, into the darkness of the mine. Behind him the rest of the men began talking again, but their light tone was forced. They would not say anything about the coughing. They knew without saying.

At the end of the day Evan rode the lift out of the mine with his brothers and a few other men. "What is on you, boy," said Evan's eldest brother, Morgan. "What did you mean by that scuffling around at tea-time? Kicking up the coal dust as though it weren't bad enough down there." Morgan was head of the family now, since their father died in a cave-in, and it seemed to Evan that Morgan took it for license to be heavy-handed and self-righteous.

"And what is wrong with trying to take care of my property?" he retorted.

They stepped off the lift and blinked in the daylight. They looked like pieces of the mine come to life, Evan thought, all of them black with the dust that would never wash off entirely, though they stood by the pump to try.

"What is wrong with being a miner," one of the other men was saying, "that you want to be a poet? You know they only let ministers and scholars in their little order—is mining not good enough for you, boyo? Think yourself better than the rest of us, do you?"

Evan rounded on the man, ready to knock him down, but Morgan's hand held him back.

"Dai's right," Morgan said, more gently. "We've been miners like our fathers before us for generations, and that's the way life is for us. We have no choice."

Somebody else coughed, and that was all Evan could stand.

"Generations it is, Morgan," he said. They all turned to stare at him and he glared back. "Generations of us. Generations of cave-ins and explosions and the black lung! How many more generations before there are none of us left? Is it wrong to be sick and tired of seeing men go down in the dark and never come up again? To be tired of seeing men cough their lungs out in black blood? Tired of hearing the women sing hymns outside the mines because they can do nothing else to help the trapped men? Tired of knowing Mam cries every night for Father and Iolo and Dewi and Huw?

"The Bible says it is a sin to spill your seed on the ground, and yet we sin this sin every day—I am tired of seeing the hands and hearts and minds of our people poured down the mines like this!" He swung the pump handle viciously, and the water spilled out on the ground and seeped in, wasted. There was shocked silence—he had voiced all the forbidden subjects. They looked at him reproachfully for reminding them of that which they wanted to ignore. He turned and ran away from them, away from the mine and the town, toward the hill nearby which still had a little oak woods on it, defying the axes of the lumber barons.

Behind him, somebody broke out of his stupor. "Stop him!" he said. "He's going up the Gorsedd!" But by then he was far ahead, and no man would follow him to that hill where, it was said, a man came down mad from a night on it—if he came down at all.

"Make me proud, Owein," his mother had said. Now Owein son of Dilys stood at the foot of the

*Mound of Arberth, ready to climb up and meet what-
ever might be there. "Whoso sitteth on the Gorsedd
Arberth shall either suffer a wound or see a wonder,"
said the land tales. It wasn't so much the seeing of
wonders he minded as the suffering of wounds. But
he had to risk the Mound. The druids, his initiators,
would be waiting for him up there, but they wouldn't
stay the night with him. Owein shivered a little under
his linen tunic despite the warm day. It was no longer
Nos G'lanhaf, but the summer-starting fire festival
was a week long, and the spirits that walked at the
exact turning of the year would walk still until moon-
dark.*

He began to climb. He could not know what
was waiting for him up there until he got there. As
the sun went down behind him, he went up before
it, worrying as he went. He needed this vision,
to convince the Oak-Knowers that he belonged
among them. But his uncle Gwyn had gone up for
the same reason, and all he'd gotten for his pains
was a broken leg that never did heal right. If Owein
went up and saw a vision, he would be fit to be a
druid; if he turned back now, he'd still be able to
take care of the herd. If he went up and was injured,
he'd be no good to anybody. Keeping wolves off
the beasts needed strong arms and legs. He stood
still for a moment. It was his choice, and his mother
would stand behind him in any case. The druids
would wait until sundown, whether he came or
not, and then they would leave without a second
thought.

He was tingling all over, as though he stood where lightning would strike. At the turning of the year, at the turning of the day, halfway up the Gorsedd Arberth, he felt as though the world's axis was right over him. The center of the spiral.

He looked up and stepped forward.

Evan sat on the hillside, watching the shadow of the hill lengthen over the town. The tailing heaps rivaled the hill for size, but they were black, always black. Nothing would grow on or around them. He turned away from them, turned his face to the green hill, wishing that he could take the whole grassy slope in his arms. He wanted to kiss every green blade. He wanted to rub his face with the clean brown earth, as though it would scrub away the black dust. How could he make the men understand him? It was this wild, fierce unreason, this love, that drove him to poems. Nowhere else could this voice in him speak.

> *This sod dearest of all, this seeded earth,*
> *That birthed, that breathes in me.*
> *The comfort of the Cymry,*
> *Best and ever-bless'd is she!*

Evan had realized only a little while ago that night was falling, and he was on the Gorsedd. But it didn't matter. He was daft already, or surely the men thought him so. And what matter if he died? Better to die quickly than the slow death he had begun dying the first day he breathed coal dust as a ten-year-old. Hard to believe that was only six years ago. He felt like an old man already, grown old without ever being a child. He got up and walked on, topping the hill just in time for the last light of the sun to flash in his face. He sat down again with the afterimage still floating in the dark behind his eyelids.

It was getting cold. The heat of the fresh bull's hide had kept Owein warm enough for a time, but now a breeze chilled the blood on his skin. The druids had killed a young bull, fed Owein some of the raw meat, and wrapped him in the bloody hide. The sharp taste of the meat still lurked around his back teeth, and he was a little dizzy. After his day and night of fasting the sudden rush of pure red meat made him almost ill. He fell into an uneasy sleep, shivering himself awake every hour.

He dozed off, then jumped suddenly awake; there was a black horse standing at his feet, swishing its tail. The hill seemed to have grown, and now he was lying at the foot of a little hillock with a spiral trail around it and the black horse looking down at him. Suddenly it gathered itself, reared, and launched itself into the air. It's going to crush me, Owein thought, watching the hooves come down at him.

The horse landed just past the top of his head, and Owein leaped up.

And was awake. Or was he still asleep, dreaming he'd awakened from a dream of being awake? He looked around for the horse, but he was alone. The branches of the single oak topping the hill, heavy with leaves, stirred and whispered.

But there was no breeze.

Evan wished he had brought a jacket. He should have known better than to stay out all night this time of year without.

This time of year. It suddenly struck him what time of year it was. It was barely two days past All Souls'. Calan Gaeaf, the old folk called it, the Winter's Calend. The hairs rose on the back of his neck and he found himself shaking not from the cold. He saw a flash of white out of the corner of his eye and jumped like a spooked deer. It would be the White Lady likeliest here, the Headless White Lady who snatched up the laggards going home after the Halloween festivities. He turned to her, trembling.

But there was nothing there. And suddenly on the night air he heard the high, imperious whinny of a horse. Out of the darkness among the trees a white mare came prancing, tossing her head, pale and shining as the absent moon. She pawed the ground while Evan stared. Nobody around here had a horse like that. Not even the mine owner had as fine. He stepped forward, his hand reaching, but she danced away from him and was gone.

He found himself facing the huge, ancient oak that topped the hill, and as he watched, it seemed to open. Evan was rooted to the spot as though bewitched. There was a glow like the white horse's glow coming from the widening crack, and soon the tree stood before him like a gate, but with a silvery, misty mirror where the door should be. He knew it was a mirror; he could see himself.

Until he realized that it was not.

Owein looked into the mirror of the tree, clearer than the best bronze mirror he'd seen at the Mayfair. But something was wrong. His twin in the mirror was black as shadow. He stepped toward it, and the reflection stepped forward. He stretched out a hand, and the reflection reached out. He shrank back, and the reflection recoiled.

The apparition in the mirror was covered in blood, and Evan shrank from the horror. Was it some kind of premonition of his death? He reached out again to it, and its hand moved tremblingly toward him. The mist in the mirror thickened, then cleared, and when a hand touched his, he shrieked.

Owein cried out when he heard the black shadow scream death at him and tore his hand from that icy grasp. He stood there hugging the bull hide to him as though it were an armor, the blood of life against the shadow of death. "Get away from me!" he shouted. "I'm not ready to die yet!"

Could Evan have heard right? It spoke Welsh. Of course it would, if it was his ghost. Evan himself had learned Welsh in secret, hanging around the older men, weaseling it out of his mother when she was tired and not thinking. Welsh was forbidden in the schools, and he'd not been about to have the shameful sign hung around his neck or be jeered at for an ignorant Taffy who couldn't be bothered to speak the King's English.

But Welsh was the language of the bards and the ovates and his dreams, so he made it his business to learn it. Still, it was not the language he would have used first. And what had the spirit said? "I'm not ready to die!" That didn't make sense.

"No more am I ready to die, boyo," Evan said in English, "but you're still taking me for all that."

The bloody spirit looked confused and—again it made no sense—frightened. Evan thought a moment, then repeated carefully in Welsh.

What strange tongues the other boy had, Owein thought. But one of them sounded like Welsh. Maybe that was what passed for language in the shadowlands. "Why should I want to take you anywhere?" Owein asked. "Are you not my black death come for me?"

"Are you not my red death come for me?" the other boy answered. And then they both looked at themselves. Owein supposed he did look hideously spectral at that.

Evan rubbed a little ruefully at his face; he'd forgotten to wash himself off in all the uproar at the pump. He looked up and saw that the other boy was looking at himself in equal embarrassment. Right, so maybe it wasn't his death over there.

"So who are you?" they asked simultaneously.

Evan answered first. "I am Evan Davies," he said.

"I am Owein fab Dilys," Owein said. "But if you are not a spirit, Efandefis, why are you all black?"

Evan felt his face flush. "If you are not a spirit, how is it that you don't know coal dust when you see it? Some kind of fine, soft, rich man's son are you?"

Owein flushed in his turn. "Don't you mock me, you black devil, I am as honest a shepherd as there is in Arberth, and a killer of wolves above that!"

Evan was confused. Who kept sheep in this valley? He couldn't think of any. And wolves he had *never* seen. While he was wondering, Owein added, "And above that again, I am on this mound to become a druid, and in all my training and all the lore, I have never heard of this 'coal.' " He couldn't hide the excitement in his voice as he said, "Is it some spirit thing?"

"It might as well be," Evan began, then choked on his words. He looked again, hard, at the other youth, and a wild idea occurred to him. "What year is it, by the Christian reckoning?"

"Mm, I have trouble with that too," Owein said. He did a calculation on his fingers. "It is five hundreds and two twenties of years since the death of their Christ."

Evan sat down slowly. 540 A.D. "Their" Christ, not "our" Christ.

"Are you ill?" Owein said anxiously. "Can I help? I know a few medicines. . . ."

Evan rubbed his hands over his face. "Owein," he said, "I am now sixteen years old, and I was born one thousand and eight hundreds and four twenties and fifteen years after the death of the Christ."

It was Owein's turn to sit down hard.

They sat in silence for a moment. Then Owein said softly, "What is it like, so many hundreds of years from now?"

"Well," Evan said, "everything nowadays is run by the force of steam, and to make the steam, my brothers and I dig coal—a sort of black rock that burns. The looms run by steam, and the railroad."

"Railroad?"

The upshot of it was, Evan had to describe to Owein all that industry had brought—including the deaths of so many of Evan's people. But Owein's eyes shone. "Magic!" he murmured, in the voice of the dreamer. "The day to come shall see all folk living by dint of magic. The world to come shall be the spirit world brought into the world of men."

Evan shook his head. But now he was beginning to wonder himself. "And what is your world like, so long ago?"

Owein shrugged. "Nothing so splendid." And he described the Bardic School and the difficult training that built strength of mind. And he told of the continuing struggle to keep the tradition alive in the face of now-hostile Christian kings, while fighting disease and famine and robber bands.

But Evan was murmuring, "How I should love to hear them, and learn at their school. What joy to live where any man may become a poet who wills and learns, and where no man dare mock a bard!"

They fell silent again, and in a moment both looked up and each met the eyes of the other. And each one thought to himself, *How much more full of wonder is that other world!*

"If I can touch your hand," Evan began—

"—then we are real to the time of the other," Owein continued—

"—and he who goes down the other side of the hill from his coming up shall be in the time of the other," Evan finished.

They stood up and clasped hands. Black horse, white horse, red youth, black youth, full moon, dark moon, summer, winter. The tree groaned over them; the worlds spun around them; the spiral paths all whirled in upon them. They gripped hands while a wind made of light stormed around them.

But Evan and Owein stood at the still center and looked at each other.

"You cannot dig coal," Evan said.

"You cannot play the harp," Owein said.

They paused a moment.

Evan said, "But now you can know the future."

Owein answered, "And now you can choose your own way."

Owein smiled and Evan smiled back. The worlds stood still.

And when they loosed hands, Evan's palm was red, and Owein's black.

"And from your vision, Owein son of Dilys, your druid name shall be Carreg Ddu."
Owein Black-Rock received from the Archdruid's hand a sickle of gold and turned to the people's cheers, holding it up to glint in the balefire light.

Evan sat dejected in the cheering crowd. His poem had not won him the chair. He rose to go, and felt a hand on his arm. Turning, he recognized one of the judges in his green ovate's robe.

"That was a fine poem, young man," the ovate said, in Welsh. "You need a few more gray hairs, though, before they'll think much of you." A smile lurked in his eyes. "My name is Rhys, Dr. Gwilym Rhys. Have you time free of work?"

"What should a common workingman's time matter to a wealthy scholar?" Evan rejoined bitterly, and was instantly sorry.

The ovate seemed not to have heard. "Your spoken Welsh is good enough," said Dr. Rhys. "But your spelling proves you cannot read it. Would you like to? I have a poem or two up at college by a fellow named Taliesin—don't suppose you know him?"

But the name of ancient Wales' greatest bard had set Evan's soul ringing like a harpstring, so loud that he thought it might be heard if he but opened his mouth, and he couldn't speak. The ovate nodded. "We start tomorrow, then?"

The harp sound inside Evan burst out unbidden. "Today?"

Dr. Rhys put a green-draped arm around Evan's shoulder and led him out of the crowd with no word, but with a smile in both eyes and lips. And the green cloth fluttered as though it hung already from Evan's shoulders.

Duffy's Jacket

by Bruce Coville

If my cousin Duffy had the brains of a turnip it never would have happened. But as far as I'm concerned, Duffy makes a turnip look bright. My mother disagrees. According to her, Duffy is actually very bright. She claims the reason he's so scatterbrained is that he's too busy being brilliant inside his own head to remember everyday things. Maybe. But hanging around with Duffy means you spend a lot of time saying, "Your glasses, Duffy," or "Your coat, Duffy," or—well, you get the idea: a lot of three-word sentences that start with "Your," end with "Duffy," and have words like "book," "radio," "wallet," or whatever it is he's just put down and left behind, stuck in the middle.

Me, I think turnips are brighter.

But since Duffy's my cousin, and since my mother and her sister are both single parents, we tend to do a lot of things together—like camping, which is how we got into the mess I want to tell you about.

Personally, I thought camping was a big mistake. But since Mom and Aunt Elise are raising the three of us—me, Duffy, and my little sister, Marie—on their own, they're convinced they have to do man-stuff with us every once in a while. I think they read some kind of book that said me and Duffy would come out weird if they don't. You can take him camping all you want. It ain't gonna make Duffy normal.

Anyway, the fact that our mothers were getting wound up to do something fatherly, combined with the fact that Aunt Elise's boss had a friend who had a friend who said we could use his cabin, added up to the five of us bouncing along this horrible dirt road late one Friday in October.

It was late because we had lost an hour going back to get Duffy's suitcase. I suppose it wasn't actually Duffy's fault. No one remembered to say, "Your suitcase, Duffy," so he couldn't really have been expected to remember it.

"Oh, Elise," cried my mother, as we got deeper into the woods. "Aren't the leaves beautiful?"

That's why it doesn't make sense for them to try to do man-stuff with us. If it had been our fathers, they would have been drinking beer and burping and maybe telling dirty stories, instead of talking about the leaves. So why try to fake it?

Anyway, we get to this cabin, which is about eighteen million miles from nowhere, and to my surprise, it's not a cabin at all. It's a house. A big house.

"Oh, my," said my mother as we pulled into the driveway.

"Isn't it great?" chirped Aunt Elise. "It's almost a hundred years old, back from the time when they used to build big hunting lodges up here. It's the only one in the area still standing. Horace said he hasn't been able to get up here in some time. That's why he was glad to let us use it. He said it would be good to have someone go in and air the place out."

Leave it to Aunt Elise. This place didn't need airing out—it needed fumigating. I never saw so many spider webs in my life. From the sounds we heard coming from the walls, the mice seemed to have made it a population center. We found a total of two working light bulbs: one in the kitchen, and one in the dining room, which was paneled with dark wood and had a big stone fireplace at one end.

"Oh, my," said my mother again.

Duffy, who's allergic to about fifteen different things, started to sneeze.

"Isn't it charming?" said Aunt Elise hopefully.

No one answered her.

Four hours later we had managed to get three bedrooms clean enough to sleep in without getting the heebie-jeebies—one for Mom and Aunt Elise, one for Marie, and one for me and Duffy. After a supper of beans and franks we hit the hay, which I think is what our mattresses were stuffed with. As I was drifting off, which took about thirty seconds, it occurred to me that four hours of housework wasn't all that much of a man-thing, something it might be useful to remember the next time Mom got one of these plans into her head.

Things looked better in the morning when we went outside and found a stream where we could go wading. ("Your sneakers, Duffy.")

Later we went back and started poking around the house, which really was enormous.

That was when things started getting a little spooky. In the room next to ours I found a message scrawled on the wall. BEWARE THE SENTINEL, it said in big black letters.

When I showed Mom and Aunt Elise, they said it was just a joke, and got mad at me for frightening Marie.

Marie wasn't the only one who was frightened.

We decided to go out for another walk. ("Your lunch, Duffy.") We went deep into the woods, following a faint trail that kept threatening to disappear, but never actually faded away altogether. It was a hot day, even in the deep woods, and after a while we decided to take off our coats.

When we got back and Duffy didn't have his jacket, did they get mad at him? My mother actually had the nerve to say, "Why didn't you remind him? You know he forgets things like that."

What do I look like, a walking memo pad?

Anyway, I had other things on my mind—like the fact that I was convinced someone had been following us out of the woods.

I tried to tell my mother about it, but first she said I was being ridiculous, and then she accused me of trying to sabotage the trip.

So I shut up. But I was pretty nervous, especially when Mom and Elise announced that they were going into town—which was twenty miles away—to pick up some supplies (like light bulbs).

"You kids will be fine on your own," said Mom cheerfully. "You can make popcorn and play Monopoly. And there's enough soda here for you to make yourselves sick on."

And with that they were gone.

It got dark.

We played Monopoly.

They didn't come back. That didn't surprise me. Since Duffy and I were both fifteen they felt it was okay to leave us on our own, and Mom had warned us they might decide to have dinner at the little inn we had seen on the way up.

But I would have been happier if they had been there.

Especially when something started scratching on the door.

"What was that?" said Marie.

"What was what?" asked Duffy.

"That!" she said, and this time I heard it too. My stomach rolled over and the skin at the back of my neck started to prickle.

"Maybe it's the Sentinel!" I hissed.

"Andrew!" yelled Marie. "Mom told you not to say that."

"She said not to try to scare you," I said. "I'm not. *I'm scared!* I told you I heard something following us in the woods today."

Scratch, scratch.

"But you said it stopped," said Duffy. "So how would it know where we are now?"

"I don't know. I don't know what it is. Maybe it tracked us, like a bloodhound."

Scratch, scratch.

"Don't bloodhounds have to have something to give them a scent?" asked Marie. "Like a piece of clothing, or—"

We both looked at Duffy.

"Your jacket, Duffy!"

Duffy turned white.

"That's silly," he said after a moment.

"There's something at the door," I said frantically. "Maybe it's been lurking around all day, waiting for our mothers to leave. Maybe it's been waiting for years for someone to come back here."

Scratch, scratch.

"I don't believe it," said Duffy. "It's just the wind moving a branch. I'll prove it."

He got up and headed for the door. But he didn't open it. Instead he peeked through the window next to it. When he turned back, his eyes looked as big as the hard-boiled eggs we had eaten for supper.

"There's something out there!" he hissed. *"Something big!"*

"I told you," I cried. "Oh, I knew there was something there."

"Andrew, are you doing this just to scare me?" said Marie. "Because if you are—"

Scratch, scratch.

"Come on," I said, grabbing her by the hand. "Let's get out of here."

I started to lead her up the stairs.

"Not there!" said Duffy. "If we go up there we'll be trapped."

"You're right," I said. "Let's go out the back way!"

The thought of going outside scared the daylights out of me. But at least out there we would have somewhere to run. Inside—well, who knew what might happen if the thing found us inside.

We went into the kitchen.

I heard the front door open.

"Let's get out of here!" I hissed.

We scooted out the back door. "What now?" I wondered, looking around frantically.

"The barn," whispered Duffy. "We can hide in the barn."

"Good idea," I said. Holding Marie by the hand, I led the way to the barn. But the door was held shut by a huge padlock.

The wind was blowing harder, but not hard enough to hide the sound of the back door of the house opening, and then slamming shut.

"Quick!" I whispered. "It knows we're out here. Let's sneak around front. It will never expect us to go back into the house."

Duffy and Marie followed me as I led them behind a hedge. I caught a glimpse of something heading toward the barn and swallowed nervously. It was big. Very big.

"I'm scared," whispered Marie.

"Shhhh!" I hissed. "We can't let it know where we are."

We slipped through the front door. We locked it, just like people always do in the movies, though what good that would do I couldn't figure, since if something really wanted to get at us it would just break the window and come in.

"Upstairs," I whispered.

We tiptoed up the stairs. Once we were in our bedroom, I thought we were safe. Crawling over the floor, I raised my head just enough to peek out the window. My heart almost stopped. Standing in the moonlight was an enormous, manlike creature. It had a scrap of cloth in its hands. It was looking around—looking for us. I saw it lift its head and sniff the wind. To my horror, it started back toward the house.

"It's coming back!" I yelped, more frightened than ever.

"How does it know where we are?" said Marie.

But I knew how. It had Duffy's jacket. It was tracking us down, like some giant bloodhound.

We huddled together in the middle of the room, trying to think of what to do.

A minute later we heard it.

Scratch, scratch.

None of us moved.

Scratch, scratch.

We stopped breathing, then jumped up in alarm at a terrible crashing sound.

The door was down.

We hunched back against the wall as heavy footsteps came clomping up the stairs.

I wondered what our mothers would think when they got back. Would they find our bodies? Or would there be nothing left of us at all?

Thump. Thump. Thump.

It was getting closer.

Thump. Thump. Thump.

It was outside the door.

Knock, knock.

"Don't answer!" hissed Duffy.

Like I said, he doesn't have the brains of a turnip.

It didn't matter. The door wasn't locked. It came swinging open. In the shaft of light I saw a huge figure. The Sentinel of the Woods! It had to be. I thought I was going to die.

The figure stepped into the room. Its head nearly touched the ceiling.

Marie squeezed against my side tighter than a tick in a dog's ear.

The huge creature sniffed the air. It turned in our direction. Its eyes seemed to glow. Moonlight glittered on its fangs.

Slowly the Sentinel raised its arm. I could see Duffy's jacket dangling from its fingertips.

And then it spoke.

"You forgot your jacket, stupid."

It threw the jacket at Duffy, turned around, and stomped down the stairs.

Which is why, I suppose, no one has had to remind Duffy to remember his jacket, or his glasses, or his math book, for at least a year now.

After all, when you leave stuff lying around, you never can be sure just who might bring it back.

Ghost Dancers

by Sherwood Smith

Edward and Charlotte, who had been watching at
the attic window since moonrise, now turned and
smiled at the other two.

"The last one seems to have arrived," Charlotte
announced.

Amelia jumped up at once. "Coo!"

Horton moved a little more slowly, as befitted the
eldest. "Let's go watch the ghost dancers, shall we?"
He gestured toward the narrow door.

"Do let's!" Charlotte laughed.

They crept down and down to the grand stairway
and sat in a row upon the steps. Amelia, who was
ordinarily the most timid, moved bravely to the very
front. Being lowest, she had the best view through
the double doors, which had been thrown back for
the evening's entertainment.

Inside the big parlor the guests danced around and
around to the fine music that came from an unseen
orchestra. Amelia watched in silent delight. She
loved the mysterious figures in their shrouding white
gowns, glimpsed between more colorful adults
dressed as devils or monks or other exotic creatures.

The faces that could be seen around masks were smiling and laughing, and those who did not dance lifted sparkling crystal glasses to their lips. Amelia adored the glow of the guests' colors and the gleam of their crystal glasses in the bright, steady light of the candle sconces on the walls. In the ceiling, the crystal chandelier caught and reflected back all the brightness from below.

The orchestra played on and on without making a mistake or taking more than a scarce few minutes' break. Behind her Amelia could feel Edward swaying. Edward loved the music best of all.

The inevitable happened, and as usual all too soon.

"Oh, here, Jan, I'll give you a hand carrying those trays!" A woman's voice separated itself from the many-throated murmur of the guests, breaking the spell.

"Oooh," Amelia sighed in disappointment.

" 'Tis still All Hallows'," Horton whispered with mocking dignity down the row to them. "Shall we repair above to our own party?"

Amelia flitted after the others as the hostess and her friend entered the hall. "Thanks, R.J.!" the hostess was saying.

"Hey! What was that!" From up the stairs Amelia heard the echoing voice of the friend, sharpened by surprise. "Did you hear that? Kind of a draft of wind and thumping! Are your kids awake?"

"I doubt it," was the laughing reply. "They've been zonked for hours. You know how kids are after marathon trick-or-treating! But this old place, like most old houses, is full of odd drafts and knocks."

"That'd give me the creeps." The women's voices now came from the direction of the kitchen.

"You get used to it." The hostess laughed again. "These old houses are more benign than any of those cramped, mean-spirited modern ones!"

"Glad *you* think so, considering what the housing market is these days. . . ." The kitchen door thumped shut behind them.

On the landing just above the kitchen, a bedroom door opened slowly. "Hear that, Jim?" There were some muffled snickers. "And Mom thinks we're asleep!"

The door across the hall opened cautiously. "Yeah, rad!" Jim replied. "Now let's go see our ghost dancers!"

"I love the little one best," Patty whispered excitedly.

"Shhh!"

Patty pressed close behind her bigger brother and sister as they crept soundlessly up the narrow stairs.

Then they sat in the dark and watched the four silvery wraiths dancing hand in hand by the light of the moon streaming in the attic window.

Wooden Bones

by Charles de Lint

"I really don't need this," Liz said.

She was standing in front of her uncle's house, looking around at the clutter that filled the front yard. What a mess. There was an old car with one door sagging open, stacks of pink insulation, tools and scrap wood, a battered RV, sheets of Styrofoam and Black Joe, a discarded sink—all the debris of a handyman's livelihood and then some, left out to the weather.

Tom Bohay, her uncle, had a renovation business that he ran from the family farm—a hundred acres set right on the Big Rideau Lake. The lake was a hundred yards from the back of the house, which was in the middle of being renovated itself; had been for the past two years, ever since the farmhouse up on the hill burned down and, rather than rebuild, her uncle decided to fix up what had been an over-sized cottage. According to Liz's mom, Tom was real good at working on other people's places, but not so hot when it came to the home front.

Staying here was going to be like living in a junkyard. Liz felt as though she were on the set of *Sanford and Son,* except it was worse, because there wasn't any urban sprawl beyond the property. No downtown or malls or anyplace interesting at all. Instead it was out in the middle of nowhere. Pasture and bush and rocky hillsides. A neighbor kept cows on the hilly pasture between the road leading into the farm and the house. If you went for a walk anywhere past the yard itself, you had to watch that you didn't step in a cow pie.

Wonderful stuff.

"I *really* don't need this," she repeated.

"Need what?" her cousin asked, coming up behind her.

Standing together, the two girls presented a picture of opposites. Annie Bohay wore her long dark hair pulled back in a ponytail. She had a roundish face, with large brown eyes that gave her the look of an owl. Her taste in clothing leaned toward baggy jeans, running shoes, and T-shirts, none of which did much for her plump figure. In contrast, Liz was bony and thin, her own jeans tight, her black leather boots narrow-toed and scuffed, her T-shirt cut off at the shoulders and emblazoned with a screaming skull's head and the words Mötley Crüe, her blond hair short and spiky.

"Any of this," she said, waving an arm that took in the whole of the farm.

"Aw, c'mon," Annie said. "It's not so bad."

Maybe not if you don't know any better, Liz thought, but she tactfully kept that to herself. After all, she was stuck here for the summer. No point in alienating her cousin, who was probably going to be her only contact with anyone even remotely her age for the next three months.

Yesterday Annie had taken her on a tour of the property. They'd gone around a wooded point that jutted out into the lake until they came to a sandy beach—the swimming was good off the dock near the house, but the shore was all rocky—and then up to a plateau that Annie called '"the Moon." The name made sense, Liz thought when they got there. The broad hilltop was a wide, flat expanse of white marble limestone, spring-fed pools, and junipers, enclosed by stands of apple trees, that had a real otherworldly feel to it.

From the Moon they went down another steep slope to a cow path leading back to the house. Instead of going back home when the path joined the lane, however, Annie took Liz the other way, up the lane with the cow pastures on either side, back to the road leading into the farm. Here there were the rusted hulks of abandoned farm machinery and the remains of outbuildings and barns that looked, to Liz's city eyes, like the skeletons of ancient behemoths, vast wooden rib cages lifting from the fields to towering heights.

The grass on either side of the lane was cropped short, and dotted with cow pies and thistles standing upright like steadfast little soldiers. At the very top of the hill where the lane met the road under a canopy of enormous trees was an old barn that had survived the years still mostly in one piece. It had a fieldstone foundation and gray weathered wood for its timbers and planking.

Inside it was mysteriously shadowed, with a thick flooring of old hay bales at one end, wooden boards at the other. What light entered came through places where side boards were missing—sudden shafts of sunlight that made the shadows even darker. Liz found the place fascinating and creepy, all at the same time.

From there they headed straight down to the lake and followed the shore back home, and that was it. The end of the tour.

Surprisingly, Liz had enjoyed herself, exploring and wandering about; but that first evening after supper, she looked out the window at the dark fields— it was *so* dark in the country—and realized that this was it. In one afternoon she'd done everything there was to do. So what was she going to do for the rest of the summer?

Because she was stuck here. Abandoned just like the rusted machinery and outbuildings up on the hill.

Things had been going from bad to worse for Liz over the past couple of years. On Christmas Eve, when she was twelve, her father had walked out on her and her mother, and they hadn't heard a word from him in the two years since. At first his departure had been a relief from all the shouting and fighting that had gone on. But then her mother started drinking, bringing boyfriends home—a different one every weekend—and Liz had ended up spending more time crashing with friends or just wandering the streets than at home.

Then her mother got a job in a hotel out in Banff.

"It's just for the summer," she'd explained to Liz. "I know it doesn't seem fair, but if you come with me, we'll end up spending all the extra money that I was hoping to save for us for this winter. You don't mind staying with Aunt Emma, do you?"

At fourteen, Liz had long since realized, you don't have any rights. And there were times you just didn't argue. Especially not after what she'd overheard her mother telling her latest boyfriend just the night before.

"What do you do with a kid like her? She's out of control, and I don't know what to do with her anymore. I've got to have some life of my own. Is that so very wrong?"

Naturally, the boyfriend told her she was doing the right thing and, "C'mon, baby. Let's party now."

Right.

It hurt. She wasn't going to pretend it didn't. But at least she hadn't cried.

I sure hope life gets better, Liz thought, standing with her cousin now in the front yard. Because if it doesn't, then I'm out of here. I can't take any more.

She could feel a burning behind her eyes, but she blinked fiercely until it went away. You've just got to tough it out, she told herself as she turned to look at Annie.

"So what do you want to do?" she asked her cousin.

Annie pointed to a heap of recently split firewood. "Well, Dad asked me to get that stacked today. Do you want to help?"

Liz's heart sank, but she kept a smile on her lips. Of course. They cooked on a wood stove, heated the place with it in the winter. Only why would anybody *choose* to live like this?

"Sure," she said. "Sounds like fun." She spoke the words cheerfully enough, but the look on her face added: About as much fun as banging my head against a wall.

There was really *nothing* to do in the evenings. The TV was a twelve-inch black-and-white that was kept in her aunt and uncle's bedroom. To watch it, you had to sit on the bed with them—not exactly Liz's scene, though Annie didn't seem to mind. Of course, they were her parents. Liz had brought some cassettes with her, but her boom box was broken and the amp here only worked on one channel. Besides, nobody cared much for Bon Jovi or Van Halen, much less the Cult or some hard-core heavy metal.

Definitely a musical wasteland.

That night, after staring at the walls for about as long as she could take, she announced that she was going out for a walk.

"I don't think that's such a good idea," her aunt began.

"Give the girl some slack," her uncle broke in. "How's she going to get into trouble out here? You just keep to the lane," he added to Liz. "It gets darker in the country than you'll be used to, and it's easy to get lost."

"I'll be careful," Liz said, willing to promise anything just to get out of there for a few moments.

Get lost, she thought when she was standing outside. Sure. As if there weren't a million side roads whichever way you turned. But it *was* dark. As soon as she left the yard and its spotlights, the night closed in on either side of her. Moonless, with clouds shrouding the stars, there wasn't much to see at all. A pinprick of uneasiness stole up her spine.

She looked back at the well-lit yard; it didn't seem nearly so bad now. Kind of comforting, really. She was of half a mind to just plunk herself down in the front seat of the old car with its door hanging ajar, when she cocked her head. What was that sound?

She turned slowly, and a glimmer of light on top of the hill near the road caught her eye. It came from the barn, a dim yellow glow against the darkness. And the sound was coming from there as well. A fiddle playing something that sounded a little like country music, only it wasn't quite the same. There was no way a bunch of hokey guys in rhinestone outfits were playing this stuff.

Curious, her fear forgotten, Liz started up the lane, crossing over the field when she was opposite the barn. She walked carefully, eyes on the ground as she tried to spot the cow pies. The fiddling was louder now, an infectious sound.

When she reached the outer wall of the barn, her nervousness returned. Who was out here, playing music in an old barn in the middle of the night? It was a little too weird. But having come this far . . .

She stood on her tiptoes to peer through a broken slat and blinked with surprise. Everything was different inside. An oil lamp lit row upon row of wooden carnival horses, all leaning against each other along one side of the barn. Their polished finish gleamed in the lamplight, heads cocked as though they were listening to the music. Their painted eyes seemed to turn in her direction. Sitting facing them, with his back to her, was the man playing the fiddle. He had a floppy wide-brimmed black hat from which two chestnut-and-pink ribbons dangled. His clothes were so patched that it was hard to tell what their original color had been.

Close as she was, with the barn magnifying and echoing the music, it sounded to Liz as though there were more than one fiddler playing. She could also hear a tap-tapping sound which, she realized as she looked more closely, came from the man's bootheels where they kept the tune's rhythm on the old barn's wooden floor.

When the tune ended, Liz wondered if she should say hello or just hang out here, listening. It was kind of neat, this—

The man turned just then and all rational thought fled. Those weren't ribbons hanging down from under his hat. They were ears. Because his face was a rabbit's: big brown eyes, twitching nose, protruding jaw. The bizarreness of what she was seeing made her head spin.

She scrambled back, a scream building up in her throat. Turning, she fled, stumbled, fell. As she tried to scrabble to her feet, a big black wave came washing over her and the world just went away as though someone had thrown its switch from on to off.

When she finally blinked her eyes open, she found herself lying on the grass in front of her uncle's house, screaming. The front door burst open and her uncle and aunt were there.

"There was . . . there was . . ." Liz tried to explain, pointing back toward the hilltop barn, but there were no lights up there now. No music drifting down the hill. And how had she gotten all the way down here anyway? The last thing she remembered was turning away from the grotesque face. . . .

She let her uncle help her into the house. Annie and her aunt put her to bed. Lying in the upstairs loft that she was sharing with Annie, she could hear her aunt and uncle arguing down below.

"I tell you she's on drugs, and I won't have it," her aunt was saying. "Not in this house. I know she's your sister's daughter, Tom, but—"

"She just got scared," her uncle said. "That's all. City kid. Probably heard a coon rustling around in the brush and thought it was a bear."

"She's trouble. I don't see why we have to look at that sullen face all summer long."

"Because she's family," her uncle said, his voice angry. "That's why. We don't turn away family."

Liz pushed her hands against her ears, shutting out the voices. The features of that rabbit-faced fiddler rose up to haunt her as soon as she closed her eyes. I don't do drugs, she thought. So I've got to be going crazy.

Liz was very subdued in the following days. She tried to stay on her best behavior—smiling, helping out where she could. She was scared about a lot of things. If her aunt and uncle kicked her out, they sure weren't going to put her on the bus back to Toronto and let her go her own merry way. They'd call her mother, and her mother was going to be really mad. She'd threatened often enough to turn Liz over to Children's Aid because she just couldn't handle her. Who knew where she'd end up if that happened?

And then there was the fiddler.

He haunted her. At first, thinking back, she decided that she'd just seen some flaky tramp wearing a Halloween mask. Only the features had seemed too real—she had an inexplicable certainty that they *were* real—and there'd been something too weird about the whole situation for her to believe that she'd just made it up. She kept hearing his music, seeing his face.

Up on the Moon with Annie one day, she thought she heard the strains of his fiddle again, but when she asked Annie if *she'd* heard anything, her cousin just gave her a strange look.

"Like what?" Annie asked.

"Some kind of music—fiddle music."

Annie grinned and leaned conspiratorially closer.

"He hides in the trees, a big old bear of a man, smelling like a swamp and playing his fiddle, trying to lure unwary travelers close so that he can chew on their bones."

Liz shivered. "Really?"

"Of course not!" Annie said, shaking her head. "That's just a story the old-timers spread around. People sometimes hear music out in the woods around here—or at least they think they do. It's been going on for years, but it's just the wind in the trees or blowing through a hole in a fence or a barn."

"These old-timers . . . do they ever tell stories about an old tramp with the head of a rabbit playing that fiddle?"

"Get serious."

But Liz kept hearing the music. Or they'd be down by the lake and she would spot a rabbit looking out at them from a cedar stand—a big rabbit, its fur the same odd chestnut color of the fiddler's ears. Its eyes too human for comfort. Watching her. Considering.

She *had* to be going crazy.

Finally, she just couldn't take it anymore. A week after the night she'd first seen him, she waited until everybody else had turned in, then got dressed and crept out of the house. Looking up the hill to the barn, she could see the dull glow of lantern light coming from between its broken side boards, but there was no music. Chewing her lip, she started up the hill.

When she reached the barn, she had to stand for a long moment, trying to calm the rapid drum of her heartbeat. This is nuts, the sensible part of her said. Yeah, she thought. I know. But I've got to see it through. Taking a deep breath, she walked around to the side of the barn that faced the road and stepped in through the doorway.

Except for the lack of music, it was all the same as it had been the other night. The oil lamp hanging from the crossbeam, throwing off its yellow light. The rows of wooden carnival horses. The fiddler, his instrument set down on a bale of hay beside him, was still dressed in his raggedy, patched clothes. His floppy hat was lying beside his fiddle. He was carving a piece of wood with a long, sharp knife and looked up to where she stood, not saying a word.

Trying not to look at the knife, Liz swallowed dryly. Now that she was here, she didn't know why she'd come. That wasn't a mask he was wearing. It was real. The twitch of the nose. The sly look in those eyes.

"Wh-what do you . . . want from me?" she managed finally.

The fiddler stopped carving. "What makes you think I want anything?"

"I . . . you . . . You're haunting me. Everywhere I turn, I see your face. Hear your music."

The fiddler shrugged. "That's not so strange. I live around here. Why shouldn't we meet in passing?"

"Nobody else sees you."

"Maybe they're not looking properly. You new people are like that a lot."

"New people?"

The rabbit-man grinned. "That's what we call you." The grin faded. "We're the ones who were here first. Everything changed when you came."

"What's your name?"

"Is a name so important?"

"Sure. Or how does anybody know who you are?"

"I know who I am, and that's enough."

Oddly enough, the more they talked, the more at ease Liz began to feel. It was like being in a dream where, because of its context, you didn't question anything. The weirdest things made sense. She sat down on a broad wooden beam across from the fiddler, her feet dangling, heels tapping against the wood.

"But what do other people call you?" she asked.

"Your people or my people?"

"Whichever."

For a long moment the fiddler said nothing. He took out a tobacco pouch and rolled a cigarette, lit it. Gray-blue smoke wreathed around his head when he exhaled.

"Let me tell you a story," he said. "There was once a girl who lived with her parents in a house in the city. One day her father went away and never came back, and she thought it was because of her. Her mother had a picture in her head as to what the girl should be, and she never let up trying to fit the girl's odd angles into the perfect mold she had sitting there in her head, and the girl thought because she didn't fit, that was her fault, too.

"But she had a will of her own, and maybe she

didn't know exactly what she wanted to be, but she wanted to be able to find out on her own what it was, not have everyone else tell her what it should be. So when someone said one thing, she did another. She wore a frown so much that she forgot how to smile. And all the time she was carrying around this baggage in her head. Useless stuff.

"The baggage was like the rot that gets into an old tree sometimes. Eventually, it just ate her away, and there was nothing left of her that she could call her own. On that day, the people around her put her in a box and stuck her in the ground, and that's where she is to this day."

Liz stared at him. A coldness sat in her chest, making it hard to breathe.

"You . . . you're talking about me," she said. "About what I've been . . . what's going to happen to me."

The fiddler shrugged. "It's just a story."

"But I can't help it. Nobody ever gives me a chance."

"The old people—my people—we make our own chances."

"Easy for you to say. You're not fourteen with everybody running your life. I don't have any rights."

"Everybody's got rights. Take responsibility for what's yours, and let the rest slide. It's not always easy, but it's not that hard once you learn the trick of it."

"But it hurts."

The fiddler nodded. "I know."

Liz stared down at her boots, trying to understand what was going on. The fiddler carefully butted out his cigarette and put the dead butt in his pocket. Picking up his instrument, he began to play.

Liz heard things in that music. Her father's voice, her mother's voice. Her aunt, her teachers. The policeman who'd caught her shoplifting. Everybody saying she was no good until she began to believe it herself, until she wore the part and made it true.

But when she closed her eyes and really listened to the music, images flooded her mind. She saw her uncle's farm as a place where two worlds met. One world was that of the new people, her people; the other was that of those who'd been here first. The old people, the first people.

Lost things from her world found a home in the world of the old people, the music told her. And in this part of that old world their keeper was a man with the face of a rabbit who didn't have a name. He looked after lost things. Like the carousel horses; sleeping at night, prancing through the fields by day. Liz knew she couldn't see them in the barn when she was in her own world, but they were here all the same. The old people made the lost welcome—for some the old world became their home; for others it was a resting place until they could go on again.

Lost things. Lost people. Like her.

It was kind of magic—maybe real, maybe not, but that didn't matter. They were what they were, just like she had to be what she was. The best that she could be—not the image that others had of her. Not weighted down with a baggage of anger and guilt.

She blinked when the music stopped. Looking up, she saw that the fiddler had laid aside his instrument once more. He had his knife out again and had gone back to carving the piece of wood he'd been working on when she first arrived.

"What kind of music is that?" she asked.

"I heard it from the first new people who came here—got my fiddle from one of them."

It had a sound like nothing Liz had ever heard before. A depth. Where heavy metal just walled away her feelings behind its head-banging thunder, this music seemed to draw those feelings out so that she could deal with them instead.

"It sounds really . . . special," she said.

The fiddler nodded. "Needs something more, though." He held up the carving and studied it in the lamplight. "Looks about right." Taking a twin to it from his pocket, he held the two curved pieces of wood between his fingers and moved his arm in a shaking motion. The pieces of wood rattled rhythmically against each other, sending up a clickety-clack that echoed comfortably in the old barn.

"Here," he said, handing them over to her and showing her how to hold them. "You give it a try."

"What are they?"

"Bones. Wooden bones. They're usually made from ribs of animals, but I like the sound of the wood, so I make them from the ribs of the old barns instead."

When Liz tried to copy his movement, one of the bones fell from her hand. She gave an embarrassed shrug. Picking up the fallen one, she started to hand them back to the fiddler, but he shook his head.

"I can't make them work," she said.

"That's because you've hardly given them a try. Take them with you. Practice. It's like everything else—takes a little work to make it go right."

Like life, Liz thought. She closed her fingers around the bones.

"All right," she said. "I will."

The fiddler smiled. "That's right. Build on the hurt. Let it temper who you become instead of wearing you down. It's not always easy, but it's—"

"Not that hard once you learn the trick of it?"

"Exactly. Time you were going."

"But—" Liz began.

Before she could finish, she felt a sense of vertigo. She shut her eyes. When she opened them again, she was standing in front of her uncle's house, blinking in the spotlights that lit up the yard, a pair of wooden bones clutched in her hand. She looked up to the old barn, dark and quiet on the top of the hill.

A dream? she asked herself. Had it all been just a dream? But she still had these. She lifted her hand, looking at the gleam of the wooden bones she was still holding.

"Will I ever see you again?" she asked.

"Look for me, and I'll be there," a voice said softly in her ear. "Listen, and you'll hear me."

She started and turned sharply, but there was no

one there. Placing the bones between her fingers the way he'd shown her, she gave an experimental shake of her hands. Still nothing. But she wasn't going to give up. Not with these. Not with anything.

The Ghost of Wan Li Road

Kara Dalkey

One hot summer's day, long ago in the ancient times of the Tsin Dynasty, in the village of Nanyang, three young men sat in the shade, discussing their fortune.

"I have so little money," said one, "I have not eaten in two days. My stomach is growling as loud as a dragon, and I fear it will soon eat me from the inside out."

"Sounds painful indeed," said the second. "What will you do?"

"I think," said the first, "that I will go to the ginkgo grove and chop some wood to sell."

The third young man, whose name was Sung Ting-Po and who was known to be very clever, said, "That won't help you. It's summer—no one will buy wood for warmth. And the wood is so dry, it will turn to splinters as soon as your ax strikes it."

The first young man shrugged and looked down at the dust between his feet.

"I am so poor," said the second young man, "that I have not bought new shoes in a year. Look, my toes and heels have worn clear through them."

"They look useless, indeed," said the first. "What will you do?"

"I will go to the lake and catch ducks to pluck their feathers. I will then sell the feathers to the pillow maker."

But Sung Ting-Po said, "The lake is dry, my friend, and no ducks swim there now. You can't pluck feathers from empty mud."

The second young man sighed and stared at his hands.

The first said, "If you are so clever, Sung Ting-Po, what will you do to earn money? You are as poor as we are."

Sung Ting-Po idly skipped a stone along the dusty ground. "I think I will try my luck at the market in Wan. Perhaps I can find a merchant who needs an assistant."

The other two stared at each other a moment, then looked at Sung Ting-Po. "Wan is very far away," said the first. "How will you get there?"

"I'll walk," said Sung Ting-Po. "If I leave this evening, when it is cool, I should reach Wan at daybreak—just when the market opens."

"No, no," said the other two. "You don't want to do that."

"Why not?" said Sung Ting-Po.

"That road," said the first, with a fearful tremor in his voice, "the Wan Li Road, is haunted by a horrible ghost!"

Sung Ting-Po started to laugh.

"It's true!" said the second. "I have seen this ghost with my own eyes."

"Me too!" said the first.

"What did you do when you saw this ghost?" asked Sung Ting-Po.

"Need you ask?" said the second. "I ran home as fast as my legs could take me. I didn't want to be caught by that ghost."

"And you?" Sung Ting-Po asked the first.

"I got down on my knees and begged the ghost not to hurt me. The ghost said he would spare my life this once, but I was never to travel the Wan Li Road again after dark or he would surely kill me."

"I see," said Sung Ting-Po with a grin. "Well, I tell you, my friends, that I am more afraid of starvation and poverty than I am of a ghost, no matter how horrible he looks. Your tales will not keep me from walking the Wan Li Road tonight." With that, Sung Ting-Po stood up, dusted himself off, and turned to go on his way.

"You should listen to us!" said the first.

"If you walk on that road, the only fortune you will gain is death," said the second.

"We'll see," said Sung Ting-Po.

The setting moon glowed in the west like a baleful dragon's eye, and the wind hissed through the dry grasses as though a thousand serpents nested there. Sung Ting-Po had been walking the Wan Li Road for hours, but it had not been tiring—all he carried with him was the cotton tunic on his back and a coiled rope at his side. Along the way he had seen nothing strange. The only sounds were the hooting of the night birds and the soft *pad-pad* of Sung Ting-Po's bare feet on the dust of the road. But it was only the hour after midnight, and he still had very far to go.

Then he noticed, out of the corner of his eye, an odd mist close to the ground by the side of the road. The mist drifted into the middle of the road ahead of Sung Ting-Po and spun itself into a white column, which then resolved into the shape of a hideous old man. Sung Ting-Po knew that this must be the ghost, because the old man had no feet. This creature stared at Sung Ting-Po with a hateful eye and opened his mouth, preparing to speak.

But Sung Ting-Po beat him to it. "Good morning!" he said to the ghost, smiling.

The ghost shut his mouth and frowned. Then he said, "Early morning it may be, but it is not good, not for you, young man."

"Why is that?" said Sung Ting-Po.

"Because," said the ghost. "I am a *ghost!*"

"Well, what a coincidence," said Sung Ting-Po. "I'm a ghost too."

"You are?" said the ghost. "You look rather substantial to me."

"Uh . . . that's because . . . I'm a *new* ghost," said Sung Ting-Po. "Just died tonight, in fact. I ate some bad lychee for dinner and it poisoned me. See, I still carry the rope with which my family bound my body while I thrashed in my death agony. It was all very unpleasant. I am now on my way to the market in Wan to haunt the merchant who sold the bad lychees to my mother."

"Well now, well now," said the ghost. "That

sounds very just. Most just indeed. I have not heard such a good reason for a haunting in many years. I would like to help you. Mind if I come along?"

"Not at all," said Sung Ting-Po.

They walked in silence together for one *li*, the ghost floating above the road while Sung Ting-Po's feet kicked up little clouds of dust as he walked.

"Say there," said the ghost, "if you *are* a ghost, why do you still have feet that touch the ground?"

"Alas," said Sung Ting-Po, "I am so new at being a ghost that my spirit still longs to connect with this earth and walk with feet upon it. I expect I shall get over it in time. After all, you clearly did."

"Ah, hum, well, yes—although I don't remember wanting to have feet to touch the ground with after I died."

"Ah, you are a superior ghost. There is much I could learn from you," said Sung Ting-Po.

"Indeed," said the ghost, "indeed, there is. You know, Wan is farther than I remembered, and the sun will be rising before long. So that we shouldn't slow from weariness and be caught in the sunlight, what do you say we take turns carrying each other?"

"A good idea," said Sung Ting-Po.

First Sung Ting-Po carried the ghost, and this was no burden to him, for the ghost was very light and insubstantial. But then came the ghost's turn to carry Sung Ting-Po.

"Ooof!" said the ghost as Sung Ting-Po clambered onto his back. "You are very heavy. Are you sure you're a ghost?"

"Alas," said Sung Ting-Po, "my soul is heavy with the sins I committed in life—I was not purged of them by a priest before I died. I sinned a great deal," said Sung Ting-Po, and he winked at the ghost.

"Ah, hum, well, even as a new ghost I was never so heavy as you," said the ghost. "But then perhaps I was not as rowdy a youth, and I spent my latter days in a temple with many priests about me. That may explain the difference."

"Undoubtedly," said Sung Ting-Po.

They continued in this way for some time until they came to a river. The ghost crossed first, floating serenely over the water like a flower petal on a summer breeze. But Sung Ting-Po splashed and sloshed his way across, making great waves in the water and getting soaked up to his waist.

As Sung Ting-Po dripped onto the far bank of the river, the ghost said, "What a mess you are and what a noise you made! Are you *sure* you're a ghost?"

Sung Ting-Po flung up his hands helplessly. "Don't blame me! I'm still new at this. I don't know how to behave as a ghost yet. I don't know anything about ghosts. Why, can you believe it, I don't even know if there is anything ghosts ought to be afraid of. Does anything bother us ghosts?"

"Ah, hum, well—you needn't worry, young man. There is almost nothing we ghosts need fear."

"*Almost* nothing?" said Sung Ting-Po. "Oh wise and ancient one, if there is something I must avoid, by all means please tell me. It would be shameful for my career as a ghost to be untimely cut short out of foolish ignorance. Pray give me the benefit of your great knowledge and experience."

"Well," said the ghost, "there is one little thing. Human spit. We don't like to be spit on by mortals. It holds us to this mortal world, and that is a terrible thing, for a ghost."

"Thank you," said Sung Ting-Po, bowing deeply. "I will bear this in mind."

And so they continued on their way down the Wan Li Road. But as the lantern lights of Wan became visible ahead of them, the sun was also beginning to rise over the eastern horizon.

"Dear me, that's too bad," said the ghost, shaking his head. "We were too slow. We cannot make it into town before daylight. We ghosts are not permitted to wander about in daylight, you know. We'll just have to come back tonight to haunt your merchant. Now we must return to our proper realm. Come along." The ghost began to fade along his left side.

"Wait!" said Sung Ting-Po. "I don't know how to get to wherever it is we have to go. Please let me hang on to your sleeve so that you can guide me to the realm beyond."

"Oh, very well," said the ghost, and he extended his right sleeve so that Sung Ting-Po could catch hold of it.

And catch hold the young man did, and Sung Ting-Po twisted the ghost's arm and clutched the ghost tightly to his chest so that he might not escape.

"I have you now!" said Sung Ting-Po.

"Let me go!" cried the ghost, and he growled and snarled and writhed in Sung Ting-Po's grasp. But Sung Ting-Po did not loosen his grip one bit.

The ghost changed himself into a slimy frog, but still Sung Ting-Po held him fast. He changed into a tiger, slashing and biting, but Sung Ting-Po did not let fangs or claws touch him. The ghost became a bear, but still Sung Ting-Po was stronger. At last, when the ghost turned into a big, black sheep, Sung Ting-Po spit on him, and twisted him around into the full light of the rising sun.

"Thank you for your lesson, most superior ghost," said Sung Ting-Po. "Now you are fixed in this shape, and tied to this world, just as you said."

"Baaaahh," said the ghost.

And Sung Ting-Po took the rope from his belt and tied it around the sheep's neck. Cheerfully, he led the transformed ghost down the road into the town of Wan.

His two companions of the previous day were very surprised when Sung Ting-Po returned to Nanyang looking well fed and wearing a new pair of shoes.

"Where have you been?" they asked. "How did you come by this good luck?"

"I went to the market at Wan by way of the Wan Li Road."

"The Wan Li Road! Didn't you see the ghost?"

"I certainly did," said Sung Ting-Po.

"Didn't he try to hurt you?"

"Not at all. In fact, he taught me some very useful

things. But you needn't worry. He won't be haunting the Wan Li Road any longer."

The other two young men looked astonished. "You killed the ghost?"

"Killed him? Don't be silly. I waited until he turned into a sheep, and then I sold him in the market in Wan. A fine, big, black sheep can fetch a very high price indeed." And with that, Sung Ting-Po continued down the street, coins jingling in his pockets, as the others watched and scratched their heads in wonder.

Night Crawler

by Anne E. Crompton

I'm the man here. I'm in charge.

And holy gazebo, this is one heck of a way to spend your fourteenth birthday!

I stand at the window of our shabby new apartment and look out at the night, snow falling past the streetlight, supposed to change to rain. The stores across the way are closed, like our grocery downstairs.

I'm the man here, so Sis asks me, over the TV racket, "What's that noise?"

"Furnace." All the weird noises in this weird place are the furnace. It sounds like a demolition crew down under the grocery.

But Sis says, "No. Listen."

I listen. I lean my forehead on the cold window glass and listen to silence, over the TV noise. I feel sick. Something's stuck in my throat. The pizza Mom's boyfriend bought is a rock in my stomach. School starts tomorrow.

I'm the man here, till Mom gets home. Tomorrow at school I'll be the New Kid, the turnip. Holy gazebo!

The kids in this town look ugly. Other towns you

get three to four uglies, the others are human. But here . . .

There goes a kid under the streetlight now. He's hunched up in the snow, he's got a parka on, I can't see his snake hook. But I know he's got one.

Every kid in town wears a snake hook. It's a big clasp you hook over your belt, with a rattlesnake coiled up to strike. His eyes are little red specks, like jewel crumbs. Realistic.

One thing is clear. I've got to get hold of one of those snakes. I don't want to walk into school with a plain buckle on my belt like a turnip. I've looked all over town for those snakes. The stores don't have them.

It's times like this I miss my dad.

Sis says again, "Listen! Hear that?"

I turn around to her. "I don't hear anything."

Sis sits curled up on the old couch watching TV. She's supposed to be in bed an hour back, but she sleeps just as well in front of the tube. She's half asleep now, popping gum instead of sucking her thumb, cuddling the Pumpkin Baby Mom's boyfriend gave her.

I turn back to the window. In its blackness I see Sis's white nightgown reflected, her pale hair, my own red hair. I lean close to my reflection.

Mom says I look like my dad. I remember him very red and very big, but maybe that's just because I was small. Now if I had him here tonight, if I could ask him, "Dad, how do you walk into a school full of uglies? How do you not be a turnip? How—"

"Hear that?" In the window I see Sis pop up straight

like the gum out of her mouth. And I do hear something.

Thumps. Downstairs, pretty loud. I open my
mouth to say "furnace," and close it. Those bumps
are not metallic.

Mom manages the grocery. That's why we moved
here. Now I'm the man, I'm in charge, and a prowler
is bumping around downstairs.

One heck of a careless prowler! He knocks over
a stack of cans.

Sis and I stare at each other. For once her jaws are
still and slack. Blue eyes wide, she clutches Pumpkin
tight. I whisper, "Shhh." She nods.

Downstairs is the prowler. Downstairs is the telephone. Any minute the prowler may prowl upstairs.
I tiptoe to the door and turn the key, softly.

Now he's dragging stuff up and down the grocery
aisles. Soft, heavy stuff. Now he's pushing something
across the ceiling under our feet. I feel the push and
drag through my socks. Sis looks about to cry. From
the door, I signal her for quiet.

And now the prowler whistles.

Holy gazebo, he doesn't care who hears him! He
gives a loud, tuneless whistle . . . or more like
a . . . hiss. And he thumps and drags. I feel he knows
we are here, a couple of turnips who can't stop him
wrecking their store. I feel he's teasing us.

Sis looks at me. I'm the man here. And I decide.
So long as the prowler doesn't bother us, we sure as
heck won't bother him! Better a turnip than a dead
ugly, huh.

In the back hall by the stairs is a stack of soup cans

in opened cartons; *was* a stack of soup cans in opened cartons. Now they're crashing and rolling all over the floor, and the prowler is rushing upstairs.

I stand by the locked door and hear him come, *rush, whoosh, drag;* WITHOUT FOOTSTEPS.

Hand on the door, I feel a great weight and force meet it, drag across it.

This is only a wood door, maybe an inch thick.

He feels softly across, around the door. He pushes it, gently, not using his force. The door bulges and creaks. Softly he says, *"Hsssssss."* The palm of my hand, flat on the door, feels his heavy drag across it.

There's no point in holding the door.

I run back to Sis and snap the table lamp off. Let him bust in and find us in the dark. But it was dark down in the grocery, and that didn't stop him. He must have a light.

This is when I want Dad. What would Dad do if he was here? He would grab a weapon, that's what. He would get beside the door with a weapon and crash the prowler on the head as he busted through.

Maybe. I remember him big and red, and stinking from cigars. Truman cigars. I remember him laughing, and swinging me around. I remember eyes like mine, but full of laughter. I don't remember any time he turned ugly.

Sis's dad, now, there was an ugly. I think I'd rather have this whistling prowler in here than him.

"Ssss!" The prowler starts off soft. But he whistles long and louder, louder, till his *"Sssss"* fills the apartment and my head. My ears want to pop, bust. Sis

and I stand rigid by the dark lamp, listening. The streetlight outside sort of lights the room. Snowflake shadows fall across the couch, the dark TV screen, Sis's crumpled face.

"Ssss! Sssss!" The whistle softens, fades out. The prowler rustles once more against the door, over the door, and draws away. We hear him drag . . . something . . . down the stairs, *bump, bump, slither* along the walls. But nothing you'd call a footstep.

The cans in the back hall roll away from him. He's gone back in the grocery.

Softly, softly, I reach down and fold back the threadbare rug.

Boyfriend showed us this little trapdoor, trap window, under the rug. He called it the peephole. You have to lie down and peep with one eye.

Sis shakes her head strongly. Her swinging hair catches the faint light. She's afraid the prowler will hear us.

Scowling, I signal her to silence. SILENCE. Soundless, I stretch out by the peephole, and peep.

Dark down there. One ray of streetlight searches the toilet-paper aisle. We didn't hear the toilet paper crash. There's rolls of it all over the floor.

The prowler knocks over the cash register. The peephole doesn't show me that far, but we hear the CRASH, *zzzzip,* as drawers fly open, the *clink-clink* as change rolls under the counter. Finally, he's getting down to business. Noisily.

Dad, where are you? If you were here now, what would you do? (Jump out the window, I bet. I bet

Mom's right and you're a real turnip, or you'd be here now with me. I wouldn't be the man here. I'd be standing with Sis watching you peep down into darkness, figure what to do!)

The grocery stinks. A cloud of stink rises through the peephole and makes me blink. I know this smell, from somewhere.

What's he doing, setting the place on fire?

Sis is on her knees, pushing at me. She wants to peek. I scowl at her—Quiet!—and let her look.

She lies on top of Pumpkin and squints down. She covers her nose with her hand and keeps on squinting. I poke her in the side. She whispers, "Detergent."

I'm the man here. I push her aside and peep.

The detergent aisle is right underneath. It's dark, the streetlight doesn't reach it. But something shines there in the dark.

Didn't I say the prowler had a light? But not a flashlight, nothing human like that. This light . . . well, the prowler shines. That's what. Holy gazebo, the prowler shines like sun on flowing water, one sparkle after another, one sparkle red and another blue. The prowler moves like flowing water, he sparkles and creeps, slides, one length meeting another, like streams meeting. And as he creeps, slides, flows, we hear his heavy dragging sound.

Sis pushes and pulls me, wanting a look. I don't budge.

The shining prowler drags himself from the dark detergents into cat food, where the streetlight glows. His head pushes into the faint light, lifts up.

It's cold in here. We need the furnace to bang on.
I need something to remind me this is the real world.

Good thing Sis doesn't see! She would screech like
the factory siren, and that would be okay. He
wouldn't hear that. But then she would faint dead
away, *boom,* on the peephole. And he would *feel*
that boom. And he would know we were up here,
in his reach. In his very, very long reach.

I know one or two things about snakes.

I know snakes are deaf. So it doesn't matter if we
talk, but we mustn't move. He can feel vibrations.

I know snakes sleep through the winter. Holy gazebo, what's he doing out on a snowy night like this?

I know there are no snakes his size in this country,
maybe in this world.

This snake must reach from the cash register by
the door to the back hall. Farther. He keeps flowing,
dragging more and more of himself into the light,
raising his head higher and higher on a swaying column of snake. In the dark he ripples blue and red.
In the light he winks purple and orange, like he's
jeweled. His eyes burn red. As he rises, rows of little
gleaming wings flap and flutter at his sides.

Now his huge head sways close to the peephole.
He breathes out a thick fog of stink. I draw back,
wipe my eyes. I cough. Can't help it. But that's okay,
he's deaf.

Not this snake! This snake doesn't know the rules.
He's out of his hole uncoiled in winter, and he hears
me cough.

He turns his head, looks up at me, pushes higher.
His huge nose aims for the peephole, blots it out.

I'm sitting two inches above that nose. Discovered.

He can't make it through the peephole. That'd be like threading a needle with a rope.

But his tongue can. Up through the peephole it licks, tall as me, forked, flaming. Holy gazebo, it's like a cold fire in the room, it lights the room. Rolling away, I see Sis back off toward the window, Pumpkin clutched in nightgowned arms. Her fearful eyes are bigger than Pumpkin's painted eyes.

The tongue flares this way and that, looking for us. On hands and knees I crawl backward. This is a small room. How far can the tongue reach?

Pressed against the peephole the serpent sighs, "*Ssss.*" And blows a great stink of smoke.

I know that stink. It's Truman cigars. This monster smokes Truman cigars. Huh!

Sis coughs. She stands glued to the window, night blackness behind her. I cough. Crawling backward, I hit the couch.

Man height, the tongue stiffens. It darkens. Darkness flows up through the peephole, the room goes dim again. I see what's happening.

The serpent is sending himself up into his tongue.

In a moment we'll have him in here with us, if I can't stop him. I'm the man here. I'm in charge.

The thing is to hit him, now, while he's weak. Huh. I mean, before he gets his whole strength up here.

I scramble up, whirl, search for a weapon. Magazine. Shoe. Plastic hair dryer. Lamp!

I grab the lamp off the table. Snakelike, the cord

whips around me. I kick it away. With both hands I hold the lamp over my head. It's good and heavy, and it's got a bulb to smash. I whirl back to face the tongue.

A man stands astride the peephole. A giant.

Like the sun, like the serpent, he shines by his own light. His red hair brushes the ceiling. Between red hair and red beard, his eyes glow brown and . . . friendly. He wears a plaid shirt and jeans, and a snake-hook belt. He breathes out Truman smoke. He asks, "You posing for the new Liberty statue?"

Right away I lower the lamp. I seem to know his husky, smiling voice.

He looks from me to Sis and back. I glance at Sis. Still plastered to the window, she doesn't look crumpled anymore. She looks like herself, only really interested, really alive. I put the lamp back on the table, and it goes part way on.

I ask Giant, "Do I know you?"

"We've met."

"I think. I think you're . . ." But I daren't say it, even though the more I study the humor-crinkled eyes and the bristly beard, the surer I am.

Sis says it. "You're his dad, huh?"

Giant nods, shakes his head, shrugs. He says, "No. Not exactly."

Not exactly? Come on, either he is my dad or he isn't, huh.

He says, "Your dad's sitting in a bar in Detroit right now. Thinking about you."

Thinking about me! Dad remembers me!

"From time to time," Giant says, as though I had said it out loud. "He thinks of you from time to time, like Christmas and your birthday. He wanted to come, but of course he couldn't."

Sis asks, "Why not?"

"It's five hundred miles. So he called me."

Aha! "My dad phoned you?"

"No." Giant shakes his head, scratches with one huge fist in his beard. "Not exactly." And I see myself, it's impossible. My dad phoned this giant serpent and said, "Visit my son"? I don't think so.

"See," says Giant, "I was here anyhow. I live here. With you."

I stare at him.

"See," says Giant, brown eyes smiling, "I am you."

I stare at him.

Sleet rustles on the window.

"Look," says Giant, "I'll show you. You were worried about school starting tomorrow, huh?"

"Yeah." Dimly, like a long time ago, I remember worrying about school starting tomorrow. But how would Giant know that, unless . . .

"I figured you wouldn't worry if you knew about me. And it's your birthday, number fourteen. You should know about me.

"There's no big deal about school starting. You just march in there like you belong. You don't look for trouble. You don't make trouble. But if you get trouble, well, I'll be there. Inside."

"Inside?"

"Inside you. Where I live."

I blink. I have to look harder to see Giant. He's fading! Now he looks like he's on black-and-white TV.

I cry, "Wait! Don't go!"

"Can't keep it up," he mutters. "Takes energy, appearing like this. The snake, he took a whale of energy! But you noticed me."

I sure did!

"Wait!" I cry. He's on black-and-white, and the tube's going. "Listen! Those kids at the school look like real uglies."

His sound's going too. "Turnips!" He whispers. "You get yourself one of these." He points a huge, fading finger at his snake hook. "You'll look ugly, too." The snake hook is the last I see of him.

He's gone. Nobody, nothing there, not even a whiff of Truman cigar. But my nose burns, and then my throat. The burn travels down my spine and coils up at the bottom. And cools.

The lamp comes on bright. Down under the wrecked grocery, the furnace kicks on like a demolition crew. Good. We're real cold in here.

Sis says, "I got you one of those."

"What?"

"Snake hook. For your birthday."

Still clutching Pumpkin, she patters over to the couch, lifts a cushion, hands me a plastic snake hook. Just what I've been looking for all week. It's a silver rattlesnake reared up, little red eyes like jewel crumbs. Realistic.

I turn it over in cold, shaky hands. "Hey," I say, "where'd you find this thing?" This wonderful, magic thing!

"You get them with gum wrappers," Sis tells me. And she laughs.

The furnace bangs. Sleety rain belts the window. Downstairs the grocery is a disaster area we have to fix, or . . . explain.

I'll fix it. I'm the man here.

Break a Leg

by Amy Lawson

Sarah heard the girls giggling outside the door, the rattling of the latch, the rasping of the lock.

She sat on the dusty, old stairs that led up to the attic of the old house that was the seventh-through-ninth-grade girls' dorm at the Beard School. She buried her head in her knees, not wanting to look around. The attic was dark and cobwebby and scary.

"Bye-bye, Sarah, have a nice time!"

"Mrs. Beard's ghost is gonna get you!"

The chorus of voices taunted her on the other side of the door, and then after one last burst of giggles, there was silence.

Sarah reached forward tentatively to try the latch. The door opened, but only a crack, just enough to allow in a sliver of light from the hallway.

How long would they leave her there? The musty attic air filled her throat, which was filled already with the ache of unshed tears. She hadn't cried in two months. How much longer could she pretend she didn't care?

It wasn't just the attic door that separated her from the other girls. They were all so sophisticated. They came from New York City and Washington, D.C., from Italy and Switzerland. Leila from Switzerland had four houses, all in exotic places. They talked about boys and relationships, they wore makeup, so perfectly, like in the magazines; their closets were stuffed with more clothes than Sarah had owned in a lifetime.

"Do you get your clothes from Ames?" her roommate had asked with a sneer the first night they were unpacking. Sarah's several outfits, some plain-colored sweaters and pants with elastic waistbands, looked drab and childish compared to the bright and fashionable clothing, scarves, and jewelry that spilled from her roommate's suitcases.

Sarah, the hick from Snake River Junction, Vermont, was not fitting in—"not adjusting" was how Miss Pitt, the dorm parent, put it when she talked to Sarah's mother on the phone.

Miss Pitt will find out what they've done, Sarah thought, *and they'll get in trouble. But they'll turn it around and take it out on me. They'll say it was all my fault.*

Because of the sheer meanness of being locked in the attic, the unshed tears began to fall. Sarah, head in her lap, began to cry.

"What's the matter, dear?" A voice from up the stairs, over her head, clucked in the darkness.

Sarah froze, stabbed through with pinpricks of fear. She kept her head down, her eyes squeezed shut. Who could it be? Who could be up in the attic? She hadn't heard anyone up there until now.

Mrs. Beard's ghost. That was the dorm joke. The old house had been her house once. "Hear those creaks, Sarah? It's Mrs. Beard's ghost," the girls were always saying.

"Don't be alarmed, dear. I'm just tidying up the mess the children always make on Halloween. Come on up the stairs and give me a hand, and maybe we could talk a little too, dear."

Sarah twisted her head upward but could not see anyone. The kindness in the voice made her sob for a moment in self-pity, but it also calmed her fear. She knew perfectly well there was no such thing as ghosts, and she thought the girls were silly when they ran around screaming every time they heard a little noise. They just weren't used to living in an old house the way she was.

Sarah stood to go upstairs, but abruptly cried out as she felt the top of her head being raked by something long and sharp.

"Oh dear," said the voice soothingly. "Be careful of the nails. They're sticking out everywhere, from the shingles on the roof, you know." The voice came closer. "Mind you bend your head. You're such a tall girl you'll be spiked to death if you don't watch it."

In the dim light coming in from the gable windows, Sarah finally made out the form of a woman. How old? Sarah could not tell—anywhere from fifty to one hundred. She was tall and quite frail, her curly hair snowy white; but in the partial light her eyes were youthful and bright. They shone with sympathy.

"Those girls giving you a hard time?"

Sarah nodded. "Yup," she said.

"It just takes time," said the woman. Her voice was warm and comfortable. "Beard is like a family."

"Yup, that's what Mr. Andrews said."

Last summer when Sarah and her parents had visited the school, the headmaster, Mr. Andrews, had smiled when Sarah's mother asked him if being away from home might be too hard on a girl like Sarah. "She's an only child," she had explained, "and there are not many kids in Snake River Junction. She's never been real sociable."

"Our school is small and we live so closely together," said Mr. Andrews, "that sooner or later even the shyest and most homesick child begins to feel at home."

But what if you were not only shy, but too tall and as big as a horse, and had crooked teeth and stringy hair and your clothes didn't have labels, and everyone told you you had a funny accent, and you didn't know anything about relationships.

And your parents were poor.

"My parents aren't even divorced," said Sarah out loud.

The woman laughed and laughed. "And that makes you a misfit," she said, nodding her head. She walked toward a heap of clothes on the attic floor. "But those girls aren't as awful as they seem. It's just a question of getting through their thick hides. Believe me, I know."

She reached down to pick up an armful of clothes and began hanging them on a rack behind her. As Sarah's eyes grew accustomed to the dark, she realized the heap of clothes was costumes. She remembered now that this was where all the kids had tramped upstairs for their Halloween costumes. She had not gone with them because she had wanted to make her own.

"Oh, look!" she cried, picking up a dress and holding it to the window. "It's beautiful! Where did all this stuff come from?"

"This is the Beard School's costume collection," said the woman. "Every year the children tear through it at Halloween, and every year they are not properly supervised so I have to pick up after them. Really, you'd think they'd take better care of them. Some of these clothes have been here since the school began ninety years ago."

"But it's dark!" Sarah exclaimed. "You've been putting them away in the dark." Panic seized her again as she looked at the woman in front of her carefully slinging a red velvet dress on a hanger.

"I'm used to this attic, and the light seems so garish—just a bare light bulb, but do turn it on if you like," said the woman. "There's a cord behind you."

Sarah pulled, and instantly the attic became a friendlier place in spite of nails studding the ceiling. Bits and pieces of girls' belongings littered the floor— a riding hat, a huge teddy bear, a winter coat. And in the light, the woman looked substantial. *A ghost wouldn't look so solid,* Sarah thought, *if there* were *such things as ghosts.*

"Here, you can help," said the woman. "The hats go in the hatboxes over there. The gloves and necklaces go in this bureau. Now let's get acquainted. You can call me Ollie. All the children do. What's your name, dear?"

"Sarah—Sarah Nicholson."

"Not related to Nick, are you?"

"Nope. No, wait a minute. Nick was what my grandfather was called," said Sarah. "He went to school here. Did—did you know him?" Sarah stared at Ollie. How old *was* she?

"Great actor, your grandfather. A natural ham."

"I'm here because of him," said Sarah. "Otherwise my parents never could have afforded it. He died and left me money on the condition that I go to school here."

"And you're not so happy about that, are you, dear?"

"Nope."

"Is that all, dear?"

Sarah shook her head and sank into a chair stored in the attic to be painted. Her misery returned. "They locked me in here," she said. "Those kids are so mean. My roommate especially. She would have died of a heart attack by now. She's always talking about Mrs. Beard's ghost."

"I know," Ollie chuckled. "But my dear, it takes some children longer than others. They're testing you, that's all. Trying you out because you're not what they're used to."

Sarah sighed. "It'll never get better for me. Never," she wailed. She looked at her watch. "And what if they don't let me out of here? It's almost time for dinner, and if I'm late, Miss Pitt will kill me."

"Go down the fire escape," said Ollie. "Then when they go to unlock you, and you're not here, they'll be awfully puzzled." Ollie's eyes gleamed mischievously.

Sarah smiled. "Yup, I will," she cried, jumping up. "What a good idea."

"But don't go just yet. I have another idea," said Ollie. She shook out a pair of wrinkled black trousers. "Shame how they treat these old things. This used to belong to our best tux. Now," she said, "it's November, isn't it? Just in time for the sign-ups for the talent show at the end of the term. School tradition. Been that way for ninety years."

"There were always lots of plays and talent shows at Beard, my grandfather said."

Ollie's eyes grew even brighter. "Oh, yes," she said. "And the best thing that could happen to a girl like you is to get onstage."

"But what could I do?" asked Sarah, amazed. "I don't have any talent."

"You are Nick's granddaughter," said Ollie. "You must have some talent. I suspect there is plenty of ham lurking in there, dear."

Sarah laughed and pointed to her stomach. "Yup," she said. "Plenty of ham all right."

"You see!" said Ollie, delighted. "That's just what I was talking about. What you have to do is go and see Miss Rose. She'll coach you, and I wouldn't be surprised if she wrote you a monologue."

"A monologue?" Sarah's voice squeaked. "You mean stand alone on stage by myself and talk?"

Ollie nodded. "I think Miss Rose will help you find just the right words. She's been at this sort of thing for a long time."

"But who is Miss Rose?"

"The drama teacher, dear. The finest that ever was."

"But Mrs. Brown is the drama teacher," said Sarah. She reached down to pick up a pink feather duster that was lying at her feet and handed it to Ollie.

"Thank you, dear. They've mixed up the props with the costumes too." She put the duster in a box behind her. "Miss Rose," she said, "has officially retired, but she keeps her office behind the stage and is always willing to coach students and lend a hand when needed."

"But when would I go to see her?" asked Sarah.

"Miss Rose is likely to be there most anytime," said Ollie. She chuckled. "She's very dedicated. Now, there's the dinner bell. You skedaddle, and if you get caught on the fire escape, don't tell 'em it was my idea. I don't want to get in trouble."

The idea of Ollie being scolded by Miss Pitt made Sarah laugh. She realized it was the first time she had laughed out loud in two months.

"Thank you, Ollie," she said. "I feel much better." She opened the attic window. "I'll make sure the attic door is unlocked so you can get out. But, hey, Ollie, did you come in this way? I never saw you in the dorm."

"I'll never tell, dear," said Ollie, smiling in a way that made Sarah wonder again how old she was.

Sarah waved good-bye and moved as quickly as she dared down the fire escape. On the ground she looked up just in time to see the attic light go out. Sarah shook her head. Ollie was working in the dark again.

Sarah made up her mind to sign up for the talent show if Miss Rose could think of anything for her to do. The most unpopular girl at the Beard School had absolutely nothing to lose.

She waited all day to go see Miss Rose. The trouble with boarding school was that every hour of your life was programmed. You never had a moment to yourself. Finally at four thirty after sports, Sarah had some free time before dinner. She checked in with Miss Pitt and headed for the theater.

The buildings at Beard were old; the theater actually had been a barn. As Sarah opened the door, the dusk-filled auditorium made her uneasy. Perhaps because it was no longer daylight saving, she felt closed in and had a passing fancy that when no one was there, animal ghosts came to feed.

In the dim light Sarah saw photographs of past plays with their dates beneath them lining the walls. Automatically she sought out the 1920s. Wasn't that when Granddad had gone to Beard? In 1924, 1925, and 1926. Her eye found him immediately—the tall, large-boned boy from Vermont, the farmer's boy. His parents had recognized his special talents and had sent him to Beard on a scholarship.

He had loved the school. His happiest days, he often had said. Sarah winced. And what if they turned out to be her most unhappy?

Walking up onto the stage, and then hesitantly making her way to the back, Sarah continued to find the atmosphere eerie and still; the stage was a place that needed lights and people. Maybe there were not only animal ghosts, but ghosts of kids who had acted on the stage as well—maybe even her grandfather. But she didn't believe in ghosts, she reminded herself, looking everywhere for Miss Rose's office.

She was about to give up, thinking she had misunderstood Ollie, when she spied a set of steps nearly hidden by a large flat of scenery. Squeezing by, she went up the steps, five of them, her heart pounding. What would she find? And would Miss Rose make her perform to prove that she could act? She faced a door, a name so faded on it she could not read the letters.

Sarah knocked. There was no answer. She started to leave when the door opened, and a tall, thin old woman stood before her. Her white hair, laced through with one or two strands of silver gray, was done up in a bun. Delicate eyebrows arched over brilliant black eyes, and a spot of color decorated each cheek.

"Yes?" she said in a fine, theatrical voice. "Can I help you?"

Sarah faltered, feeling awkward before the woman's delicate grace. "Y-yes," she said. "Ollie—you know Ollie—" Sarah's courage failed. Perhaps Ollie did not exist; perhaps she had hallucinated the whole thing.

"Ollie!" The woman's face creased into a thousand wrinkles. She even seemed to reflect Ollie's kindness. "Of course, she must have sent you."

"Are you Miss Rose?" asked Sarah bluntly.

"Indeed, yes! And, you are?"

"Sarah Nicholson."

Miss Rose peered at her and then stepped back, waving one arm in a sweeping dramatic gesture. "You're Nick's daughter," she exclaimed. "The living likeness." Her voice became flutelike in surprise.

"Granddaughter," said Sarah. "His granddaughter."

"Yes, of course," said Miss Rose. "Do come in, Sarah. You are here for the talent show, am I right? How nice to work with Nick's daughter—*granddaughter*. I'm sure talent stays in the blood."

Sarah looked around. The small office was jammed with books on acting, and scripts cluttered a small desk. Above the desk on the wall was a smiling mask with rosy cheeks and doll-like lashes curling out from empty eyes.

"Sit down, Sarah, and tell me about yourself."

Sarah sat in a chair near Miss Rose's desk, and in

the time left found herself talking and talking to Miss Rose about the farm in Vermont, about skating on the pond in winter, about her father reading to her at night in his slow, methodical voice, about her mother's quilts and how the quilt she had at boarding school eased the homesickness at night.

For once Sarah did not dread going to the evening meal, where everyone at the table either insulted or ignored her.

"Thanksgiving dance is coming up," said the boy next to her. "Got a date, Sarah?"

The day before, Sarah would have blushed and kept her eyes down. Tonight she smiled sweetly at the boy and said, "Yup. As a matter of fact, I do."

"Who?" asked the boy, as every pair of eyes at the table turned toward her.

"You," said Sarah. "You'll go with me, won't you?"

The kids at the table squealed with laughter. "No way," said the boy in disgust, but Sarah could feel a change. She had made the other kids laugh, not just *at* her, but a little bit *with* her.

"You signed up for the talent show," Sarah's roommate said one night.

"Yup," said Sarah. "I did."

"Well, what are you going to do?" asked the roommate. "Don't people from Vermont ever talk?"

"Nope," said Sarah.

"Yup—nope—is that all you can say? Oh. You

were joking." The roommate had blond hair that she bounced when she was embarrassed. She smiled at Sarah in spite of herself. "Please tell me, Sarah. What are you going to do?"

"A monologue," said Sarah.

"A what?"

"A monologue. A speech you make alone on stage."

"You're going to do that?"

"Yup," said Sarah.

"What is the speech? From Shakespeare or something?"

"Nope."

"*Sarah!*"

"I'm writing it," said Sarah. "At least I'm writing part of it, and Miss Rose is helping me."

"Who is Miss Rose?"

"She used to teach drama here, and now she coaches kids and helps them out."

"Oh," said the roommate. She was quiet for a moment. "I can't believe you're doing that. Won't you just die getting up onstage in front of all those people?"

"Maybe," said Sarah.

"We've got to do something about your hair," said the roommate. "You can't go onstage looking like that."

"But what can I do?" sighed Sarah.

"Makeover time," the roommate screamed, sticking her blond head out the door. Girls collected in Sarah's room like ants suddenly appearing on a drop of jam.

"Miss Rose," said Sarah one afternoon in Miss Rose's office, "where is Ollie? And who is she, anyway? No one has heard of her, and I only saw her that one time in the attic."

Miss Rose's laugh was pleasant. "Oh, Ollie," she said. "She's mostly retired now and she's not around very much. She used to help out with the plays, and she does love those old costumes. She hates to see them ruined."

"Then she really does exist?"

Miss Rose laughed again, the flute in her voice. "Oh yes," she said. "Very much so. Why, Sarah, you saw her with your own eyes."

"Yup, I know," said Sarah, "but that night was so weird. As if she just appeared when I needed her or something."

"She's like that," said Miss Rose. "She seems to sense when a child's in trouble. Now, dear, let's get on with it, shall we? Dress rehearsal today."

Dress rehearsal. Even though no one except for Miss Rose would be watching her this time, Sarah felt a tingling in her fingers and toes. Stage fright seemed to start at the ends and work its way to the pit of her stomach.

"I'll sit here," said Miss Rose from the back of the barn, "and you give it a run-through." Her voice filled the room as though it belonged and was comfortable there. "Remember to look over the heads of your audience. Avoid eye contact with your young friends. They will only try to make you giggle, and there's nothing more tiresome than watching adolescents giggling onstage."

"Giggle?" said Sarah. "More like pass out."

As Sarah waited in the wings on the night of the performance, she was more excited than frightened. She could hear the audience on the other side of the curtain. They were excited too—laughing and chattering. How different the barn was with all the lights on and with so many people.

The acts began: skits, dances, songs, a few halting piano pieces, and then, "The next act is bound to bring tears to your eyes," she heard the M.C. saying. "Our one and only Vermonter, Ms. Sarah Nicholson, in 'The Letter Home.' "

The crowd applauded, and Sarah could hear the screaming and yelling from a section near the front. The kids in her dorm were rooting for her.

"Break a leg, dear," she heard a voice say in the darkness behind her. For a moment she was not sure who was speaking—Ollie or Miss Rose—but when she turned, no one was there.

Sarah walked out onstage. "Talent stays in the blood," Miss Rose had said. Well, perhaps it did, for while Sarah could recite her monologue as automatically as a prayer, now onstage before an audience, suddenly she could feel each word she said, provide each word with exactly the right gesture, with exactly the right shift of her eyes.

Sarah knew, too, the monologue was perfect for her. They had written it together, she and Miss Rose.

It was a letter to Ma and Pa from the country hick away from home at boarding school.

Dear Ma and Pa, [she began]
Well, here I am at boarding school at last, but it shore was a long ride down from the farm. Daisy didn't much like being hitched up to the wagon, and she kept gettin' distracted by the other cows along the way until Silas finally had to jump down and tie my best red bandanna around her eyes. It was too bad, because I was plannin' on wearin' that bandanna to the first dance here, but it smells kind of cowlike now, and anyhow, I found out they don't wear those kinds of things here. Come to think of it, they dress kind of funny—they don't go in much for boots and overalls. . . .

At first the audience thought she was serious, just as they were supposed to. She could feel their embarrassment, hear them squirming in their seats hoping she would be finished soon. And then slowly, as they began to get it, there was a chuckle here, a guffaw there, until the trickle of laughter turned into a rainstorm.

Sarah tried to find Miss Rose after the show, but she was nowhere to be found, and the office was locked.

"Sarah, got a sec?" Mr. Andrews called her into his office. "Sit down a moment. Just want to compliment you on your fine performance the other night," he said. "You've got some talent there. Must be a family trait. It was your grandfather, wasn't it, who did a lot of acting at Beard?"

"Yup," said Sarah. "He did."

"And Miss Pitt tells me things are going much better for you in the dorm."

"Yup," said Sarah. "That's right."

"I'm so delighted," said Mr. Andrews. "Sooner or later, everyone at the Beard School—"

But Sarah was not listening. She was staring at the portrait behind Mr. Andrews' head.

"Who is that?" she interrupted him. "The woman with the curly white hair?"

"Olivia Beard," said Mr. Andrews, turning to look. "The founder of our school."

"The founder? Ollie didn't tell me that," said Sarah.

"I beg your pardon?" Mr. Andrews laughed. "You do have quite a sense of humor."

Sarah felt the blood rushing to her face. "You're going to tell me that Ollie is dead, aren't you?"

"Ollie—Mrs. Beard—of course she's dead," said Mr. Andrews. "She died in 1972."

"I sort of thought so all along," said Sarah, almost in a whisper. "But Miss Rose told me—" Sarah paused for a moment. "Miss Rose . . ." she said, her voice trailing off.

"Miss who?" asked Mr. Andrews.

"Miss Rose," said Sarah. "The drama teacher. You know. She's retired, but she still helps out and coaches kids."

Mr. Andrews shook his head. "Who has been fill-
ing your head with fairy tales, Sarah?"

"Miss Rose," said Sarah, insistent. "You must
know who I mean. She has an office behind the
stage." Wasn't it enough that she had been alone in
an attic with one ghost? Did she now have to find
out that she had been spending hours and hours with
another one?

"The kids have been playing a joke on you,
Sarah," said Mr. Andrews. "Don't take it to heart,
though. They're really on your side now. There never
has been a Miss Rose at Beard."

"Oh," said Sarah, stunned. Those last words,
"Break a leg, dear," had sounded so real in her ears.
How could Miss Rose have been a ghost? But then
she remembered: She had not been sure who had
spoken them—Miss Rose or Ollie. Sarah forced herself to look up at the portrait of Olivia Beard. There
was something about the brightness of her eyes, the
delicate arch of her eyebrows . . . but of course! The
truth finally dawned.

"Olivia Beard was a great actress in her time,"
mused Mr. Andrews, following Sarah's gaze. "And
she certainly encouraged the children here to get up
onstage."

"Yup," said Sarah slowly as she tried to grasp what
had happened to her, "she sure was a great actress—
my grandfather told me," she added hurriedly. "And
she sure does—did—encourage kids to get up onstage."

"Even at the end," said Mr. Andrews, "she'd go

to all the performances. She didn't like to give up the ghost."

"Nope!" said Sarah, laughing. "I guess she didn't," and as she stared again at Ollie's portrait, she thought how there had been one other ghost who had helped her, silently and invisibly. She wouldn't be at all surprised if one day she walked into the barn and found Granddad acting there on the stage.

Chair Person

by Diana Wynne Jones

What happened to the old striped armchair was Auntie Christa's fault.

The chair had stood in front of the television for as long as Simon and Marcia could remember. As far as they knew, the cushion at the top had always been tipped sideways, and it had never been comfortable to sit in. The seat was too short for Dad and too low for Mum and too high for Simon or Marcia. Its arms were the wrong shape for putting things on. Perhaps that was why there was a coffee stain on one arm and a blot of ink on the other. There was a sticky brown patch on the seat where Simon and Marcia had once had a fight for the ketchup bottle. Then one evening the sideways cushion at the top wore out. Whatever the chair was stuffed with began to ooze out in a spiky brown bush.

"The armchair's grown a beard," said Simon.

"It looks as if someone's smashed a hedgehog on it," Marcia said.

Dad stood and looked at it. "Let's get rid of it," he said. "I've never liked it anyway. I tell you what— we can sit the "guy" in it on Guy Fawkes night. That will make a really good bonfire."

Marcia thought this was a very good idea. Now that she thought about it, she had never liked that chair either. The purple and orange and pale-blue stripes on it never seemed to go with anything else in the room. Simon was not so sure. He always liked things that he *knew,* and he had known that chair all his life. It seemed a shame to burn it on the bonfire. He was glad when Mum objected.

"Oh, you can't throw it out!" Mum said. "It's got such a personality!"

"But it's worn out," said Dad. "It wasn't new when we bought it. We can afford to buy a much nicer one now."

They argued about it, until Simon began to feel sorry for the old chair and even Marcia felt a little guilty about burning a chair that was old enough to have a personality. "Couldn't we just sell it?" she asked.

"Don't *you* start!" said Dad. "Even the junk shop wouldn't want a mucky old thing like—"

At that moment Auntie Christa came in. Auntie Christa was not really an auntie, but she liked every-one to call her that. As usual, she came rushing in through the kitchen, carrying three carrier bags and a cardboard box and calling, "Coo-ee! It's me!" When she arrived in the living room, she sank down into the striped armchair and panted, "I just had to come in. I'm on my way to the community hall, but my feet are killing me. I've been all afternoon col-lecting prizes for the children's party for The Caring Society on Saturday—I must have walked *miles*! But you wouldn't *believe* what *wonderful* prizes people have given me. Just look." She dumped her cardboard box on the arm of the chair—the arm with the ink blot—in order to fetch a bright-green teddy bear out of one of the carrier bags. She wagged the teddy in their faces. "Isn't he *charming*?"

"So-so," said Dad, and Marcia added, "Perhaps he'd look better without the pink ribbon." Simon and Mum were too polite to say anything.

"And here's such a lovely clockwork train!" Auntie Christa said, plunging the teddy back in the bag and pulling out a broken engine. "Isn't it exciting? I can't stay long enough to show you everything—I have to go and see to the music for the senior citizens' dance in a minute—but I think I've just got time to drink a cup of tea."

"Of course," Mum said guiltily. "Coming up." She dashed into the kitchen.

Auntie Christa was good at getting people to do things. She was a very busy lady. Whatever went on at the community hall—whether it was Youth Club Disco, Children's Fancy Dress, Mothers' Choir, Dog Training, Soup for the Homeless, or a Bring and Buy Sale—Auntie Christa was sure to be in the midst of it, telling people what to do. She was usually too busy to listen to what other people said. Mum said Auntie Christa was a wonder, but Dad quite often muttered "Quack-quack-quack" under his breath when Auntie Christa was talking.

"Quack-quack," Dad murmured as Auntie Christa went on fetching things out of her bags and telling them what good prizes they were. Auntie Christa had just got through all the things in the bags and was turning to the cardboard box on the arm of the chair when Mum came dashing back with tea and biscuits. "Tea!" Auntie Christa said. "I can always rely on a cup of tea in this house!"

She turned gladly to take the tea. Behind her, the box slid into the chair.

"Never mind," said Auntie Christa. "I'll show you what's in there in a minute. It will thrill Simon and Marcia. Oh, that reminds me! The African Aid Coffee Morning has to be moved this Saturday because the Stamp Collectors need the hall. I think we'll have the coffee morning here instead. You can easily manage coffee and cakes for twenty on Saturday, can't you?" she asked Mum. "Marcia and Simon can help you."

"Well—" Mum began, while Dad looked truly dismayed.

"That's settled then," said Auntie Christa and quickly went on to talk about other things. Dad and Simon and Marcia looked at one another glumly. They knew they were booked to spend Saturday morning handing around cakes and soothing Mum while she fussed. But it was worse than that.

"Now you'll never guess what's in the box," Auntie Christa said, cheerily passing her cup for more tea. "Suppose we make it a competition. Let's say that whoever guesses wrong has to come and help me with the party on Saturday evening."

"I think we'll all be busy—" Dad tried to say.

"No refusing!" Auntie Christa cried. "People are so wicked, the way they always try to get out of doing good deeds! You can have one guess each. And I'll give you a clue. Old Mr. Pennyfeather gave me the box."

As old Mr. Pennyfeather kept the junk shop, there could have been almost anything in the box. They all thought rather hard.

Simon thought the box had rattled as it tipped. "A tea set," he guessed.

Marcia thought she had heard the box slosh. "A goldfish in a bowl," she said.

Mum thought of something that might make a nice prize and guessed, "Dollhouse furniture."

Dad thought of the sort of things that were usually in Mr. Pennyfeather's shop and said, "Mixed-up jigsaw puzzles."

"You're all wrong, of course!" Auntie Christa said while Dad was still speaking. She sprang up and pulled the box back to the arm of the chair. "It's an old-fashioned magician's kit. Look. Isn't it thrilling?" She held up a large black top hat with a big shiny blue ball in it. Water—or something—was dripping out of the hat underneath. "Oh dear," Auntie Christa said. "I think the crystal ball must be leaking. It's made quite a puddle in your chair."

Dark liquid was spreading over the seat of the chair, mixing with the old ketchup stain.

"Are you sure you didn't spill your tea?" Dad asked.

Mum gave him a stern look. "Don't worry," she said. "We were going to throw the chair away anyway. We were just talking about it when you came."

"Oh good!" Auntie Christa said merrily. She rummaged in the box again. "Look, here's the magician's wand," she said, bringing out a short white stick wrapped in a string of little flags. "Let's magic the nasty wet away so that I can sit down again." She tapped the puddle in the chair with the stick. "There!"

"The puddle hasn't gone," said Dad.

"I thought you were going to throw the hideous old thing away anyway," Auntie Christa said crossly. "You should be quite ashamed to invite people for a coffee morning and ask them to sit in a chair like this!"

"Then perhaps," Dad said politely, "you'd like to help us carry the chair outside to the garden shed?"

"I'd love to, of course," Auntie Christa said, hurriedly putting the hat and the stick back into the box and collecting her bags, "but I must dash. I have to speak to the vicar before I see about the music. I'll see you all at the party for The Caring Society, the day after tomorrow at four thirty sharp. Don't forget!"

This was a thing Simon and Marcia had often noticed about Auntie Christa. Though she was always busy, it was always other people who did the hard work.

Now Mum had told Auntie Christa they were going to throw the chair away, she wanted to do it at once.

"We'll go and get another one tomorrow after work," she told Dad. "A nice blue, I think, to go with the curtains. And let's get this one out of the way now. I'm sick of the sight of it."

It took all four of them to carry the chair through the kitchen to the back door, and they knocked over most of the kitchen chairs doing it. For the next half hour they thought they were not going to get it through the back door. It stuck, whichever way they tipped it. Simon was quite upset. It was almost as if the chair were trying to stop them throwing it away. But they got it into the garden in the end. Somehow, as they staggered across the lawn with it, they knocked the top off Mum's new sundial and flattened a rosebush. Then they had to stand it sideways in order to wedge it inside the shed.

"There," Dad said, slamming the shed door and dusting his hands. "That's out of the way until Guy Fawkes Day."

He was wrong, of course.

The next day Simon and Marcia had to collect the key from next door and let themselves into the house, because Mum had gone straight from work to meet Dad and buy a new chair. They felt very gloomy being in the empty house. The living room looked queer with an empty space where the chair had been. And both of them kept remembering that they would have to spend Saturday helping in Auntie Christa's schemes.

"Handing around cakes might be fun," Simon said doubtfully.

"But helping with the party won't be," said Marcia. "We'll have to do all the work. Why couldn't one of us have guessed what was in that box?"

"What *are* the children who need The Caring Society, anyway?" asked Simon.

"I *think*," said Marcia, "that they're the ones who have to let themselves into their houses with a key after school."

They looked at one another. "Do you think we count?" asked Simon. "Enough to win a prize anyway? I wouldn't mind winning that magic set. It was a real top hat, even if the crystal ball did leak."

Here they both began to notice a distant thumping noise from somewhere out in the garden. It suddenly felt unsafe being alone in the house.

"It's only next door hanging up pictures again," Marcia said bravely.

But when they went rather timidly to listen at the back door, the noise was definitely coming from the garden shed.

"It's next door's dog shut in the shed again," Simon said. It was his turn to be brave. Marcia was scared of next door's dog. She hung back while Simon marched over the lawn and tugged and pulled until he got the shed door open.

It was not a dog. There was a person standing inside the shed. The person stood and stared at them with his little head on one side. His little fat arms waved about as if he weren't sure what to do with them. He breathed in heavy snorts and gasps as if he weren't sure how to breathe.

"Er, hn hm," he said as if he weren't sure how to speak. "I appear to have been shut in your shed."

"Oh—*sorry!*" Simon said, wondering how it had happened.

The person bowed, in a crawlingly humble way. "I—hn hm—am the one who is [*snuffle*] sorry," he said. "I have made—hn hm—you come all the way here to let me out." He walked out of the shed, swaying and bowing from foot to foot.

Simon backed away, wondering if the person walked like that because he had no shoes on. He was a solid, plump person with wide hairy legs. He was wearing a most peculiar striped one-piece suit that came only to his knees.

Marcia backed away behind Simon, staring at the person's stripy arms. He waved them in a feeble way as he walked. There was a blot of ink on one arm and what looked like a coffee stain on the other. Marcia's eyes went to the person's plump striped stomach. As he came out into the light, she could see that the stripes were pale blue, orange, and purple. There was a damp patch down the middle and a dark sticky place that could have been ketchup once. Her eyes went up to his sideways face. There was a beard on the person's chin that looked rather as if someone had smashed a hedgehog on it.

"Who *are* you?" she said.

The person stood still. His arms waved like seaweed in a current. "Er, hn hm, I am Chair Person," he said. His sideways face looked pleased and rather smug about it.

Marcia and Simon of course both felt awful about it. He was the armchair. They had put him in the shed ready to go on the bonfire. Now he was alive. They hoped very much that Chair Person did not know that they had meant to burn him.

"Won't you come inside?" Simon said politely.

"That is *very* kind of you," Chair Person said, crawlingly humble again. "I—hn hm [*snuffle*]—hope that won't be too much trouble."

"Not at all!" they both said heartily.

They went toward the house. Crossing the lawn was quite difficult, because Chair Person did not seem to have learned to walk straight yet, and he talked all the time. "I believe I am—hn hm—Chair Person," he said, crashing into what was left of the sundial and knocking it down, "because I think I am. [*Snuffle.*] Oh dear, I appear to have destroyed your stone pillar."

"Not to worry," Marcia said kindly. "It was broken last night when we—I mean, it was broken anyway."

"Then—hn hm—as I was saying," Chair Person said, veering the other way, "that this is what [*snuffle*] wise men say. A person who thinks is a person." He cannoned into the apple tree. Most of the apples Dad had meant to pick that weekend came showering and bouncing down onto the grass. "Oh dear," said Chair Person. "I appear to have loosened your fruit."

"That's all right," Simon and Marcia said politely. But since Chair Person, in spite of seeming so humble, did not seem very sorry about the apples and just went on talking and weaving about, they each took hold of one of his waving arms and guided him to the back door.

"Only the finest [*snuffle*] apples," said Chair Person as he bashed into both sides of the back door, "from the finest—hn hm—orchards go into Kaplan's Peasant Pies. This is one of many [*snuffle*] facts I know. Er, hm, very few people have watched as much television as I have," he added, knocking over the nearest kitchen chair.

Marcia picked the chair up, thinking of the many, many times she had gone out of the living room and forgotten to turn the television off. Chair Person, when he was an armchair, must have watched hours of commercials and hundreds of films.

Simon turned Chair Person around and sat him in the kitchen chair. Chair Person went very humble and grateful. "You are—hn hm—treating me with such kindness," he said, "and I am going to cause you a lot of [*snuffle*] trouble. I appear to need something to eat. I am not sure what to do about it. Do I—hn hm—eat *you*?"

"We'll find you something to eat," Simon said quickly.

"Eating people is wrong," Marcia explained.

They hurried to find some food. A can of spaghetti seemed easiest, because they both knew how to do that. Simon opened the can and Marcia put it in a saucepan with the gas very high to get the spaghetti hot as soon as possible. Both of them cast nervous looks at Chair Person in case he tried to eat one of them. But Chair Person sat where he was, waving his arms gently. "Hn hm, Spiggley's tasty snacks," he said. "Sunshine poured from a can." When Marcia put the steaming plateful in front of him and Simon laid a spoon and a fork on either side of it, Chair Person went on sitting and staring.

"You can eat it," Simon said kindly.

"Er, hn hm," Chair Person said. "But this is not a complete meal. I shall have to trouble you for a napkin and salt and pepper. And I think people usually [*snuffle*] eat by candlelight with soft music in the background."

They hurried to find him the salt, the pepper mill, and a paper towel. Simon fetched the radio and turned it on. It was playing country and western, but Simon turned it down very low and hoped it would do. He felt so sorry for Chair Person that he wanted to please him. Marcia ran upstairs and found the candlesticks from Mum's dressing table and two red candles from last Christmas. She felt so guilty about Chair Person that she wanted to please him as much as Simon did.

Chair Person was very humble and grateful. While he told them how kind they were being, he picked up the pepper mill and began solemnly grinding pepper over the spaghetti. "Er, hn hm, with respect to you two fine, kind people," he said as he ground, "eating people is not wrong."

Simon and Marcia quickly got to the other side of the table. But Chair Person only took up the fork and raked the spaghetti into a new heap, and ground more pepper over that. "There are tribes in South [*snuffle*] America," he said, "who believe it is quite correct to—hn hm—eat their grandparents. I have a question. Is Spiggley's another word for spaghetti?"

"No," said Marcia. "It's a name."

Chair Person raked the spaghetti into a different-shaped heap and went on grinding pepper over it.

"When the [*snuffle*] grandparents are dead," he said, "they cook them and the whole tribe has a feast."

Marcia remembered seeing something like this on television. "I watched that program too," she said.

"You—hn hm—will not know this," Chair Person said, raking the spaghetti into another new shape and grinding another cloud of pepper over it. "Only the sons and daughters of the dead man are allowed to eat the brains." This time he spread the spaghetti flat and ground pepper very carefully over every part of it. "This is so that [*snuffle*] the wisdom of the dead man can be passed on to his family," he said.

By this time the spaghetti was gray. Simon and Marcia could not take their eyes off it. It must have been hot as fire by then. They kept expecting Chair Person to sneeze, but he just went on grinding pepper and explaining about cannibals.

Simon wondered if Chair Person perhaps did not know how to eat. "You're supposed to put the spaghetti in your mouth," he said.

Chair Person held up the pepper mill and shook it. It was empty. So he put it down at last and picked up the spoon. He did seem to know how to eat, but he did it very badly, snuffling and snorting, with ends dangling out of his mouth. Gray juice dripped through his smashed-hedgehog beard and ran down his striped front. But the pepper did not seem to worry him at all. Simon was thinking that maybe Chair Person did not have tastebuds like other people, when the back door opened and Mum and Dad came in.

"What happened to the rest of the sundial?" said Mum. "I leave you alone just for—" She saw Chair Person and stared.

"What have you kids done to those apples?" Dad began. Then he saw Chair Person and stared too.

Both Simon and Marcia had had a sort of hope that Chair Person would vanish when Mum and Dad came home, or at least turn back into an armchair. But nothing of the sort happened. Chair Person stood up and bowed.

"Er, hn hm," he said. "I am Chair Person. Good [*snuffle*] evening."

Mum's eyes darted to the ink blot on Chair Person's waving sleeve, then to the coffee stain, and then on to the damp smear on his front. She turned and dashed away into the garden.

Chair Person's arms waved like someone conducting an orchestra. "I am the one causing you all this trouble with your apples," he said, in his most crawlingly humble way. "You are so kind to—hn hm—forgive me so quickly."

Dad clearly could not think what to say. After gulping a little, he said in a social sort of voice, "Staying in the neighborhood, are you?"

Here Mum came dashing back indoors. "The old chair's not in the shed anymore," she said. "Do you think he *might* be—?"

Chair Person turned to her. His arms waved as if he were a conductor expecting Mum to start singing. "Your—hn hm—husband has just made me a very kind offer," he said. "I shall be delighted to stay in this house."

"I—" Dad began.

"Er, hn hm, needless to say [*snuffle*]," said Chair Person, "I shall not cause you more trouble than I have to. Nothing more than—hn hm—a good bed and a television set in my room."

"Oh," said Mum. It was clear she could not think what to say either. "Well, er, I see you've had some supper—"

"Er, hn hm, most kind," said Chair Person. "I would love to have some supper as soon as possible. In the meantime, a [*snuffle*] flask of wine would be most—hn hm—welcome. I appear to have a raging thirst."

Marcia and Simon were not surprised Chair Person was thirsty after all that pepper. They got him a carton of orange juice and a jug of water before they all hurried away to put a camp bed in Simon's room and make Marcia's bedroom ready for Chair Person. Marcia could see that Mum and Dad both had the same kind of dazed, guilty feelings about Chair Person that she had. Neither of them quite believed he was really their old armchair, but Mum put clean sheets on the bed and Dad carried the television up to Marcia's room. Chair Person seemed to get to people that way.

When they came downstairs, the fridge door was open and the table was covered with empty orange juice cartons.

"I—hn hm—appear to have drunk all your orange juice," Chair Person said. "But I would be willing to drink lemon squash instead. I happen [*snuffle*] to know that it has added glucose, which puts pep into the poorest parts."

He sat at the table and slurped lemon squash while Marcia helped Mum get supper. Simon went to look for Dad, who was hiding behind a newspaper in the living room. "Did you buy a new armchair?" Simon asked.

"Yes," said Dad. "Hush. That thing in the kitchen might get jealous."

"So you *do* believe he is the armchair?" Simon said.

"I don't *know*!" Dad groaned.

"I think he is," Simon said. "I'm quite sorry for him. It must be hard to suddenly start being a person. I expect he'll learn to speak and behave like a real person quite soon."

"I hope you're right," said Dad. "If he just learns to stop waving his arms in that spooky way, I shall be quite pleased."

For supper, Chair Person ate five pizzas and six helpings of chips. In between, he waved his arms and explained, "I—hn hm—have a large appetite for my size, though I do not always need to [*snuffle*] eat. I am strange that way. Could I trouble you for some Mannings' fruity brown sauce? I appear to have eaten all your ketchup. I think I shall enjoy my—hn hm—life with you here. I suggest that tomorrow we go on—hn hm—a short tour of Wales. I think I should go to [*snuffle*] Snowdon and then down a coal mine."

"I'm sorry—" Dad began.

"Er, hn hm, Scotland then," said Chair Person. "Or would you rather charter an airplane and take me to France?"

"We can't go anywhere tomorrow," Mum said firmly. "There's Auntie Christa's party in the evening and the coffee morning for African Aid before that."

Chair Person did not seem at all disappointed. He said, "I shall enjoy that. I happen to—hn hm—know a great deal about Africa. At the end of the day, it must be [*snuffle*] said that not nearly enough is being done to help Africa and the Third World. Why in Kenya alone . . ." And he was talking almost word for word—apart from the snuffles—the way last night's television program on Africa had talked.

Before long, Simon and Marcia both had had enough. They tiptoed away to Simon's room and went to bed early.

"I suppose he's here for good," Simon said.

"He hasn't any other home," Marcia said, wriggling her way into the uncomfortable camp bed. "And he *has* lived here for years in a sort of way. Do you think it was the stuff that dripped from the crystal ball that brought him alive? Or Auntie Christa tapping him with the wand? Or both?"

"Perhaps she could look after him," Simon said hopefully. "She does good works. Someone's going to have to teach him all the things that aren't on television."

They could hear Chair Person's voice droning away downstairs. It was a loud voice, with a bleat and bray to it, like a cow with a bad cold. After an hour or so it was clear that Mum and Dad could not stand any more of it either. Simon and Marcia heard them coming to bed early, too. They heard Chair Person blundering upstairs after them.

"Er, hn hm—oh dear!" his voice brayed. "I appear to have broken this small table."

After that there was a lot of confusing moving about and then the sound of running water. Chair Person's voice bleated out again. "Tell me—er, hn hm—is the water supposed to run all over the bathroom floor?"

They heard Mum hurry to the bathroom and turn the taps off. "There are such a lot of things he doesn't know," Marcia said sleepily.

"He'll learn. He'll be better tomorrow," Simon said.

Chair Person ate four boiled eggs and half a packet of shredded wheat for breakfast. He drank what was left of the milk with loud slurping sounds while he told them about oil rigs and then about shipbuilding. "Er, hn hm," he said. "Studies at the dockyards reveal that less than ten [*snuffle, slurp*] percent of ships now being built are launched by the queen. Oh dear, I appear to have drunk all your—hn hm—milk."

Dad jumped up. "I'll buy more milk," he said. "Give me a list of all the other things you want for the coffee morning, and I'll buy them, too."

"Coward!" Mum said bitterly when Dad had gone off with orders to buy ten cake mixes, milk, and biscuits. She was in a great fuss. She told Chair Person to go upstairs and watch television. Chair Person went crawlingly humble, and went away saying he knew he was—hn hm—being a lot of trouble. "And I hope he stays there!" said Mum. She made Simon help in the kitchen and told Marcia to find twenty chairs—which were all the chairs in the house—and put them in a circle in the living room. "And I suppose it's too much to hope that Auntie Christa will come in and help," Mum added.

It *was* too much to hope. Auntie Christa did turn up. She put her head around the back door as Simon was fetching the sixth tray of cakes out of the oven. "I won't interrupt," she said merrily. "I have to dash down to the community hall. Don't forget you're all helping with the party this evening." And away she went and did not come back until Mum and Simon had heaped cakes on ten plates and Dad and Marcia were counting coffee cups. "You *have* done well!" Auntie Christa said. "We must have African Aid here every week."

Dad started to groan, and then stopped, with a thoughtful look on his face.

The doorbell began ringing. A lot of respectable elderly ladies arrived, and one or two respectable elderly men, and then the vicar. They each took one of the twenty seats and chatted politely while Simon and Marcia went around with cakes and biscuits and Mum handed out coffee. When everyone had a cup and a plate of something, the vicar cleared his throat—a bit like Chair Person but nothing like so loudly.

"Er, hm," he said. "I think we should start."

The door opened just then and Dad ushered in Chair Person.

"Oh *no!*" said Mum, looking daggers at Dad.

Chair Person stood, pawing at the air, and looked around the respectable people in a very satisfied way. He had found Dad's best shiny brown shoes to wear and Simon's football socks, which looked decidedly odd with his striped suit. The respectable people stared, at the shoes, the socks, the hairy legs above that, at the stain on his striped stomach and then at the smashed-hedgehog beard. Even Auntie Christa stopped talking and looked a little dazed.

"Er, hn hm," brayed Chair Person twice as loudly as the vicar. "I am—hn [*snuffle*]—Chair Person. How kind of you all to come and—hn hm—meet me. These good people"—he nodded and waved arms at Dad and Mum—"have been honored to put up with me, but they are only small, stupid people who do not matter."

The slightly smug smile on Dad's face vanished at this.

"I shall—hn hm—talk to people who matter," said Chair Person. He lumbered across the room, bumping into everything he passed. Ladies hastily got coffee cups out of his way. He stopped in front of the vicar and breathed heavily. "Could I trouble you to move?" he said.

"Eh?" said the vicar. "Er—"

"Er, hn hm, you appear to be sitting in my seat," said Chair Person. "I am Chair Person. I am the one who shall talk to—hn hm—the government. I shall be running this meeting."

The vicar got out of the chair as if it had scalded him and backed away. Chair Person sat himself down and looked solemnly around.

"Coffee," he said. "Er, hn hm, cakes. While the rest of the world starves."

Everyone shifted and looked uncomfortably at their cups.

In the silence, Chair Person looked at Mum. "Hn hm," he said. "Maybe you have not noticed that you've not given me—hn hm—coffee or cakes."

"Is *that* what you meant?" said Mum. "I thought after all the breakfast you ate—"

"I meant—hn hm—that we are here to feast and prove that we at least have enough to eat," said Chair Person.

Auntie Christa said loudly, "We are here to talk about Africa, Mr. Chair Person."

"Er, hn hm," said Chair Person. "I happen to know a lot about Africa. The government should act to make sure that the African—hn hm—elephant does not die out."

"We were not going to talk about elephants," the vicar said faintly.

"The [*snuffle*] gorilla is an endangered animal too," said Chair Person. "And the herds of—hn hm—wildebeests are not what they were in the days of Dr. Livingstone, I presume. Drought afflicts many animals—I appear to have drunk all my coffee—and famine is poised to strike." And he went on talking, mixing up about six different television programs as he talked. The vicar soon gave up trying to interrupt, but Auntie Christa kept trying to talk, too. Every time she began, Chair Person went "ER, HN HM!" so loudly that he drowned her out, and took no notice of anything she said. Marcia could not help thinking that Chair Person must have stood in the living room picking up hints from Auntie Christa for years. Now he was better at not letting other people talk then Auntie Christa was.

In the meantime, Chair Person kept eating cakes and asking for more coffee. The respectable people, in a dazed sort of way, tried to keep up with Chair Person, which meant that Simon and Marcia were kept very busy carrying cups and plates. In the kitchen Mum was baking and boiling the kettle non-stop, while Dad grimly undid packets and mixed cake mix after cake mix.

By this time Simon was finding it hard to be sorry for Chair Person at all. "I didn't know you thought you were so important," he said as he brought Chair Person another plate of steaming buns.

"This must be—hn hm—reported to Downing Street," Chair Person told the meeting, and he interrupted himself to say to Simon, "That is because I—er, hn hm, always take care to be polite to people like you who don't [snuffle] count. I shall make you feel good by praising these cakes. They are [snuffle] country soft and almost as Mother used to make." And turning back to the dazed meeting, he said, "Ever since the days of the pharaohs—hn hm—Egypt has been a place of [*snuffle*] mystery and romance."

There seemed nothing that would ever stop him. Then the doorbell rang. Unfortunately, Dad, Mum, Marcia, and Simon were all in the kitchen when it rang, pouring the last of the cake mix into paper cases. By the time Marcia and Dad got to the front door, Chair Person had got there first and opened it.

Two men standing outside holding a new armchair. It was a nice armchair, a nice plain blue, with a pleasant look on the cushion at the back where Chair Person's face had come from. Marcia thought Mum and Dad had chosen well.

"I—er, hn hm—I said take that thing away," Chair Person told the men. "This house is not big enough for [*snuffle*] both of us. The post is—hn hm—filled. There has been a mistake."

"Are you sure? This is the right address," one of the men said.

Dad pushed Chair Person angrily aside. "Mind your own business!" he said. "No, there's no mistake. Bring that chair inside."

Chair Person folded his waving arms. "Er, hn hm. My rival enters this house over my dead body," he said. "This thing is bigger than [*snuffle*] both of us."

While they argued, Auntie Christa was leading the coffee-morning people in a rush to escape through the kitchen and out the back door.

"I do think," the vicar said kindly to Mum as he scampered past, "that your eccentric uncle would be far happier in a home, you know."

Mum waited until the last person had hurried through the back door. Then she burst into tears.

Simon did not know what to do. He stood staring at her.

"A home!" Mum wept. "I'm the one who'll be in a home if someone doesn't *do* something!"

Chair Person got his way over the new chair, more or less. The men carried it to the garden shed and shoved it inside. Then they left, looking almost as bewildered and angry as Dad.

Marcia, watching and listening, was quite sure now that Chair Person had been learning from Auntie Christa all these years. He knew just how to make people do what he wanted. But Auntie Christa did not live in the house. You could escape from her sometimes. Chair Person seemed to be here to stay.

"We'll have to get him turned back into a chair somehow," she said to Simon. "He's not getting better. He's getting worse and worse."

Simon found he agreed. He was not sorry for Chair Person at all now. "Yes, but *how* do we turn him back?" he said.

"We could ask old Mr. Pennyfeather," Marcia suggested. "The magic set came from his shop."

So that afternoon they left Mum lying on her bed upstairs and Dad moodily picking up frost-bitten apples from the grass. Chair Person was still eating lunch in the kitchen.

"Where does he put it all?" Marcia wondered as they hurried down the road.

"He's a chair. He's got lots of room for stuffing," Simon pointed out.

Then they both said, "Oh *no!*" Chair Person was

blundering up the road after them, panting and snuf-fling and waving his arms. "Er, hn hm, wait for me!" he called out. "You appear to have [*snuffle*] left me behind."

He tramped beside them, looking pleased with himself. When they got to the shops, where all the people were, shoppers turned to stare as Chair Person clumped past in Dad's shoes. Their eyes went from the shoes to the football socks, and then to the short striped suit, and then on up to stare wonderingly at the smashed-hedgehog beard. More heads turned every time Chair Person's voice brayed out, and of course he talked a lot. There was something in every shop to set him going.

At the bread shop, he said, "Er, hn hm, those are Sam Browne's lusty loaves. I happen to know [*snuffle*] they are nutrition for the nation."

Outside the supermarket, he said, "Cheese to please, you can [*snuffle*] freeze it, squeeze it and—er, hn hm—there is Tackley's Tea, which I happen to know has over a thousand holes to every bag. Flavor to [*snuffle*] savor."

Outside the wine shop his voice went up to a high roar. "I—hn hm—see Sampa's Superb Sherry here, which is for ladies who like everything silken [*snuffle*] smooth. And I happen to know that in the black bottle there is—hn hm—a taste of Olde England. There is a stagecoach on the—hn hm—label to prove it. And look, there is Bogan's—hn hm—Beer, which is, of course, for men only."

By now it seemed to Simon and Marcia that everyone in the street was staring. "You don't want to believe everything the ads say," Simon said uncomfortably.

"Er, hn hm, I appear to be making you feel embarrassed," Chair Person brayed, louder than ever. "Just tell me [*snuffle*] if I am in your way and I will [*snuffle*] go home."

"Yes, do," they both said.

"I—er, hn hm—wouldn't dream of pushing in where I am [*snuffle*] not wanted," Chair Person said. "I would—hn hm—count it a favor if you tell me [*snuffle*] truthfully every time you've had enough of me. I—er, hn hm—know I must bore you quite often."

By the time he had finished saying this, they had arrived at old Mr. Pennyfeather's junk shop. Chair Person stared at it.

"We—er, hn hm—don't need to go in there," he said. "Everything in it is old."

"You can stay outside then," said Marcia.

But Chair Person went into another long speech about not wanting to be—hn hm—a trouble to them and followed them into the shop. "I—er, hn hm—might get lost," he said, "and then what would you do?"

He bumped into a cupboard.

Its doors opened with a *clap* and a stream of horse brasses poured out: *clatter, clatter, CLATTER!*

Chair Person lurched sideways from the horse brasses and walked into an umbrella stand made out of an elephant's foot,

which fell over—*crash CLATTER*—
against a coffee table with a big jug on it,
which tipped and slid the jug off—*CRASH, splinter, splinter*—
and then fell against a rickety bookcase,
which collapsed sideways, spilling books—
thump, thump, thump-thump-thump
and hit another table loaded with old magazines and music,
which all poured down around Chair Person.
It was like dominoes going down.

The bell at the shop door had not stopped ringing before Chair Person was surrounded in knocked-over furniture and knee deep in old papers. He stood in the midst of them waving his arms and looking injured.

By then Mr. Pennyfeather was on his way from the back of the shop, shouting, "Steady, steady, steady!"

"Er, hn hm—er, hn hm," said Chair Person, "I appear to have knocked one or two things over."

Mr. Pennyfeather stopped and looked at him in a knowing, measuring kind of way. Then he looked at Simon and Marcia. "He yours?" he said. They nodded. Mr. Pennyfeather nodded too. "Don't move," he said to Chair Person. "Stay just where you are."

Chair Person's arms waved as if he were conducting a very large orchestra, several massed choirs, and probably a brass band or so as well. "I—er, hn hm, er, hn hm—I—er, hn hm—" he began.

Mr. Pennyfeather shouted at him. "*Stand still! Don't move, or I'll have the springs out of you and straighten them for toasting forks!* It's the only language they understand," he said to Simon and Marcia. "STAND STILL! YOU HEARD ME!" he shouted at Chair Person.

Chair Person stopped waving his arms and stood like a statue, looking quite frightened.

"You two come this way with me," said Mr. Pennyfeather, and he took Simon and Marcia down to the far end of his shop, between an old ship's wheel and a carved maypole, where there was an old radio balanced on a tea chest. He turned the radio up loud so that Chair Person could not hear them. "Now," he said, "I see you two got problems to do with that old magician's box. What happened?"

"It was Auntie Christa's fault," said Marcia.

"She let the crystal ball drip on the chair," said Simon.

"*And* tapped it with the magic wand," said Marcia.

Mr. Pennyfeather scratched his withered old cheek. "My fault really," he said. "I should never have let her have those things, only I'd got sick of the way the stuff in my shop would keep getting lively. Tables dancing and such. Mind you, most of my furniture only got a drip or so. They used to calm down after a couple of hours. That one of yours looks as though he got a right dousing—or maybe the wand helped. What was he to begin with, if you don't mind my asking?"

"Our old armchair," said Simon.

"Really?" said Mr. Pennyfeather. "I'd have said he was a sofa, from the looks of him. Maybe what you had was an armchair with a sofa opinion of itself. That happens.''

"Yes, but how can we turn him *back?*" said Marcia.

Mr. Pennyfeather scratched his withered cheek again. "This is *it*," he said. "Quite a problem. The answer must be in that magic set. It wouldn't make no sense to have that crystal ball full of stuff to make things lively without having the antidote close by. That top hat never got lively. You could try tapping him with the wand again. But you'd do well to sort through the box and see if you couldn't come up with whatever was put on the top hat to stop it getting lively at all.''

"But we haven't got the box," said Simon. "Auntie Christa's got it.''

"Then you'd better borrow it back off her quick," Mr. Pennyfeather said, peering along his shop to where Chair Person was still standing like a statue. "Armchairs with big opinions of theirselves aren't no good. That one could turn out a real menace.''

"He already *is*," said Simon.

Marcia took a deep, grateful breath and said, "Thanks awfully, Mr. Pennyfeather. Do you want us to help tidy up your shop?''

"No, you run along," said Mr. Pennyfeather. "I want him out of here before he does any worse.'' And he shouted down the shop at Chair Person, "Right, you can move now! Out of my shop *on* the double and wait in the street!''

Chair Person nodded and bowed in his most crawlingly humble way and waded through the papers and out of the shop. Simon and Marcia followed, wishing they could manage to shout at Chair Person the way Mr. Pennyfeather had. But maybe they had been brought up to be too polite. Or maybe it was Chair Person's sofa opinion of himself. Or maybe it was just that Chair Person was bigger than they were and had offered to eat them when he first came out of the shed. Whatever it was, all they seemed to be able to do was to let Chair Person clump along beside them, talking and talking, and try to think how to turn him into a chair again.

They were so busy thinking that they had turned into their own road before they heard one thing that Chair Person said. And that was only because he said something new.

"*What* did you say?" said Marcia.

"I said," said Chair Person, "I appear—er, hn hm [*snuffle*]—to have set fire to your house."

Both their heads went up with a jerk. Sure enough, there was a fire engine standing in the road by their gate. Firemen were dashing about unrolling hoses. Thick black smoke was rolling up from behind the house, darkening the sunlight and turning their roof black.

Simon and Marcia forgot Chair Person and ran.

Mum and Dad, to their great relief, were standing in the road beside the fire engine, along with most of the neighbors. Mum saw them. She let go of Dad's arm and rushed up to Chair Person.

"All right. Let's have it," she said. "What did you do *this* time?"

Chair Person made bowing and hand-waving movements, but he did not seem sorry or worried. In fact, he was looking up at the surging clouds of black smoke rather smugly. "I—er, hn hm—was thirsty," he said. "I appeared to have drunk all your orange juice and lemon squash and the stuff [*snuffle*] from the wine and whiskey bottles, so I—hn hm— put the kettle on the gas for a cup of tea. I appear to have forgotten it when I went out."

"You fool!" Mum screamed at him. "It was an electric kettle anyway!" She was angry enough to behave just like Mr. Pennyfeather. She pointed a finger at Chair Person's striped stomach. "I've had enough of you!" she shouted. "You stand there and don't *dare* move! Don't *stir*, or I'll—I'll—I don't know what I'll do, but you won't like it!"

And it worked, just like it did when Mr. Penny- feather shouted. Chair Person stood still as an over- stuffed statue. "I—hn hm—appear to have annoyed you," he said in his most crawlingly humble way.

He stood stock-still in the road all the time the firemen were putting out the fire. Luckily only the kitchen was burning. Dad had seen the smoke while he was picking up apples in the garden. He had been in time to phone the fire brigade and get Mum from upstairs before the rest of the house caught fire. The firemen hosed the blaze out quite quickly. Half an hour later Chair Person was still standing in the road and the rest of them were looking around the ruined kitchen.

Mum gazed at the melted cooker, the crumpled fridge, and the charred stump of the kitchen table.

Everything was black and wet. The vinyl floor had bubbled. "Someone get rid of Chair Person," Mum said, "before I murder him."

"Don't worry. We're going to," Simon said soothingly.

"But we have to go and help at Auntie Christa's Caring Society children's party in order to do it," Marcia explained.

"I'm not going," Mum said. "There's enough to do here—and I'm not doing another thing for Auntie Christa—not after this morning!"

"Even Auntie Christa can't expect us to help at her party after our house has been on fire," Dad said.

"Simon and I will go," Marcia said. "And we'll take Chair Person and get him off your hands."

The smoke had made everything in the house black and gritty. Simon and Marcia could not find any clean clothes, but the next-door neighbors let them use their bathroom and kindly shut up their dog so that Marcia would not feel nervous. The neighbors on the other side invited them to supper when they came back. Everyone was very kind. More kind neighbors were standing anxiously around Chair Person when Simon and Marcia came to fetch him. Chair Person was still standing like a statue in the road.

"Is he ill?" the lady from Number 27 asked.

"No, he's not," Marcia said. "He's just eccentric. The vicar says so."

Simon did his best to imitate Mr. Pennyfeather. "Right," he barked at Chair Person. "You can move now. We're going to a party."

Though Simon sounded to himself just like a nervous person talking loudly, Chair Person at once started snuffling and waving his arms about. "Oh—hn hm—good," he said. "I believe I shall like a party. What [*snuffle*] party is it? Conservative, Labor, Alliance, Democrat, or Republican? Should I be—hn hm—sick of the moon or over the parrot?"

At this, all the neighbors nodded to one another. "*Very* eccentric," the lady from Number 27 said as they all went away.

Simon and Marcia led Chair Person toward the community hall, trying to explain that it was a party for children who needed caring for. "And we're supposed to be helping," Marcia said. "So do you think you could try to behave like a proper person for once?"

"You—hn hm—didn't have to say *that!*" Chair Person said. His feelings were hurt. He followed them into the hall in silence.

The hall was full of children and quite nicely decorated with bunches of balloons. Simon and Marcia knew most of the children from school. They were surprised they needed caring for—most of them seemed just ordinary children. But the thing they looked at mostly was the long table at the other end of the room. It had a white cloth on it. Much of it was covered with food: jellies, cakes, crisps, and big bottles of Coke. But at one end was the pile of prizes, with the green teddy on top. The magic set, being quite big, was at the bottom of the pile. Simon and Marcia were glad, because that would mean it would be the last prize anybody won. They would have time to look through the box.

Auntie Christa was in the midst of the children, trying to pin someone's torn dress. "There you are at last!" she called to Simon and Marcia. "Where are your mother and father?"

"They couldn't come—we're awfully sorry!" Marcia called back.

Auntie Christa rushed out from among the children. "Couldn't come? Why *not?*" she said.

"Our house has been on fire—" Simon began to explain.

But Auntie Christa, as usual, did not listen. "I think that's extremely thoughtless of them!" she said. "I was counting on them to run the games. Now I shall have to run them myself."

While they were talking, Chair Person lumbered into the crowd of children, waving his arms importantly. "Er, hn hm, welcome to the party," he brayed. "You are all honored to have me here because I am [*snuffle*] Chair Person and you are only children who need caring for."

The children stared at him resentfully. None of them thought of themselves that way. "Why is he wearing football socks?" someone asked.

Auntie Christa whirled around and stared at Chair Person. Her face went quite pale. "Why did you bring *him?*" she said.

"He—er—he needs looking after," Marcia said, rather guiltily.

"He just nearly burned our house down," Simon tried to explain again.

But Auntie Christa did not listen. "I shall speak to your mother very crossly indeed!" she said, and ran back among the children, clapping her hands. "Now listen, children. We are going to play a lovely game. Stand quiet while I explain the rules."

"Er, hn hm," said Chair Person. "There appears to be a feast laid out over there. Would it [*snuffle*] trouble you if I started eating it?"

At this, quite a number of the children called out, "Yes! Can we eat the food now?"

Auntie Christa stamped her foot. "No you may *not!* Games come first. All of you stand in a line, and Marcia bring those beanbags from over there."

Once Auntie Christa started giving orders, Chair Person became quite obedient. He did his best to join in the games. He was hopeless. If someone threw him a beanbag, he dropped it. If he threw a beanbag at someone else, it hit the wall or threatened to land in the jelly. The team he was on lost every time.

So Auntie Christa tried team Follow My Leader and that was even worse. Chair Person lost the team he was with and galumphed around in small circles on his own. Then he noticed that everyone was running in zigzags and ran in zigzags too. He zagged when everyone else zigged, bumping into people and treading on toes.

"Can't you stop him? He's spoiling the *game!*" children kept complaining.

Luckily, Chair Person kept drifting off to the table to steal buns or help himself to a pint or so of Coke. After a while Auntie Christa stopped rounding him back into the games. It was easier without him.

But Simon and Marcia were getting worried. They

were being kept so busy helping with teams and fetching things and watching in case people cheated that they had no time at all to get near the magic set. They watched the other prizes go. The green teddy went first, then the broken train, and then other things, until half the pile was gone.

Then at last Auntie Christa said the next game was Musical Chairs. "Simon and Marcia will work the record player and I'll be the judge," she said. "All of you bring one chair each into the middle. *And you!*" she said, grabbing Chair Person away from where he was trying to eat some jelly. "This is a game even you can play."

"Good," Simon whispered as he and Marcia went over to the old, old record player. "We can look in the box while the music's going."

Marcia picked up an old scratched record and set it on the turntable. "I thought we were never going to get a chance!" she said. "We can give them a good long go with the music first time." She carefully lowered the lopsided stylus. The record began:

> *Here we go gathering* click *in May,*
> Click *in May, nuts in* click . . .

and all the children danced cautiously around the chairs, with Chair Person prancing in their midst, waving his arms like a lobster.

Simon and Marcia ran to the table and pulled the magician's box out from under the other prizes. The crystal ball was still leaking. There was quite a damp patch on the tablecloth. But when they opened the box, the wand was lying on top, still wrapped in flags. Simon snatched it up. Marcia ran back and lifted the stylus off the record. There was a stampede for chairs.

Chair Person, of course, was the one without a chair. Simon had expected that. He followed Chair Person and gave him a smart tap with the wand as Chair Person blundered up the line of sitting children. But the wand did not seem to work. Chair Person pushed the smallest girl off the end chair and sat in it himself.

"I saw that! You were out!" Auntie Christa shouted, pointing at him.

Chair Person sat where he was. "I—er, hn hm—appear to be sitting in a chair," he said. "That was the [*snuffle*] rule as I understand it."

Auntie Christa glared. "Start the game again," she said.

Simon tapped Chair Person on the head with the wand before everyone got up, but that did not seem to work either. "What shall we *do?*" he whispered to Marcia as they hurried back to the record player.

"Try it without the flags," Marcia whispered back. She lowered the stylus again.

Here we go gathering click *in May,* the record began as Simon dashed over to the table, unwrapping the string of flags from the wand as he went. He was just putting the flags back in the box when the table gave a sort of wriggle and stamped one of its legs.

Simon beckoned Marcia madly. The box must

have been standing on the table for quite a long time. The stuff from the crystal ball had leaked down into the table and spread along the tablecloth to the food. The tablecloth was rippling itself in a sly, lazy way. As Marcia arrived, the jelly spilled its way up to the edge of its cardboard bowl and peeped timidly out.

"It's *all* getting lively," Simon said.

"We'd better take the crystal ball to the toilet and drain it away," Marcia said.

"No!" said Simon. "Think what might happen if the toilet gets lively! Think of something else."

"Why should *I* always have to be the one to think?" Marcia snapped. "Get an idea for yourself for once!" She knew this was unfair, but by this time she was in as bad a fuss as Mum.

Here the record got as far as *Who shall we* click *to* click *him away?* and stuck. *Who shall we* click, *who shall we* click, *who shall we* click . . .

Marcia raced for the record and took it off. Simon raced among the stampede toward Chair Person and hit him with the unwrapped wand. Again nothing happened. Chair Person pushed a boy with a leg brace off the end chair and sat down. Auntie Christa said angrily. "This is *too* bad! Start the game again."

Marcia put the stylus down on the beginning of the record a third time. "I'd better stay and do this," she said. "You go search the box—quickly, before we get landed with Table Person and Jelly Person as well!"

Simon sped to the table and started taking things out of the magician's box—first the flags, then the dripping hat with the crystal ball in it. After that came a toy rabbit, which was perhaps meant to be lively when it was fetched out of the hat. Yet for some reason it was just a toy. None of the things in the box was more than just wet. Simon took out a sopping leather wallet, three soaking packs of cards, and a dripping bundle of colored handkerchiefs. They were all just ordinary. That meant that there *had* to be a way of stopping things getting lively, but search as he would, Simon could not find it.

As he searched, the cracked music stopped and started and the table stamped one leg after another in time to it. Simon glanced at the game. Chair Person had found another way to cheat. He simply sat in his chair the whole time.

"I'm counting you out," Auntie Christa kept saying. And Chair Person went on sitting there with his smashed-hedgehog chin pointing obstinately at the ceiling.

Next time Simon looked, there were only two chairs left beside Chair Person's, and three children. "We'll have tea after this game," Auntie Christa called as Marcia started the music again.

Help! thought Simon. The wobbling, climbing jelly was half out of its bowl, waving little feelers. Simon turned the whole box out onto the jigging table. All sorts of things fell out. But there was nothing he could see that looked useful—except perhaps a small, wet pillbox. There was a typed label on its lid that said DISAPPEARING BOX. Simon hurriedly opened it.

It was empty inside, so very empty that he could

not see the bottom. Simon put it down on the table and stared into it, puzzled.

Just then the table got livelier than ever from all the liquid Simon had emptied out of the magician's box. It started to dance properly. The tablecloth got quite as lively and stretched itself in a long, lazy ripple. The two things together rolled the hat with the crystal in it across the tiny, empty pillbox.

There was a soft *whop*. The hat and the crystal were sucked into the box. And they were gone. Just like that. Simon stared.

The table was still dancing, and the tablecloth was still rippling. One by one, and very quickly, the other things from the magician's box were rolled and jigged across the tiny pillbox. *Whop* went the rabbit, *whop* the wand, *whop-whop* the string of flags, and then all the other things *whop whop whop,* and they were all gone too. The big box that had held the things tipped over and made a bigger *whop*. And that was gone as well, before Simon could move. After that the other prizes started to vanish *whop whop whop.* This seemed to interest the tablecloth. It put out a long, exploring corner toward the pillbox.

At that, Simon came to his senses. He pushed the corner aside and rammed the lid on the pillbox before the tablecloth had a chance to vanish too.

As soon as the lid was on, the pillbox was not there anymore. There was not even a whisper of a *whop* as it went. It was just gone. And the tablecloth was just a tablecloth, lying half wrapped across the few prizes left. And the table stood still and was just a table. The jelly slid back into its bowl. Its feelers were gone and it was just jelly.

The music stopped, too. Auntie Christa called out. "Well done, Phillippa! You've won again! Come and choose a prize, dear."

"It's not fair!" somebody complained. "Phillippa's won *everything*!"

Marcia came racing over to Simon as he tried to straighten the tablecloth. "Look, look! You *did* it! Look!"

Simon turned around in a dazed way. There were still two chairs standing in the middle of the hall after the game. One of them was an old shabby striped armchair. Simon was sure that was not right. "Who put—?" he began. Then he noticed that the chair was striped in pale blue, orange, and purple. Its stuffing was leaking in a sort of fuzz from its sideways top cushion. It had stains on both arms and on the seat. Chair Person was a chair again. The only odd thing was that the chair was wearing football socks and shiny shoes on its two front legs.

"I'm not sure if it was the wand or the pillbox," Simon said.

They pushed the armchair over against the wall while everyone was crowding around the food.

"I don't think I could bear to have it on our bonfire after this," Marcia said. "It wouldn't seem quite kind."

"If we take its shoes and socks off," Simon said, "we could leave it here. People will probably think it belongs to the hall."

"Yes, it would be quite useful here," Marcia agreed.

Later on, after the other children had gone and Auntie Christa had locked up the hall, saying over her shoulder, "Tell your mother and father that I'm not on speaking terms with either of them!" Simon and Marcia walked slowly home.

Simon asked, "Do you think he knew we were going to put him on our bonfire? Was he having his revenge on us?"

"He may have been," said Marcia. "He never talked about the bonfire, did he? But what was to stop him just *asking* us not to when he was a person?"

"No," said Simon. "He didn't have to set the house on fire. I suppose that shows the kind of person he was."

We'll Do Lunch

by Jymn Magon & Mark Zaslove

THE MOSQUITO MEN OF MASLOG-5
A screenplay by Jeffrey Howard

FADE-IN:

<u>EXTERIOR—OUTER SPACE—NIGHT</u>

[OPENING MUSIC: SOMETHING GRANDIOSE AND JOHN WILLIAMS-ESQUE]

ESTABLISHING SHOT—A million stars glitter against the black curtain of deep space. Suddenly, a large, skeletonlike SPACE VESSEL zigzags into shot. <SFX: LOUD METALLIC DRONE, BLENDED WITH A HIGH-PITCHED BUZZ>

TRACK ON VESSEL—Despite its size, it moves with the effortless grace of a dragonfly . . . or a mosquito.

PUSH IN—on the front viewports (which on this ship look like insect eyes).

CROSS-DISSOLVE TO:

For a glossary of film script terms, see page 184.

INTERIOR—ALIEN VESSEL

PAN ACROSS—an ELABORATE COMMAND CONSOLE, displaying otherworldly controls and switches.

Through the front viewports, the blue-white planet Earth hangs defenselessly in the black void.

PAN OVER—to a series of ornately barred cages.

HOLD ON—last cage in the row. A spindly INSECT ARM reaches INTO SHOT, opens the small cage door, and extracts a FURRY CREATURE that looks a little like a six-legged guinea pig. It <SQUEALS FURIOUSLY>.

CLOSE ON FURRY CREATURE—It squirms helplessly as a long, tubular SNOUT enters shot and pierces its body like a needle. <SFX: RODENTLIKE SCREAM> The snout begins NOISILY SUCKING the insides out of the helpless creature, until all that's left is a furry "fig"—a dried-out husk.

CUT TO:

—CREDITS—

They roll over the following sequence:

EXTERIOR—SUBURBS—NIGHT

LONG SHOT—Beneath the spangled sky sits a cozy TWO-STORY HOUSE. It lies serenely on the very edge of town, bordered by a large grassy field and woods. <SFX: CRICKETS>

SLOW PUSH IN ON HOUSE—There is a light burning in an upstairs window. We begin to hear the faint sounds of hard-driving ROCK MUSIC as we get closer. [MUSIC: MÖTLEY CRÜE OR BON JOVI]

PUSH IN—further to reveal the bedroom of fifteen-year-old TONY HOOPER. Through the window we can see POSTERS of BMX bike racers tacked to the walls; several TROPHIES adorn a dresser. In the middle of the floor sits Tony, dressed in faded jeans and a T-shirt emblazoned with the motto: "Put Something Exciting Between Your Legs—Redline Bikes."

PUSH TIGHT—Tony's busily cleaning a BICYCLE CHAIN in a large Tupperware bowl of gasoline, humming along with the radio station on his boom box. <MUSIC INCREASES>

INTERIOR—TONY'S ROOM

MEDIUM SHOT—of Tony as he bounces to the beat. <MUSIC IS LOUD NOW>

TONY
<sings along with music>

—END CREDITS—

A moment later, the radio gives a <SQUELCH> of static.

CLOSE—BOOM BOX—<SFX: STATIC>

ON TONY—He frowns and pounds the radio with his fist.

TONY
Come on, you piece of Japanese junk!

But the <STATIC> only gets worse. Suddenly, Tony is bathed in a YELLOW-GREEN GLOW from outside his window! He leaps to his feet, staring out into the night.

TONY'S POINT OF VIEW—A FIREBALL streaks down across the sky, leaving a dazzling trail of "pixie dust" that scintillates as it fades (from red to yellow to blue).

<SFX: DIVING ROCKET SCREAM; BLARING RADIO STATIC>

The fireball finally plows into Earth somewhere off in the woods outside Tony's house. There's a blinding FLASH, followed by a <RUMBLE> and then an <EXPLOSION>.

CLOSE ON TONY—He shields his eyes from the searing light.

TONY

JEEEEZ!!!

The light subsides and the static disappears. <SILENCE> Everything's back to normal. Tony lowers his hands and gapes out the window.

TONY

Whoa! . . .

WIDER ANGLE—Tony grabs his denim jacket and dashes for his bedroom door, under—

TONY
I gotta check this out!!

WIPE TO:

"That's all I need!!!" Mr. Nat Smith, Hollywood producer of large reputation though slight stature, slapped the script on his desk as though he were swatting a mosquito with it. "Another *Invaders from Mars* rip-off!!"

He stabbed a finger out and buzzed his secretary, rubbing his temples all the while. "Ms. Jones. Bring me a fistful of Tylenol, will ya?"

Smith leaned back in his leather armchair, asking himself for the forty-second time how he got talked into judging this high school script contest. Yeah, yeah . . . the next wave of talented screenwriters and all that b.s. Hah! The only talent these kids ever showed was a gift for copying plots from the Late Late Show. He fingered the script again. *"And then Tony stumbled onto the Mothership!* I do quality movies, I don't need this!"

Ms. Jones flitted into the room, making a show of balancing a glass of water and two white tablets at the same time. "Another bad screenplay, Mr. Smith?" she squeaked.

"Five-cent words with five-million-dollar special-effects budgets! Who do people think I am, George Lucas? Just once, I'd like to see a writer with a little imagination." He knocked back the Tylenol, while Ms. Jones hovered around him.

"Awful, huh?"

A sputtered swallow was answer enough, but Smith continued, softening a little: "Well, at least this kid can put all the words in the right order, I suppose. Who knows? Maybe he'll become the next William Goldman." Then he glanced at the amateur screenplay and wrinkled his nose. "But the title of this turkey really makes me itch."

Ms. Jones made what she thought was an appropriate giggle at the pun. "Oh, Mr. Smith, you're so funny."

"Did Redford's agent call back yet?"

"Yes, Mr. Smith. Ten minutes ago."

"What!!! Well, get him on the phone!" He waved Ms. Jones out as though she were an annoying insect. "Pronto!"

Six important calls and a dozen promises of "We'll do lunch, babe" later, Mr. Smith's head was still humming. What a morning. And he still wasn't even halfway through this kid's script. Well, he'd remedy that: Smith picked up the screenplay and flipped to somewhere near the middle.

---

firing a look over to the barricaded stairwell door. Tony continues punching the elevator button frantically.

TONY
Come on! Come on!

CLOSE ON—ELEVATOR PANEL. Floor 32 lights up.
<SFX: DING>

ANGLE ON TONY—He glances up at the elevator panel, vastly relieved.

> TONY
> Saved!

He waits impatiently for the elevator door to open . . . which it finally does. Tony takes a hasty step forward and—

CLOSE-UP—MR. CLISBY, standing in the elevator! [MUSIC: STING]

> MR. CLISBY
> I got tired of the stairs.

> TONY (O.S.)
> YAAHH!!!

BACK ON TONY—His worst fear come true, he turns and runs down the empty darkened corridor. Clisby races after.

TRACKING SHOT —Tony is running for his life! He skids around a corner and keeps pumping. He glances over his shoulder.

TONY'S POV—Mr. Clisby is only ten paces behind, arms outstretched, grasping at him.

WIDE—Tony ducks into an office and slams the door.

INTERIOR—DARKENED OFFICE

ON TONY—He locks the door, panting painfully. As Clisby pounds on the door, Tony steps backward away from it, fearing it might give way at any second. He continues backing until he bumps into the floor-to-ceiling WINDOW. Tony turns and looks down, eyes widening.

TONY'S POV—A dizzying shot of the city lights and traffic, far below! [MUSIC: SOMETHING LIKE THE *Vertigo* THEME]

BACK ON TONY—He's terrified. Just then <SFX: CRASH!>, he spins round to see . . .

ANGLE ON DOOR—It flies open! Clisby stalks into the room.

> MR. CLISBY
> Game's over, kid. You lose.

REVERSE ANGLE—Tony moves away from the window, grabbing a swivel chair from behind the desk. He rolls it in front of himself like a shield.

> TONY
> Leave me alone! I haven't told
> anyone about you!!

Mr. Clisby continues to advance on Tony, menacingly.

> MR. CLISBY
> That's right, kid. And I'm here
> to make sure you never will.

CLOSE ON CLISBY—With a sinister grin he peels back his hairpiece to reveal a metallic green-black scalp.

ON TONY—A look of utter shock and revulsion.

BACK ON CLISBY—[NOTE: a series of elaborate makeup shots follow, similar to Rick Baker's werewolf transformation in *The Howling*]

1. Clisby's nose elongates grotesquely. <SFX: DISGUSTING STRETCHING SOUND>
2. An extra pair of black spindly insect arms <RIP> through his business shirt.
3. A large hypodermic-like rod pokes through the facial tissue, continuing to grow. The flesh splits up across the forehead. <SFX: TEARING>
4. Scene by scene, Mr. Clisby reveals his true MOSQUITO MAN form!

TWO-SHOT OF TONY and CLISBY/MOSQUITO MAN—The metamorphosis is complete; the slavering alien is hideous. Tony looks petrified with fright . . .

> MR. CLISBY
> (gurgling voice now)
> . . . And I mean that from the bottom
> of *your* heart!

. . . but as Clisby lunges his needle tube at the boy's chest, Tony quickly ducks. The alien drives the deadly nose into the back of the chair.

CLOSE ON TONY—crouched. The needle thrusts through the Naugahyde, missing his face by an inch. With a determined look, Tony grabs the nose with one hand and pushes the chair forward with the other.

ANGLE ON CLISBY—Tony's maneuver manages to tumble the alien facedown onto the chair. The boy rolls the chair away from the desk.

ANOTHER ANGLE—With a mighty shove, Tony sends the chair *and* Mr. Clisby right through the huge office window. It <SHATTERS> spectacularly!

LONG SHOT—The Mosquito Man falls, kicking and flailing.

> MR. CLISBY
> YEEEEAAAAAaaaaaahhh! . . .

ON TONY—resting on all fours. His valiant effort has left him exhausted. He rolls onto his back, relieved.

> TONY
> (panting)
> At last . . . it's over.

<SFX: THE WHINE OF WINGS!>

> MR. CLISBY (O.S.)
> *Is* it now?

Tony rolls over to see . . .

TONY'S POV—The Mosquito Man is hovering just ten feet away. He has sprouted WINGS!

Mr. Smith let the script slip through his sweaty

fingers and onto the decorator rug. He was shaken; his heart pounded quickly like the beat of hummingbird wings. "This kid's got some imagination," gasped the film executive. He sat back in his chair, contemplating his options.

If he didn't get to this kid first, some other studio might. Universal loved films in this teenage vein; they'd buy it for Spielberg, who'd make it into a blockbuster! *Millions of people* would see the film! His own superiors wouldn't like that—they'd be out for blood then.

Smith made his decision.

His fingers skittered to the call button again. "Ms. Jones—get our young Shakespeare on the phone, if you can."

The metallized buzz of Ms. Jones words came back with a hint of surprise. "The high schooler?"

"That's right." Smith retrieved the fallen manuscript and read the title page again. "Name's Jeffrey Howard. Goes to school in North Hollywood. Should be easy to get hold of."

He flipped to the last few pages of the screenplay. "Oh, and I think I'll have an early lunch. I'm kinda hungry."

"Yes, Mr. Smith."

EXTERIOR—OUTSIDE MOTHERSHIP—NIGHT

CLOSE-UP—of a Motocross helmet: head covered, face covered, only Tony's eyes can be seen through the slits of his mask.

TONY
Okay—

PULL BACK TO REVEAL:

Tony in full riding gear, sitting astride his BMX bike like the Lone Ranger on Silver. A KNAPSACK bulging with items is strapped to his back; a PLUMBER'S HELPER has been clamped to his handlebars, punching forward like a lance.

TONY (CONT'D)
—here we go. . . .

IN THE FOREGROUND can be seen the MOTH-ERSHIP, lights glowing, boarding ramp lowered. Tony begins pedaling for all he's worth, speeding forward, up the ramp and into the bowels of the enemy craft.

TONY (O.S.)
Yeeeiiiiaaaaaaaaa!!!

QUICK CUT TO:

INTERIOR—MOTHERSHIP

MOSQUITO MEN are everywhere, scurrying about, preparing for lift-off: pressing buttons, moving crates full of warm-blooded Earth creatures, etc. It looks like a beehive!!! <SFX: INTENSE BUZZING>

TONY (CONT'D)
Yeeeiiiaaaaa!!!

ON TONY—Like a blazing streak he rockets into the ship. Taken by surprise, the Mosquito Men are caught in a state of confusion.

ANOTHER ANGLE—Tony jams on his *front* brake, does a "forward" wheelie, and pirouettes—smacking two Mosquito Men upside the head with his back tire. <SFX: HARD SMACKS!!>

ON MOSQUITO MEN—as they go down for the count.

TONY
Two points!!

ON TRIO OF MOSQUITO MEN—as they rush toward Tony, multi-arms clutching for his throat.

MOSQUITO MEN
<infuriated buzzing>

TONY—reaches into his knapsack and pulls out . . . a D-CON FOGGER (one of those bug-killing spray bombs). He yanks the cap off and detonates it like a grenade, under—

TONY
Take a hit of this, suckers!

THE MOSQUITO MEN—are doused with a fog of insecticide. They <SCREAM> in pain and shrivel up, limp, falling to the floor.

ON TONY

TONY
<laughs>
(notices more Mosquito Men charging)
Uh-oh! Wheels, don't fail me now.

He pedals like a madman, zooming just past the outstretched claws of the aliens.

CLOSE—A CLAW glances off Tony's helmet, leaving a ragged gash.

BACK ON TONY—FOLLOWING—as he speeds away from his pursuers and up into the upper parts of the ship. He hangs a right down a side corridor and runs right smack-dab into—

TONY
Bug boys!!!

TONY'S POINT OF VIEW—Two Mosquito Men swoop down on him, wings <HUMMING>!!!

REVERSE ANGLE—WIDE—Tony jumps his bike into the air and bails out, kicking the two-wheeler forward!!! The bike flies into the Mosquito Men <SFX: SQUISH> knocking them out of the air.

TONY—rolls to his feet and dashes through a side door.

TONY
Better duck in here.

INTERIOR—BREEDING ROOM

The room is one huge STAGNANT POOL about three

feet deep! The water's dark green, overgrown with SCUM, and smells like a zookeeper's heel.

TONY
Yeeuuuk!! Must be E.T's bathroom.

With true bravery, Tony steels himself and takes a step into the muck. <SQUELCHING SFX> as Tony slushes through the gunge to a door at the far side of the pool.

WATER LEVEL POV—RIPPLES begin beneath the surface of the pool. LEPROUS WHITE SHAPES speed through the water!!!

WIDER—<A BUZZING MEWLING> begins and a swarm of MOSQUITO MEN LARVAE wriggle toward Tony, nipping at his legs. [These things are pale, white, wormlike, undulating, disgusting squirmies about two feet long, with little sucker mouths each filled with a circular row of teeth.]

TONY
Jeez!!!

ANOTHER ANGLE—Tony frantically begins slapping the larvae from his legs. They come away, ripping his jeans and swallowing the material. Streaks of blood appear on the boy's legs. He begins running toward the far door, more and more larvae chasing him, feeding on his skin!!

> TONY
> (frantic)
> Get off! Get off!!!

TIGHT—Tony's sweating! Fear is etched on his face.

<SPLASH!!!> Tony falls!

> TONY
> Nooooo!!!

CLOSE—THE LARVAE move in for the kill!!! In the
nick of time, Tony violently wrenches his knapsack
open and pulls out . . .

CLOSE-UP—a CAN OF DRĀNO!!! He dumps the
contents in the pool, which begins BUBBLING and
HISSING!!!

ON LARVAE—they <SQUEAL IN PAIN> and begin
writhing and tearing at themselves!!!

TONY scrambles to his feet and rushes to the exit
door. His legs are bare from the knees down and
bleeding.

> TONY
> Made it!!

ON POOL—larvae are all floating on the surface,
motionless, bloated, dead. It's a disgusting sight.

> CUT TO:

INTERIOR—ENGINE ROOM

This place looks like the boiler room of the *Titanic*,
only high tech. Knobs, gadgets, tubes, glowing thing-

ies, buzzing hums, zapping electricity, etc. In the center of the room is a well-like funnel that is luminescing like a supernova. It is the MAIN REACTOR.

PAN AROUND ROOM—a couple of Mosquito Men are busy with their takeoff procedures. HALT PAN on shadowy corner: Tony is hiding in it.

>TONY
>(whispering to self)
>Boy, I'm sure glad I saved this
>from last Fourth of July. . . .

CLOSE—out of his pocket he pulls an M-80!!! (A very *large* firecracker.)

WIDER—TONY kisses the M-80 and tries to light it. Unfortunately, his Bic doesn't flick.

>TONY
>C'mon!

Flicks it again. Nothing.

CLOSE—Bic—still nothing, under—

>TONY (O.S.)
>C'mon! C'mon!!!

It lights!

> TONY
> Banzai!!!!

Tony races out to the Reactor Well and, before the surprised Mosquito Men can react, lobs his M-80 into the depths . . .

> TONY
> (to Mosquito Men)
> Hope you get a bang out of it.

. . . and races out of the room.

HOLD ON REACTOR WELL—an <EXPLOSION> rings out, starting a chain reaction!!! The alien technicians are fried by SHORTING WIRES—<ELECTRICAL SFX>.

> MOSQUITO TECHNICIANS
> <buzzy screams>

> CUT TO:

INTERIOR—CORRIDORS

Tony races down the passageways, which are beginning to shake, rattle, and roll. ARCING SPARKS are sizzling everywhere. It's Dante's *Inferno*. The floors buckle beneath his feet, as the ship heaves and EXPLOSION AFTER EXPLOSION rips her up. Mosquito Men are <SCREAMING> and being crushed by falling girders. [NOTE: Like the end of *Aliens*]

ON TONY—He dodges a falling piece of metal and jumps a pile of Mosquito Men.

TONY
Just a little farther.

TONY'S POV—The exit ramp of the mothership beckons. Freedom is only ten yards away, and there are no Mosquito Men in sight.

CLISBY (O.S.)
You're not leaving the party so
soon, are you?

UP SHOT—a <BUZZING> grows and Clisby (in Mosquito Man form) unfolds from the ceiling and hangs upside-down. SIX CLAWS shoot out and grab Tony, lifting him into the air and slamming him against the wall.

TONY
Let go, Clisby! Your whole
ship's gonna blow!

The alien forces the boy's head sideways, exposing the right ear.

MR. CLISBY
Perhaps . . . but not before I suck
your brains out first.

TONY'S POV—as Clisby's proboscis inches toward Tony's ear . . .

WIDER—Tony clutches desperately at the evil alien's snout, but it pushes closer and closer and closer.

TONY grabs a CAN OF RAID from his knapsack, stuffs the nozzle up Clisby's nose, and sprays!!!
<SFX: FSSSSTT!>

> TONY
> Suck *this*, needle nose!!!

Clisby <CHOKES, SPUTTERS> and dies!!!

> CUT TO:

EXTERIOR—MOTHERSHIP

Tony races out of the ship just as it FIREBALLS into oblivion!!! It's Hiroshima and the Fourth of July all rolled into one!!!

ON TONY—battered and smudged, but alive!!

> TONY
> I made it. . . .
> (yells for joy)
> I made it!!!!

WIDE—as the embered remains of the alien ship float down, Tony heads for home, wearing a grin that only heroes know. He's saved the world from the dreaded Mosquito Men of Maslog-5.

> FADE OUT.

> THE END

___

Smith held the script thoughtfully to his cheek, caressing his skin with the paper. "Quite an imagination. . . ."

The shrill whine of the intercom broke Smith's reverie. "I have Jeffrey Howard on the line, Mr. Smith," pipped Ms. Jones. "He seems terribly excited."

Smith snatched up the phone. "Jeffrey! A plea-sure . . ." A buzz of excitement roared from the re-ceiver. "Whoa! Slow down, son! Yes, I thought your script showed a great deal of creativity."

The receiver chattered again. Mr. Smith smiled.

"Of course I'm interested, Jeff. In fact, maybe you'd like to come to my office. We'll talk about your future!" A further burst of excitement from the other end of the line. "Yes, today would be just fine by me. How about noon?" A pause. "We'll . . . *do lunch.*"

As the movie producer hung up, a disgusting, stretching sound ripped through the room. His face elongated. His skin tore. His jacket slit open, and the whine of wings was heard.

Ms. Jones peeked her head in and smiled. Nothing to worry about; Mr. Smith was simply changing for lunch.

A note from the authors: Film scripts have a language all their own, and many of the terms may be unfamiliar to the reader. So here are a few definitions to help the story move smoothly.

CLOSE: Close-up shot.

CROSS-DISSOLVE TO: The new scene overlaps old one.

CUT TO: Jump to the next scene.

ESTABLISHING SHOT: A camera angle (usually a LONG SHOT) that establishes where the scene is taking place (for example, the exterior of a factory at dusk).

FADE IN: The transition from a black screen to the first image.

FADE OUT: The reverse of fade in.

HOLD ON: Stop a pan or push to call audience's attention to a particular object or person.

LONG SHOT: Put the camera a long way from the action.

MEDIUM SHOT: Put the camera in the middle distance.

O.S.: Off screen.

PAN OVER or PAN ACROSS: Rotate the camera slowly from one subject to another.

POV: Point of view--as if seen from that character's (or object's) angle.

PUSH IN or PUSH TIGHT: Zoom in to get closer.

REVERSE ANGLE: Opposite of previous shot.

SFX: Sound effects.

TRACK ON: follow the movements of a character.

TWO-SHOT: Two characters in shot.

UP SHOT: Angle of shot, looking upward.

WIPE TO: An old scene is wiped off the screen to reveal a new one.

Buddy Morris, Alias Fat Man

by Melissa Mia Hall

Diets stink. Buddy Morris hated diets. He hated artificial sweeteners, fake butter, diet colas, and salads. But he was tired of being "tubby bubby," something his bratty sister Charla delighted in calling him, or "pigola commoda," a weirdo name his brother Frank, now thankfully away at college, used to call him.

At fourteen, Buddy Morris had decided to slim down, once and for all. No more apple danish, potato chips, candy bars, french fries, and no more—as hard as it might be—*Cockydoodledoos*. *Cockydoodledoos* was a honey and sugar-coated cereal with chocolate chips, raisins, and chewy bits of toffee that Buddy adored, worshiped, and prayed to practically every morning of his life. He loved it and now, for over six weeks, he had gone without it. He had lost almost twenty pounds.

Everyone had noticed. Charla had not called him "tubby bubby" for a whole week. At school, Noreena Brown had actually smiled at him in front of superjock Roy Swanson and had said, oh sweet love—"Hi, Bud. You sure are looking good these days."

Yep—he smiled at his image in the bathroom mirror—those old chipmunk cheeks were definitely collapsing. His jeans were getting baggy too. He sighed blissfully. By the time Thanksgiving came around, he would be down two whole sizes. He pictured himself at Macy's picking out a whole new wardrobe. He pictured Noreena impulsively kissing him in the school cafeteria with the entire football team watching. She'd swoon at his feet, well, maybe not, maybe she'd just impulsively kiss him on the cheek and whisper in his ear, "Bud, I just can't help myself, I think I'm in love with you—" That's it. Bud the stud.

"Buddy? Buddy—can you go with me to the store today?"

Buddy's smile froze on his lips. Then it shrank to a thin line.

"The supermarket?"

"I *need* your help. I've got the committee meeting in two hours. I wouldn't ask you to go but you're such a help. Please?"

"Mom—" Buddy had to get out of going to Golden Savers. It was a dangerous place full of temptations. "I've got homework."

"You told me you did your homework." She looked at her watch. "Just do me this favor, okay? We're wasting time."

"Well, okay, I guess so."

"Could you change your shirt before we go?"

Buddy looked down at the faded blue "Fat Man" T-shirt Frank had given him for his birthday a couple of years ago. He hadn't done it to be mean. Buddy actually called himself "Fat Man." It was a routine he'd done for ages—he'd go "dadadadadadadada—fat man" to the *Bat Man* theme song. It always got a laugh. But it was true, ever since he'd started losing weight, the t-shirt had lost some of its original appeal. "I'll change," Buddy said, heading for his bedroom.

His mother watched him anxiously. "Hurry up, okay, the auxiliary waits for no one."

Mrs. Connie Morris propped the frozen-food door open with one shoulder and examined the rainbow of ice cream items. "Are you sure you don't want some frozen yogurt, Buddy, or at least some chocolate ice milk?"

"Mom, it says right there on the glass: 'Please make your selection before opening the door.' See how you're fogging the glass up?"

"Oh." Connie grabbed a quart of chocolate-chip ice cream and slammed the door. She sighed as Buddy wedged some cartons of low-fat unfrozen yogurt next to the gallon of skim milk and the tub of Slim Jim cottage cheese. "Lord, Buddy, it's getting to where you scare me."

"I'm just thinking nutritionally now, like you've been trying to teach me to do for years." Buddy rearranged the groceries so the water-packed tuna-fish cans wouldn't bruise the bananas.

"It's not that I mind, honey, it's just that I don't want you to go overboard." Together they trundled the cart through the bakery-delicatessen area, bravely ignoring the boxes of iced brownies, neatly packaged cheesecakes, ready-made pizza, and worse, the free samples of Vermont cheddar cheese and imported sausage. "I'm really proud of how you're succeeding with this diet—"

"No, Mom, it's not a *diet*, it's like my nutritional way of thinking—common sense, you know?"

"But you're losing weight so fast. It's like I'm losing my baby—like that—before my eyes." She snapped a finger and grinned.

"Mom—" Buddy rolled his eyes. "I'm not a baby, for crying out loud." He looked around to see if anyone had heard her. With his luck, old Roy boy would be in the next aisle thumbing through *Sports Illustrated.*

"I'm sorry." Connie stopped the cart suddenly. She stared mindlessly toward the cosmetics aisle. "What was it I had to get?"

Buddy glowered at the crowded cart. He didn't like being nutritional, but since he'd come this far, he was going all the way. He was going to be so good-looking that by the time Christmas came around, Noreena would be asking Santa to put old Bud Morris in her stocking. Buddy stunned even himself with his wit sometimes. His glower turned into a sloppy grin. Noreena had long golden legs and strawberry-blond hair, big brown eyes. His sister called her an autumn blonde. Noreena was a cheerleader. Noreena was the most beautiful girl in the whole school.

Buddy stood in the front of the Cover Girl display. There was a mirror to the left of it. He caught his expression. A way to go, Buddy boy, before you can come on like Mark Harmon or even Michael J. Fox. As his granddad would say, "a fur piece to go." At least ten pounds. His mother rifled through the eyeshadow compacts. Buddy tried to be cool about it, but he began to fidget—didn't she have some sort of big-deal meeting to get to?

Connie noticed. "Say, I forgot to get the cereal, Buddy—would you go get it? And don't forget instant oatmeal for Dad and my raisin bran."

"What brand?"

"I don't care; we don't have any cereal coupons this week."

"Okay."

Buddy headed off without the cart. His Nikes plopped down with a sudden lethargic heaviness. He'd entered the store with such courage and self-righteous fervor. Now every aisle seemed loaded with temptation. And he was hungry. Lord, he was *so* hungry. Potato chips, onion dip, chocolate. Every step he took brought him closer to the cereal aisle. *Cockydoodledoos.* Here he was, fourteen, almost fifteen, and still he had a craving for a childish cereal with a bird on it that was a cross between the Kellogg's rooster and Godzilla. He could taste the cereal in his mouth, *crunch-crunch-yum.* With lots of milk, *whole* milk, and an extra dollop of sugar, not Nutrasweet.

As last he arrived at the cereal aisle. He drove himself directly to the instant oatmeal, tucked it under his arm, and then turned toward the first raisin bran he could find, avoiding the stacks of *Cocky-*

doodledoos. Naturally, it was on sale. He felt his cheeks flush and perspiration break out on his neck. Maybe if he read the ingredients again just to make sure it was nutritionally unsound. Buddy sighed. He definitely knew there were more than three hundred calories per serving. A lot more.

But he'd lost twenty pounds. He could eat it without milk. *Cockydoodledoos* were crunchier without milk and almost as good. Now the perspiration turned into plain old sweat, and it dripped down from his armpits.

An elderly woman carefully maneuvered her cart around him. Buddy stepped aside. He lost his balance and knocked a box of *Cockydoodledoos* onto the floor. It seemed to glow. He *had* to pick it up. What if the old lady came back and ran into it, toppling her cart or something? She could break a hip, all due to his negligence. The box of *Cockydoodledoos* joined his armload of more nutritional offerings. Buddy felt a surge of relief. It wasn't important. He was in control, *Noreenally* speaking, he chortled to himself. Yep.

At the check-out counter, Connie noticed the *Cockydoodledoos* but didn't say anything. Instead she read the headlines on the *National Enquirer* and handed the coupons to the cashier, avoiding eye contact with Buddy. She waited till they got out to the car.

"You know, Buddy, I thought that was a good idea, getting that cereal. For a while there I was getting worried."

"I'm still going to stick to the weight thing—I mean, I'm going to do it. I'm gonna get"—his next words died on his lips—"really good-looking, handsome even." It sounded so dumb.

"Oh, Buddy." Connie put on her seat belt and put the key in the ignition. "Listen to me—let me tell you a story about your dad and how he quit smoking. They say you can go cold turkey. Well, maybe some people can, but your dad couldn't. He did it. Eventually. So don't get in such a rush—what's the hurry? You want to get it off and keep it off. I'd hate to see you become a diet yo-yo like my aunt Caroline." She reached over with one hand and mussed his hair. "Okay, baby?"

Buddy cringed.

"Sorry, again," Connie said. "You're my big handsome son, not my baby, and I'm very proud of you, Buddy."

"Thanks, Mom." He was radical, bad, premium cool. "Only from now on, could you call me Bud?" Bud-lite. That's right. He fiddled with the radio station till he found a blast of Bruce Springsteen.

"Okay, Bud." she smiled.

Five pounds later and he had yet to crack open that box of *Cockydoodledoos*. In another week he could just drop them in the garbage can; they'd be too stale to eat. But maybe he'd just have a handful, a little snack. It had been a difficult day at school. Real difficult. Like so difficult he'd wanted to hang himself in his locker or at least hide in there till the last period of the day was over. Noreena and Roy had been telling everyone they were officially an item: item as in steady teddy, peanut butter and jelly, and Bud, you're a crud.

He looked down at his tight new stone-washed jeans. He ran his fingers through his expertly styled hair. "And I look so good." But it didn't matter.

He got one of Charla's Cokes (nondiet) and fished around for a clean bowl. He found a spoon, then put it away. He didn't need a bowl or a spoon. He got the cereal out of the cabinet and carefully opened it. The aroma of *Cockydoodledoos* filled his nostrils. It was light, fresh, tasty. He reached into the box and grabbed a handful of cereal and jammed it in his mouth. It tasted wonderful. He'd forgotten how good it really was, even without milk. Then he felt a terrible guilt. He folded the foil wrapper up tightly and closed the box. It sat there on the kitchen table, bright and sassy, the *Cockydoodledoo* monster bird laughing at him silently. He swallowed a huge gulp of Coke.

The phone rang and Bud jumped to answer it. Paul. "Can I come over?" Bud begged him.

They ordered in a large pizza with everything on it. They ate that, then they ate a bag of chips with a tub of onion dip. After that, they split an apple pie. After that, they ate a couple of candy bars. Bud thought he was going to die, he was so full, but he was happy. They went down to the video-rental place and got a couple of John Hughes movies and then discussed everything but girls. Until it was time for Bud to go home.

Paul rewound the last cassette and Bud grabbed his pack, loaded down with some Stephen King paperbacks Paul had loaned him.

"So what're you doing for Thanksgiving?"

"Oh, the usual scene over at Grandma's—what about you?"

"Oh, the usual."

"You okay?"

"Sure, but I don't think I'll ever eat again."

Paul, perpetually stick thin, suddenly looked embarrassed. "Sorry if I nuked your diet."

"It's okay as long as I don't make it a habit." But it wasn't okay. Bud felt nauseous even though he'd taken some antacid. "I haven't eaten that much for days. Months."

"Yeah." Paul popped the cassette out of the VCR and put it back in its case. "Say, about Noreena. You know about her and that limp-brain Roy—"

"Sure." Bud started edging toward the front door. It was getting late and he was tired.

"That's why, isn't it?"

"Why what?" Bud muttered. Sometimes Paul was as nosy as Charla.

"Noreena. You've been getting thin for Noreena."

"Get out of here." Bud made it to the porch, but Paul was right after him like an over-eager beagle.

They stood outside under the yellow porch light.

"Women."

"Yeah."

"I wouldn't do anything for that stuffed-shirt priss butt. And that name—*Noreena*? And she thinks she's better than—" Paul went silent for a moment. "Christie Brinkley?"

"Let it go," Bud said, his heart breaking.

"Get outta here," Paul said, whacking his best friend a good one. "Nerdo Fat Man—"

Bud did his Fat Man routine briefly, without his old gusto, but it still made them both smile. Then he took off on his ten speed.

Some nights last forever, especially ones when you can't sleep. At all. Buddy kept checking the clock, and a couple of times saw the green digits change right before his eyes. He went to the bathroom a lot. He burped, tossed, turned, burned. For Noreena.

It was just a crush. He'd get over it. He'd live. Marsha Henry had told Janet Smith that he'd really changed, that he was better than cute. Almost handsome. Roy was handsome. Blond hair, blue eyes, and big shoulders. Bud's shoulders were too narrow. He'd made his mom buy him a jacket with padded shoulders. He pushed the sleeves up and he looked great in it. Even Charla had said he was getting really good-looking, taller, smarter-looking. Good, smart, almost handsome. "I bet someday you'll be voted the Boy Most Likely to Succeed," his computer teacher had told him. "I *want* to be Most Handsome," Bud said, to his pillow.

He needed to sleep; tomorrow was Thanksgiving. He had to sleep. He squinched his eyes shut and tried to sleep. But he couldn't stop thinking about Noreena, and suddenly it was after three A.M., then four A.M., and a horrendously savage hunger pang made him sit bolt up in bed. He'd never been so hungry in his life. He had to eat. He grabbed his aching, ever-so-hollow stomach and knew he had to fill it with some *Cockydoodledoos*. With milk. They had only skim milk in the house—white-tinted water. But it would have to do.

He grabbed his voluminous terry-cloth robe and wrapped up in it. The house was so cold. He padded quietly into the kitchen. The oven light was on. It was freezing in the kitchen. The refrigerator door was ajar. Maybe Dad? Charla? As he approached it, the door swung open wider, as if an invisible hand were responsible, a big fat white hand. His hand.

Maybe he wasn't hungry after all.

Oh, but he was. Another hunger pang swiped him in the gut, and he staggered toward the refrigerator. The door practically came off its hinges, swinging open so wide that the milk seemed to be tipping over, about to spill onto the blue tiles.

He reached out and picked up the jug. Whole milk. Mom had been to the store. He noticed there was an awful lot of food in the refrigerator, preparations for Thanksgiving: cranberry sauce; Jell-O salad; broccoli-rice casserole; a roll of sausage; a ton of cheese, including Vermont cheddar; a chocolate-cream pie with bits of chocolate sprinkled over the whipped cream.

Bud shut the refrigerator and set the milk on the

table. The turkey was already cooking. That's why the oven light was on. He could smell the strong turkey smell. The oven door was open slightly. He moved to shut it, and the oven door pushed back at his touch. He jumped back. The door slammed shut. Forget that. Space City. He was tired, that's all.

He turned around and headed for the cereal cabinet. The door was open, and the *Cockydoodledoo* bird leered up at him, its beak dripping milk. And teeth? Bud shook his head and grabbed the box anyway. He was too hungry to care. He opened the box shakily and started eating with trembling hands. He kept eating and eating, but he couldn't taste anything. It seemed so pointless. He put the box down and turned to go back to bed. Then the claws of the bird reached around him from the back and grabbed him so tightly he couldn't breathe. He tried to scream, but the cereal was in his mouth. The scream came out a strangled gurgle, and then he spat out bits of *Cockydoodledoo* everywhere. The claws clutched him around the middle, tighter and tighter, practically cutting him in two. They were claws painted an electric pink. It hurt so bad.

"Bud the Stud," a soft voice cackled in his ear.

"Noreena?" Bud cried.

"Rise and shine, Bud, it's Turkey day!" Charla poked at the swaddled form in the tangled bedclothes. Buddy opened one bleary eye and gratefully sat up on his pillow. Just like in the movies—it had all been a bad dream.

Charla smiled at her brother. "Geez, Fat Man, pretty soon you're going to have to beat off all the girls with a stick."

Bud got out of bed and stared at the mirror. "I am kinda handsome, aren't I?" He struck a beefcake pose that made Charla gag, but he could see her eyes, see that she agreed, and it scared him. Charla ran out of the room after making a semiobscene gesture, and Bud continued to stare at himself. Then he took off the ragged football jersey he slept in and saw the scabby claw marks around his middle.

"*Cockydoodledoo,*" he sighed.

The Scarlet *Batling*

by Addie Lacoe

Bugan stiffened as Amanda turned in at the native Filipino arts shop.

"I need you," Amanda urged. "What if they only speak Tagalog?"

This was Bugan's first week working as a live-in house girl for Mr. Armstrong and his daughter. A thousand pesos, or about fifty dollars, a month seemed like a fortune compared to what she could earn weaving in the mountain barrios of northern Luzon. But she hadn't anticipated that "doing whatever needs to be done" would include shepherding Amanda through the streets of Manila, carrying her bags and enduring a place like this. Bugan's mother had warned her against the godless American *kandangyan*, but the Armstrongs had been nice enough—till now.

"What's this?" Amanda picked up a carved wooden figure, seated, with his elbows on his knees.

"*Hipag*," the shopkeeper replied.

"A war deity," Bugan translated.

"I speak English," the man interrupted. "The Igorots, the 'mountain people,' smear it with blood to summon the god it represents."

Amanda shivered. "That's grotesque."

"But fascinating," the man said. "And exotic, no?"

Amanda's attention was drawn to another figure—this one carved from soapstone, a man and a god. "And that?"

"A *pili*," he said. "It guards a man's property and 'bites' his enemy. Very rare. Very quaint, yes?"

Bugan didn't think her people's customs were grotesque or exotic or quaint, and they were hardly as simple as the man implied, but Bugan didn't want to argue. She wanted *out*. These were not contented, well-fed, and revered gods. She could feel their spirits' anger at being put on display and sold like so many coconuts.

The shop was full of tourist items too—key chains, trinket boxes, oversized ladles—but among the colorful baskets and the patterned fabrics of woven *dami*, or beaten bark, there were genuine relics, shiny with use—a pair of *bulul* from an Ifugao granary and a *tinagtagu* from the Kankanay tribe. It was not wise to treat these with disrespect nor stay too long in their presence without making obeisance.

"May I see those?" Amanda pointed to the jewelry case. "The long red earrings with the slivers of mother-of-pearl."

The proprietor brought them out and Amanda held them, scarlet and iridescent, swishing and flashing, against her blond hair. "They're beautiful." She looked to Bugan. "What do you think?"

Bugan dropped the bag she had been carrying. The assortment of gifts Amanda had bought to send back to America spilled onto the dirty red concrete floor.

"For goodness' sake. Be *careful*, Bugan."

It took Bugan a moment to recover herself enough to bend down and gather up the treasures. "I'm sorry, Missy." Her voice broke in a squeak.

"No real harm done." Amanda turned back to the earrings, removing the studs she had been wearing and inserting the first of the new pair. "I love them," she said. "They're so unusual. How much?"

"Twenty-five hundred pesos," the man said. "For you—one hundred twenty American dollars."

Bugan fought down the urge to bolt from the place. She didn't want to lose her job by offending her employer. "The earrings, Missy." Bugan tried to sound calm. "These are *men's* ear pendants."

Amanda laughed. "They're not Daddy's color." Amanda was already putting on the second earring. "But twenty-five hundred is a lot."

Bugan *had* to make her understand. "These are Ilongot *batling*."

"That's right," the dealer said. "You'll believe me, then, when I tell you they're authentic—probably hundreds of years old. You'll not soon find such a bargain elsewhere." He held up a hand mirror.

Amanda shook her head, watching the earrings dance and sparkle in the light.

Bugan could see she would have to be blunt. "They're head-hunting trophies."

"Eeew!" Amanda nearly threw the earrings to the counter in her haste to get them off.

But the proprietor was not put off so easily. "Think

of what a conversation piece they'll be. It's not as if they were made out of anything human, after all. They're only hornbill and shell. Very skillfully made."

Amanda still cringed, repulsed by what Bugan had said. But the man's words held her. She didn't leave the shop.

"They summon the *amet*," Bugan insisted, "the spirit of the beheaded. And they are the focus point for all their previous owners."

"That's nothing but superstition," the man taunted. "Only the natives believe such nonsense—the ones you see picnicking in the graveyard, leaving crumbs for the ghosts."

"I'm not superstitious," Amanda retorted.

Bugan could see her weakening. "The Ilongot were the last to give up head-hunting," she said. "This spirit might be newly dead and still very angry. Or else this man bought them from *grave robbers*."

"Are you Ilongot?" The proprietor addressed Bugan directly for the first time.

"No." She stood straighter in response to his intimidating stare. "I am Ifugao," she said proudly. Couldn't he tell one tribe from another?

"Then you don't know."

Bugan felt shamed. There were many things she did not know, but she had grown up knowing about *this*.

The dealer continued. "An Ilongot woman wouldn't marry a man who didn't own a pair of *batling*. They are very lucky."

He lies, Bugan thought. The *batling* represented

concentrated anger and focused energy. Perhaps they were lucky for an Ilongot warrior, but anger was not an auspicious influence to bring to the hearth of an American, a traditional Ilongot enemy. Still, she held her peace.

Amanda touched an earring. "They *are* gorgeous," she said.

"And only twenty-*three* hundred pesos." The shopkeeper grinned. His long, betel-stained teeth were a crude parody of the *batling*.

Amanda let him put the earrings back in her ears.

"You'll entertain your friends with these foolish fables," he said.

Amanda took out her wallet.

To Bugan the proprietor said, "I'll give you fifteen hundred pesos for your bracelets."

Bugan glowered at him. She could never give up the powerful protective jewelry that had belonged to generations of her ancestors. Their spirits hovered near their earthly possessions, and she would surely need their help and that of the whole host of Ifugao gods. She *must* persuade Amanda to get rid of the damnable *batling* before they could destroy the entire family.

Despite Bugan's increased chicken blood and rice sacrifices, dinner was a total disaster. Up till now she had received nothing but delighted compliments for her meals, strange though they were to her own taste. But this time Mr. Armstrong pushed his plate away after the first two bites.

His voice was controlled. "I know it's hard, Bugan,

but if you'll follow my mother's recipes exactly and not substitute your native ingredients, the dumplings won't be so gummy. The gravy should be thicker than this, and the corn bread should hold together when it's cut."

He didn't raise his voice, but his words cut Bugan. She was a *good* cook. Everyone said so. Surely the spirits had sabotaged her meal. And these Americans had no taste, anyway. Neither Mr. Armstrong nor Amanda would even *try* the purple-yam ice cream, which was the only dish that Bugan was positive had turned out the way it was supposed to. "I will fix you something else." Bugan's cheeks burned with humiliation at her failure.

"I don't have time to wait, now," Mr. Armstrong said. "Amanda and I have to go out tonight."

Bugan took his words as a personal rebuke for dinner's being an hour late. She choked back the impulse to blame Amanda, to blame the earrings. He would not understand any more than Amanda had. "I will try harder tomorrow," she said.

Mr. Armstrong waved away her apology. "Don't worry about it," he said. "It's not a big deal."

Bugan bristled. To her it *was* a "big deal." It was so unfair that he should think the bad dinner was her fault. It was the spirits. Bugan had never before lost her way on the bus or had her pocket picked or had a chicken die before she got it home. She had been in a terrible state before she even *started* to cook. Bugan spent the rest of the evening sobbing in her room.

The earrings' mischief had begun.

* * *

The next morning Bugan's eyes were still red from crying, almost as red as the *batling*. "Please, Missy," she begged, "don't wear the earrings to school today. They're unlucky." She restrained herself from using the word *lethal*. "I can perform rituals to placate the spirits."

Amanda had one of the earrings in place already, as she sat before her vanity mirror. "No," she said. "I told you I'm not superstitious. And after all the compliments I got on them last night, I simply *have* to wear them today."

"You may wear my *lingling-o*." Bugan started to take them from her ears. "They're silver and even more precious to me than my bracelets."

Amanda touched Bugan's hand to stop her. "I know you mean well."

"I don't want to see any harm come to you, Missy." She could hardly bear to see those abominations dangling from Amanda's ears.

"I don't believe the same things you do, Bugan."

"I believe enough for both of us. Let me do this just in case."

Amanda laughed. "You'll dip them in crocodile grease or bat's blood or something even worse."

Bugan felt the heat of anger rise inside. Her village rites were not to be ridiculed. "These are ancient, sacred practices," she said.

"No," Amanda said. "This is the twentieth century. You'll see. When nothing awful happens you'll be glad to be free of those backward traditions."

Bugan clenched her teeth. She was outraged by

Amanda's superior, scoffing tone. She fought back the anger by telling herself that Amanda was not herself. This discord was the *batling's* fault. But what retribution would the spirits exact for such blasphemy? "You must be more careful in what you say."

Amanda smiled. "You worry too much."

Amanda was late getting home from school, and Bugan was almost sick with worry. Without the earrings, the efficacy of her spells was in grave doubt. If she had been nearer to home, she could have enlisted the help of the village priest, with his ritual paraphernalia. A combination of male and female magic was the most powerful kind. But she did what she could. In a thicket she found a small tree fern that she carved into a special *anito*, a household god. She embedded stones in it for eyes and mouth, built a little *komis* shelter for it, and supplied it with a tiny shield and spear and jewelry of white wood before placing it at the end of the Armstrongs' driveway and activating it with the proper ceremonies.

Bugan ran to meet Amanda as she came within sight of the house. But somehow her relief was tainted with anger at Amanda's thoughtlessness in not calling home to say she'd be late.

Amanda sat down at the kitchen table. "See how wrong you were about these earrings being unlucky," she said. "I got so many compliments on them. And my algebra paper came back with an 'A' and there's a new, good-looking Spanish boy in my English class."

Bugan saw little comfort in Amanda's assurances. An angry spirit could hardly have changed the results of a test that had been taken days earlier. Nor could it have foiled the long-planned move of a family to their neighborhood. She offered Amanda a fudge brownie.

Amanda took a bite and made a face.

"Are you late getting home because you stayed to talk to this new boy?" That might be a good omen.

"No, I was helping the biology teacher clean up a mess in the lab. Two specimens fell off the shelf last period—all by themselves—and spilled formaldehyde all over. The whole school stank."

Bugan hardly dared ask, "What were these specimens?"

Amanda wrinkled her nose. "A carabao heart and a pig's brain. Ugh."

Bugan gasped. Both were sacrificial animals. It was as if some spirit had exacted its own offering. "This is very bad, Missy."

"Don't be silly," Amanda insisted. "We got out of a whole period of biology because of it, and I got extra credit for helping out."

"I mean, this shows the great power of the earrings."

Amanda stood up. "I won't listen to nonsense like that," she said. "Coincidences happen all the time." And she walked out without even finishing her brownie.

Bugan picked up the gloppy black thing to throw it away. The nuts protruded in an odd arrangement where Amanda's bites had sculpted it. Bugan looked closer and shrieked. It was the image of her *anito*.

Bugan burned her tree-fern *anito*. It had obviously been weakened and corrupted by the enemy. Any spirit that could mock her idol by creating one of its own in the black dough was obviously a very dangerous and frightening being. Bugan donned the ceremonial clothing she reserved for only the most important occasions—a short jacket and *tapis*. Also a cloth headband and a knotted belt. Next she put on all the protective jewelry she had in addition to her coiled brass bracelets and *lingling-o*: a shell hip ornament, heavy silver-and-feather earrings that hung to her shoulders, and nine necklaces of glass, wood, crystal, and carnelian beads. It was her best armor. She could only hope it would be enough.

That evening Mr. Armstrong broke the news that his company was moving to South Korea because of the unstable political climate in the Philippines. "I'm just as glad to go," he said. "And there's a pay raise in it."

But Amanda was beside herself. "We can't move. I only just started to make new friends. My stateside transcript finally caught up with me. And I don't know a *word* of Korean." She threw herself onto the sofa. "I won't go."

Bugan's own sudden anger at the prospect of losing her job was overshadowed by Amanda's outburst. Bugan could hardly believe her ears. Amanda had seemed like a model daughter till now. She wasn't defiant or rude to her elders like those other "spoiled" rich foreigners.

"Amanda, be reasonable."

"You could find another company here."

The sudden argument flared. Bugan felt herself drawn into the atmosphere of accusations and impossible demands. Mr. Armstrong and Amanda couldn't have been listening to one another. Spirits were flooding their home with contention and anger. Bugan was protected somewhat from the effects by her charmed jewelry, but not entirely. She concentrated on reflecting her own anger back to its source—the *batling*.

If only Mr. Armstrong could be persuaded to burn the earrings as Bugan had burned the *anito*.

"If I may be permitted," she tried. "It is the earrings that are the cause of these problems."

"Bugan, *please*," Mr. Armstrong said.

Amanda only whimpered, fondling the smooth, scarlet bangles. "If Mother were here . . ." she mewled, touching off Mr. Armstrong's defensiveness. The family that, only two days earlier, had seemed so close and understanding seemed to be falling apart.

Bugan felt somehow responsible for these poor, blind foreigners, innocent to the spirit world. There was only one solution. Before the angry spirits could totally possess the Armstrongs, Bugan would have to steal the earrings and dispose of them herself.

She waited in her downstairs bedroom until the sky was propitious. The waning moon didn't rise till after one o'clock in the morning, but Bugan could not have slept if she'd tried. She could hear the earrings rattling in the jewelry box in Amanda's room, directly over her head. It was not her imagination. Many times she had heard her own jewelry rustle in the dark of night. But the sound above her was not the comforting talk of friendly, sympathetic souls.

Bugan stilled her own charms by pressing them tight against her body as she crept up the stairs to Amanda's room, murmuring a prayer. In a sack tucked into her belt she had matches and a ceramic mortar and pestle. When she found the earrings she would first burn them in the mortar, destroying the soft cartilage of the hornbill. Then she would grind the shell to powder and spread the powder and ash, along with the brass fittings, over a hundred square kilometers.

She reached Amanda's door and eased it open. Not even starlight penetrated the drawn curtains. Bugan inched along the opposite wall.

Amanda's breathing was like the soughing of wind through trees, but the jewelry box was still, as if wary of Bugan's approach, silently lying in wait. Bugan touched the bureau top, searching for the wooden box lined with felt in which Amanda kept her peculiar dead jewelry. Bugan had cleaned the room enough times that she knew every square centimeter of it. Her fingers located the case. But she hesitated to open it, for fear that the earrings might blaze forth like the noonday sun. Better to take the whole thing with her and open it in the light. She eased the box off the bureau, holding it gingerly at arm's length.

Then the contents of the box shifted in her hand. *Thump.*

In a panic she almost dropped it. Instead she followed it, as it seemed to sink of its own accord, to the floor.

Thump again.

The springs beneath Amanda's mattress screeched, and Amanda's voice demanded, "Who's there?"

Bugan hugged the floor at the foot of Amanda's bed. She scarcely knew what frightened her more— being discovered by Amanda or being eaten alive by the spirit of the *batling.*

A third thump seemed to come from downstairs. But Bugan was not deceived.

Amanda turned on her bedside lamp, slid from bed, and was out the door to her room before Bugan's eyes had fully adjusted to the brightness.

Now was her chance. In the light the *batling* were vulnerable. She invoked an Ifugao spirit to bind the enemy Ilongot. Then she gingerly opened the box. The scarlet earrings were right on top. Still, she was loath to touch them. She found a rattail comb on Amanda's bureau, lifted the *batling* into her mortar, and pinned them there with the pestle.

In the next room Bugan heard Mr. Armstrong grumble, "It's nothing, Amanda. Go back to bed."

Bugan heard Amanda returning. She had no time. She put the box back in place and hid under the bed.

Amanda rummaged in her closet. Bugan heard her unzip the leather covering from her tennis racket and swing it, whistling through the air. Then Amanda turned out the light and tiptoed out.

In the darkness, again, the *batling* made a new, more sinister scratching sound, like rats.

Bugan scraped her back along the springs in her frantic escape from under the bed. She felt two of her necklaces catch and snap. Beads clattered to the floor behind her as she scrambled into the protective moonlight.

Fury welled up in Bugan. The *batling* had killed her ancestral jewelry. Their spirits seemed to scatter in the air, even as the beads rolled across the floor and fell through the cracks between the planks.

Bugan forced herself to breathe deeply, focusing her energy and her reason for the confrontation. She wanted nothing more than to give up, to put the earrings back and escape. But she had to finish what she had begun. Once aroused, the *batling* would haunt her forever, would hound her to death. She reached for her matches. They were gone. She must have lost them under the bed. But going back into the pitch darkness in search of them was unthinkable. She'd get more in the kitchen.

"Amanda, you were right. I hear noises too." Mr. Armstrong whispered through Amanda's door.

Bugan was trapped. Then she thought of the huge coconut palm growing right next to the house. She stepped to the window and looked down. Bugan had never tried this. The tree seemed dangerously far away as she crouched on the windowsill.

"Amanda," Mr. Armstrong called louder.

Bugan sprang. Her *tapis* split from the stretch of her legs, and she hit the tree with more force than she had expected. Her hip ornament cracked. A semicircle of white shell plummeted through the void like the moon gone mad, taking with it the spirits of a hundred Ifugao women. Bugan's eyes were blinded with grief and fear. She *must* destroy the *batling*. She slid to the ground, the mortar seemingly welded to her hand.

She ducked between the stilts below the house just in time to hear Mr. Armstrong frantically calling from the window above her. "Amanda!"

"Daddy," Amanda called back from within the house.

Bugan ran to the front door. It was locked.

Mr. Armstrong's voice descended the stairs inside, "Amanda, you're safe."

"The Tantocos have a telephone to call the police," Amanda said.

"I'll go," Mr. Armstrong said. "You turn on all the lights and stay inside."

Given time Bugan could have started a fire in a wet rice paddy with nothing but tinder and flint, but matches were faster, and the *batling* were strong. They had already murdered too many of her defensive spirits. Bugan hid beneath the house again and watched Mr. Armstrong leave. She heard Amanda lock the door behind him, then go upstairs and secure her bedroom window.

Bugan *had* to get in. Frustration and anger simmered inside her. Part of her said, "You barely know

these foreign invaders. Save yourself while you can."
Another part said, "If you do not succeed in destroying the *batling*, its evil will roam the earth in search
of you."

Bugan steeled herself against the diversion of her
purpose. She put the mortar through the glass of the
kitchen window.

A scream rang out. It might have been Bugan's
own, but she reached inside, unlocked the window,
and climbed through.

In the kitchen she struck a safety match along the
top of the stove. It went out the moment she plunged
it into the mortar. She tried again and again. A spirit
breath seemed to extinguish the flame each time.

"I have my father's gun," Amanda cried from upstairs. "Whoever you are, I'm warning you."

Please, not yet. Bugan looked to her ancestral gods
for help. The gas stove! It lit, first try. She clamped
the earrings in a pair of tongs and held them over
the flame. The tongs heated up, and Bugan reached
for a towel to wrap around the handles.

"I hear you," Amanda shouted. "I'm coming
down."

Amanda's threat distracted Bugan just enough that
she didn't notice the corner of the towel catch fire
until the flame leaped up and licked her wrist. "Ach!"

She dropped the *batling* into the stove. Green fire
spewed up and engulfed the towel. Bugan tried to
pick it up and throw it in the sink, but the flame blew
back at her and caught the fringe of her jacket.

Bugan struggled to free herself, ripping open the

clasp at her neck. She threw off her clothes, only to realize that in doing so she had spread the fire to the tablecloth. She was losing control.

Smoke brought tears to her eyes. Her throat ached. And she couldn't get her breath. Still she fought back.

"Fire!" It was Amanda's voice. "Bugan! Is that you?"

"Run, Missy," Bugan choked. She swept the tablecloth off the wooden table onto the concrete floor.

Amanda rushed in and threw a pot upside down over the spire of flame ascending from the stove toward the wooden cabinets.

Bugan doused a smoldering stack of newspapers with water, while Amanda pulled the curtains from the window and snuffed out the herbs that hung, dry and brittle, overhead. Both of them were coughing uncontrollably.

The front door opened, and a draft from it ignited a spark in a rattan storage basket. Bugan stomped it out.

Mr. Armstrong and a policeman rushed in only seconds after the draft they had caused. Amanda threw herself into her father's arms, while the policeman helped Bugan stumble outside.

Amanda hugged her father, tears of joy in both their eyes.

As Bugan lay gasping on the lawn, the feathers in her earrings singed, her heart was at peace.

The house smelled of smoke, and the kitchen walls were black with soot. But Bugan cared only for the blood-red glob she found in the bottom of the stove. She pounded what remained of the *batling* into powder and sealed it in a *punamhan* box. The very next day, without even saying good-bye to the Armstrongs, Bugan fled Manila and headed home, scattering pinches of the powder over the miles of trail through Ilongot territory.

For months she worried that the Armstrongs would discover her theft and call the authorities. But when Amanda somehow managed to track her down and write to her from Korea, she had nothing but praise for the way Bugan had saved their home from fire.

And she never even asked what had become of the scarlet *batling.*

Skinning a Wizard

by Mary Frances Zambreno

Jermyn Graves spent the day doing accounts in the outer premises of his aunt's small magic shop and waiting for the customers who didn't come anymore. Just at sunset, his aunt poked her nose in from the back, and sniffed.

"*More* numbers, Jerry? Why, when we've more important things to do?"

He sighed. "Do we? Aunt Merovice, if we don't make some money soon, we'll be behind on *last* month's rent as well as this, and what the sales tax people will say—"

From inside the shop there came a muffled thud. Merovice Graves uttered a shriek and a curse that were not at all muffled, and vanished. Closing the ledger, Jermyn followed her into the back room.

"*Now* what's gone wrong?" he asked tiredly.

His aunt shoved a pallid, puddingy pot into his face.

"Look at this!" she demanded. "Just look! If the crucible hadn't given way, the whole tripod could have gone up."

Coughing, Jermyn batted away clouds of steam. "What—what happened?"

"The precipitate failed because we didn't buy the mercury. I *told* you how fatal it is to try to congeal *athame inferiori* without the best ingredients! If you'd attach a familiar like a *proper* wizard, you'd know!"

Jermyn sighed again, privately this time. He was eighteen, well past the age for a wizard to call a familiar, and it just wasn't going to happen for him. Even Pol, Merovice's own great orange tabby, despised him. The truth was, he took after his mother's side of the family, where magic ran thin in the male line—and only Merovice had never seemed able to accept that.

"We can't afford mercury at the moment," he said, firmly taking the ruined precipitate from her hands and setting it safely on the floor. "We can't afford anything at the moment, and that's the trouble. Ever since you argued with old Foul Weather Fulke and got yourself cursed, we haven't had a client worth the name. We're behind on the rent; we can't afford to pay for fresh supplies; and the larder's been bare of everything but oatmeal and stewed prunes since midweek last. Aunt Merry, what are we going to *do?*"

Merovice drooped visibly.

"Who would have thought the old blowhard had it in him?" she muttered, refusing to look up. "He's always been strictly a weather wizard. I thought maybe he'd rain cats and dogs on the shop for a week, and that would be that. I didn't think he could manage a full-scale curse on my own magic working."

"Well, he did," Jermyn said, grateful that she'd at least gotten off the subject of his own shortcomings. "Come on, Aunt, it isn't that bad."

"It is, and all," she said. "Here's me without a real magic to my soul, scared to work even the simplest spell for fear it will go sideways, and dragging my only kith and kin down into the gutter with me— though, mind you, that wouldn't be necessary if you'd just call a familiar and free the whole of your own magic for use! Fulke wouldn't dare curse both of us, even if he could—it's against guild bylaws to blight a whole family. You could handle him easily if only you—"

"Aunt Merovice, you know I can't!" he said. He might have known she'd circle *back* to the subject. "I've tried. There isn't a cat on the dockside I haven't Spoken, not a litter born I haven't visited. It just doesn't work!"

"You could try again," she said. "It needn't be a cat, you know, though cats are best. If you—"

"No!" His own vehemence startled him, but Merovice could always put him in the wrong. "Fulke is the problem now, not me. Maybe if one of us went to him and apologized—"

"Apologize!" she said loudly. "*Apologize*, is it?"

"Aunt Merry, we can't go on—"

"Oh, and can't we? Listen to me, Jerry-lad. If I've told you once, I've told you twice a day—a sorcerer doesn't apologize. No, there's more ways to skin a wizard than one, and we'll just have to try a few. Now."

Jermyn's mouth went dry. "Aunt, you aren't going to try a Great Magic in your condition!"

"My condition is not to the point at all. Get me my Book."

"But Aunt—"

"Not a word. You're talking of apologizing—I've let this matter drag on too long, it's clear. Past time we got it settled. Go!"

He went. There was no arguing with Merovice in this mood. When he returned with the large, dark volume in his arms, she had her crystal set out on its cloth and took no notice of him. The crystal was blank; no picture.

"Tchah," she said. "Here, Jerry, you do it, and give me the Book. I want to see Fulke."

"But you said—"

"I say lots of things. We need him *here* to make this work, and he isn't likely to come by without an invitation."

Jermyn had worked with his aunt's crystal before, but not often: it required all his attention to feel his way delicately into the spiderweb network of energies, and even more to broadcast an image of the person he wanted to see. But in a few moments the crystal misted over, and the mist solidified into the bearded, bespectacled face of Siegfried Fulke, the weather wizard.

"Who calls?" Fulke asked abruptly. "Oh, it's you, Jermyn. Blast it, you've got a touch like a galumphing elephant. Can't you learn a little restraint?"

"I'm sorry," Jermyn started.

"Never mind him, nephew," Merovice said briskly. "I told you, a wizard never apologizes."

"If you call this snirp a wizard, then your family has fallen farther than I'd thought," Fulke retorted. "I've half a mind—"

"Obviously you have, you mold-eaten excuse for a sorcerer. If you'd ever had more than half a mind, you wouldn't have cursed me illegally."

Fulke looked amused. "I? Curse you illegally? Come now, Merovice, don't judge everyone by your own standards."

"A curse that threatens the bearer's life is illegal, and you know it."

"I haven't threatened your life."

"You have. If this goes on much longer, I'll starve to death, and my nephew with me."

He snorted. "If you truly believe that, then why haven't you called me into Claims Court?"

"Because I don't wish to make a public spectacle of myself for your amusement," she snapped. "Instead, we choose to issue formal challenge."

His eyes sharpened under shaggy brows. "You wouldn't dare."

"I just did," she said.

"I refuse it. Jermyn isn't even a guild member."

"We'll reenter it in the Guild Hall."

"I'll lodge a protest."

"Then we *will* see you in court."

He snorted again. "You're bluffing."

"Care to wager? Jermyn, break contact. Look lively now!"

Caught off-balance, Jermyn almost lost the crystal entirely when he reached back into it. He could hear Fulke's roar of anger as he severed bright connections and quickly shielded the whole.

"That's done it," he said, sighing. "I'll have a headache for a week, and so will he."

"Serves him right. You go take some camomile, and wash your hands and face. And take this back to my room while you're about it."

She shoved the Book at him. Nonplussed, he almost dropped it. "Aren't you going to use it?"

"Power defend us, lad, did you think I was going to work a Great Magic with a curse on me? That was just to worry Fulke—he saw me with my Book in my hands. He'll wonder if something has gone wrong with his curse. He'll want to come see about that for himself, now I've challenged."

"Then what *are* we going to do?"

"Not me, Jermyn. You."

"Me?" he squeaked. "Aunt, I'm not a magic worker!"

"You're not a wizard—yet," she corrected him. "If you weren't a magic worker at all, you wouldn't be able to do anything. Not even wake my crystal."

"Yes, but I haven't got anything like Fulke's power! I'm an herbalist—a bookkeeper!"

"You're my nephew," she told him sternly. "If you'll do as I tell you and use what powers you have, everything will work like—like a guild-sanctioned charm. Now hurry up and put my Book away."

Whatever Merovice had in mind, she didn't seem

to need the crystal anymore, or the bones, or the cauldron. Or her familiar, he hoped, since Pol had deserted the shop on the day the curse was laid. He'd come back when he was good and ready, Merovice declared, but in the meanwhile there was no sense in trying to make a cat share your discomforts. Cats were many things, but willing to live on oatmeal and stewed prunes wasn't one of them.

When Jermyn got back, she had the small saucepan out with water boiling in it. She watched the bubbles carefully as she scattered a few flakes of some brownish powder across them.

"The spell's set in it already," she said calmly. "It's an herbal, none of my own magic involved, so it should work. Breathe through your mouth."

"What? I don't—" The fumes caught him mid word, and he gasped, wishing he'd taken her advice without asking: hydrogen sulfide, essence of rotten eggs, almost made him choke. "Aunt, what is *that* for?"

"For Fulke, of course. What he did to me stinks, and I want the world to know. Besides, there're simpler magics than Great Ones, Jermyn, and not a weather wizard living who can work with his nose blocked up from a bad smell."

"I see." He didn't really, but it didn't feel like the right time to ask for an explanation. "What do you want me to do?"

"To start, move the long mirror over, facing me. That's right, just tilt it so we can see the door in it from here."

They usually kept the full-length scrying mirror facing the door to the outer premises, in case a nosy customer tried to peek in where he shouldn't. Jermyn wrestled the stand into a ninety-degree turn. It was heavy; he got more than one lungful of stink by breathing incautiously as he worked.

"Is this all right?"

She glanced up. "Perfect. You stand to the left, facing it."

Jermyn did as he was told. "Now what do we do?"

"We wait." She sat back and crossed plump hands in front of her. "It shouldn't be long."

"Until what?"

"Until Fulke gets here, of course. I told you he was coming. Now, as soon as you see him in the mirror, I want you to hold his image in your mind exactly as you did when you called him in the crystal. Can you do that?"

"I—I suppose so." A mirror was only another kind of glass, after all. "What good will that do?"

"It will keep him still—freeze him in place, just long enough for me to get my little concoction settled nicely onto him. An herbal takes time, but only compared to a *real* spell. You should be able to hold him long enough."

"What if he brings another curse?"

"I'm counting on it. A heavy magic weighing him down can only help you keep him steady while I fix the spell. When he realizes he can't get the odor off without our help, he'll trade. Just don't be slow when he strikes at me."

"What if I am?"

She fixed him with a piercing eye. "Don't be."

Jermyn swallowed. "Aunt, I still think we should try an apology. . . . "

Merovice ignored him. The hours that followed were among the worst in Jermyn's memory. He and his aunt waited through twilight, past lamplighting, and into full night together, crouched silently in the shadowed room. Every time he tried to say something, an admonitory hiss from his aunt held him still; every time she twitched, he jumped. Then, just as the moon was rising into a sky full of stars outside the room's single window, there was a noise like a hollow *thump* in the shop's outer premises. Jermyn started uncontrollably; the outer door opened and closed.

Merovice shook her head in the moonlight. "Through the front door. Tchah. Just like a weather wizard, no imagination. Why the guild doesn't downgrade them, I'll never know."

The inner door opened slowly, and Jermyn stared at the shining silver expanse of the mirror.

"Aunt," he croaked, "he isn't there!"

"What? But he has to be!"

Something was there, all right. Jermyn could feel the hairs on the back of his neck prickle as the squeaky floorboard just left of the threshold creaked and went quiet under an oddly familiar whisper of sound. Oh, of course!

"He's here, Aunt! He's—"

A flicker of light reached out at him from the emptiness by the doorway. Gasping, he threw himself sideways. His aunt's eyes darted about, searching for something she couldn't see. Wishing with all his heart for even a hint of real magic, Jermyn fell against the edge of the crucible from the day's experiment. With a desperate heave, he hurled its soggy contents straight at the source of the flickering light.

Fulke, the weather wizard, stood there; head, shoulders, and hood of his cloak of invisibility outlined in sticky goo. Merovice cried out in relief, then started to giggle like a girl.

"An eyes-aside! Well *done*, Jermyn. Oh, Fulke, I didn't know you were such a coward."

The wizard glared at her as best he could, and took a long step forward.

"A coward, am I?" he said, a trifle thickly. "You pseudo-Gaelic hedgewitch, I'll show you who is the coward!"

He was right in front of the mirror; Jermyn could see the reflection move as he started to strip off the soiled cape. His free hand was already raised, and before Jermyn could even think about fixing the image into the glass, Merovice tossed the contents of the small saucepan.

It caught the edge of the cape, and spattered all over the floor. Jermyn goggled as Fulke shook out the cape to one side. It was too fast! She knew how awkward he was with the crystal—why hadn't she given him a chance to try?

Fulke sneered. "Is that the best you can do? Really, Merovice."

His hand reached out into empty air, opened, and closed around a spell. Whatever it was, it couldn't be good: Merovice stood frozen. Her eyes went sideways, and Jermyn knew she was waiting for him to do something, but he *couldn't.*

"Remember this, Merry," Fulke said gloatingly. "Remember this, the next time you decide to speak against me in Council."

"No!" Jermyn cried incoherently, and flung himself between the weather wizard and his aunt.

There was a sudden hissing noise, and an even worse odor than that which had emanated from Merovice's saucepan filled the room. Jermyn's chest felt tight, as if he were going to explode. Hardly aware of what he was doing, he gestured with his right hand as he'd seen his aunt do a thousand times. Light streamed from his own fingers, and caught Fulke full in the body. The wizard cried out in shock and staggered backward—to fall directly into the suddenly smoky surface of the tall mirror behind him.

Jermyn stared: in seconds, even the image had dwindled to nothing.

He licked his lips. "Where—where is he?"

"On the other side of the mirror until he finds a glass surface to bring him out again," Merovice said, glowing with delight. "And he's taken a *lovely* smell in with him too. Oh, my very dear, I always knew you could do it if you just put your mind to it!"

"I don't understand. What did I do?"

"Powered Fulke straight out of here, and freed your own magic. Can't you feel it?"

Now that he thought, he did feel different. Sort of—electric. "Where did the stink come from?"

"You did it, of course, when my own little plan went astray. What is it, butyl mercaptan?"

"I don't know."

"Not know? Tosh, boy, no magic's that unconscious. Where's your familiar?"

"My what?"

"Your *familiar*," she repeated, beginning to sound irritated. "I sensed your reaching for one as soon as Fulke raised his hand to me. I knew it would take only some strong emotion for you to Call. Your mother's family was all like that—they needed to *feel* things."

A sudden, dreadful suspicion gripped Jermyn. "My mother's family—Aunt Merovice, did you do this on purpose?"

"Did I do what on purpose?"

"Get into all this trouble with Fulke, of course."

"Me?" She was the picture of sweet innocence. "Why would I do a thing like that?"

"To force me to protect you. Aunt Merry, if you *did*—"

"Really, Jermyn, don't be silly," she said, but she wasn't looking at him, and he didn't believe her. "Would any experienced magic worker risk getting her own abilities cursed? And anyway, it worked."

"Of all the despicable, managing— You might have gotten us both killed! What if I hadn't been able to call?"

"You were. And Fulke wouldn't kill anyone. He's too white-livered."

Jermyn ignored the interruption. "Or what if Fulke's cloak of invisibility had fooled us? It almost did, you know. If I hadn't fallen into the broken crucible—"

"So there, that is a point." She looked thoughtful. "About the eyes-aside, I mean. I wasn't expecting that. Still and all, you handled it, didn't you? I always knew you had good stuff in you. You're my nephew, and there must be *something* of your father, my brother, about you. And it's finished now, lad, so no sense complaining. Where's our new cat? I do hope he gets along with—"

There was a loud, protesting *meow* from the window, where a large orange tomcat stood on the sill.

"Pol!" Merovice said happily. "I knew you'd come back! Poor boy, *how* I've missed you."

Pol was in no mood to be cosseted. He hissed, glaring at the floor in pure feline fury. Bewildered, Jermyn looked down. There, clumsily brushing up against his boots, was a fat, furry creature with a long bushy tail and a pointed nose. It looked a little like a black-and-white cat, but it wasn't. Automatically, he knelt and extended his hand to be sniffed.

"A skunk?" Merovice said, as outraged as her cat. "You can't have a skunk for a familiar!"

"But I do," Jermyn pointed out. Beady black eyes gazed up at him adoringly. "At least, I seem to. Why are you so upset? You said yourself, familiars don't *have* to be cats."

"Of course not, but it's always an animal with some—with some dignity! A bird of prey, or—not a skunk!"

"I think she's rather nice," Jermyn said, sitting cross-legged on the floor to consider the matter. "Useful, too."

"Useful!"

"Well, you saw what she did to Fulke." The skunk set short forepaws on his shin and with some difficulty began to hoist herself into his lap. "Or smelled it, I should say."

"A familiar isn't supposed to be useful."

"Pol catches rats," Jermyn replied. He knew he was being obstreperous, but he didn't care: after all the frustrated years of trying, this was *his* familiar and *his* magic, and he was going to enjoy himself. No matter how he offended Merovice's propriety *or* her plans for him. "I imagine Delia could too. And I don't imagine she'd mind having to eat oatmeal and stewed prunes while she did it, either."

"Delia? Who is Delia?"

"My new familiar." Carefully, he settled the skunk across his knees and began to tickle her under the chin. She liked that.

"But Delia is a lady's name. You can't give it to a skunk."

"I just did," he said.

"Why?"

"Because she looks like a Delia, I suppose. Doesn't she?"

Merovice regarded her nephew helplessly. After a moment, she began to laugh, deep-throated little chuckles that made Pol twitch his tail in annoyance over irrational human behavior.

"Delia, is it?" she said at last, wiping streaming eyes. "Well, I suppose she does look like a Delia, if you say so. And I suppose it's no bad way to get your own back at Pol for all the years he's snooted and scorned you, by making him share houseroom with that—that creature. Yes, and at me, too," she added honestly, "for the way I've bullied you in your own interest. But oh, Jermyn—however are we going to explain her to the neighbors?"

"You'll think of something," he said cheerfully, as happy as he could ever remember being in his life. "You're an experienced magic worker, after all."

Delia just burrowed closer into his stroking hand, and softly began to snore.

Leaves

by Mary K. Whittington

High on a branch of the tallest maple tree, one lone leaf trembled in the autumn wind. Meech willed the yellow scrap to fall, to join the ankle-deep carpet of leaves beneath the trees that crowded old Mrs. Foss' wide front yard. Smiling, he kicked up great rustling swashes of leaves, watched them float groundward. They could stay there forever, for all he cared. Crazy old Mrs. Foss would never make him rake her leaves again. She'd died last month.

Seven autumns he'd worked for her, since he was six and barely able to handle a rake. Mom praised him for being neighborly, but that wasn't the reason he continued to do the job. Mrs. Foss paid him four dollars, more spending money than he ever had at one time.

Still, he dreaded the raking weeks in advance. To begin with, Mrs. Foss always waited until every one of the leaves had fallen, until it took him a whole day to rake them up. Then, she ordered him to come on the one Saturday he'd made plans, like playing football with the guys. Usually, if he could postpone the game until Sunday, he'd wake up to pouring rain.

And no matter what Meech did, Mrs. Foss was never satisfied. From early morning until late afternoon on raking day, she watched him from the corner window of the sprawling gray house, her ugly old housecoat wrapped tightly about her thin shoulders. When she wasn't spying, she yelled at him.

"You, Meacham. Don't forget to rake down by the creek. And you've missed two leaves near the hedge." She punctuated each word with a bony finger jabbed in his direction. "You, boy, don't you know how to use a rake? I should hire someone else, I should."

Meech, trying without success to ignore her, almost agreed. But he thought of his four dollars, gritted his teeth, and kept raking.

When Meech was ten, Dad got hurt at the mill and could not work for several months. Meech told Mrs. Foss he needed more pay, and she promised him a raise. All day, while he raked and hauled leaves, he imagined his mother's face, happy and proud, when he told her he was giving all that money to her, to help out with the groceries. And then Mrs. Foss only paid him one extra dollar. The old witch. Her dead husband had left her plenty of money. Meech had hated her ever since.

From then on, when he finished raking, he almost had to force himself to go to the back of the house and knock on the door. There she met him, wearing her faded green housecoat, torn and unwashed. Meech tried not to focus on the daubs of egg and the brown stains on the front. Her hair, dull and dirty, hung in different lengths as if she'd attempted to cut it herself, and she smelled like mildew. Taking shallow breaths, he watched her dig into her pocket with a shriveled hand, its nails long, yellow, and curved. She extracted a wad of gray tissues, found a limp five-dollar bill among them, and thrust it at him. Without saying thank you, she closed the door in his face, leaving him holding his pay by one damp corner. After he got home, he'd put the bill into the pocket of a pair of dirty jeans going into the next wash.

Strange, Meech thought, kicking leaves before the vacant house, how he could have hated Mrs. Foss so much. She probably hated him, too, maybe because she was jealous of his being young and healthy while she could only move with pain. Sometimes, when he had found himself starting to feel sorry for her, a thought he hid deep within stirred. He should help her, five dollars or no five dollars. But then the hate rose and stilled the traitor thought.

"Meacham." A whisper, like the sound of leaves falling, startled him. He glanced over his shoulder at the corner window. His heart lurched. Behind the glass something moved. He made himself look, and breathed relief when he recognized the reflection of the last leaf floating past the window. And the voice? Imagination, that's what. Nothing was going to scare him.

The maples fenced him in, interbranched above him, their empty twigs twisted against the sky. She'd loved those trees, Mrs. Foss had, probably the only living things she'd ever loved. More than once he had looked out his bedroom window in the morning to see her hobbling among them, touching a trunk here, a branch there, the hem of her housecoat wet with dew. She had cared for them like she would her children, if she'd ever had any, making sure the trees had enough water in the summer, that their leaves got raked every autumn.

Now, he crunched his way between the trees, heading home. At the gap in the hedge he paused and looked back at the lonely gray house, the maples guarding it, and the fir trees behind, separating the property from the community cemetery, where Mrs. Foss lay buried.

Shouldering through the hedge, Meech went in to dinner.

In the middle of the night, the chimes of the grandfather clock downstairs woke Meech from a dream. Someone had been chasing him through leaves, which whirled about him in slow motion. Awake now, he listened for the clock's comforting tick, strained to catch sounds of his father snoring two rooms away, his mother talking in her sleep, the house creaking. He heard nothing. Sitting up in bed, he eased himself over the edge of the mattress to the floor, felt the braided rug beneath his bare feet, rose, and went to the window.

Below was the dark mass of the hedge between Mrs. Foss' yard and his. The moon, nearly full, silvered the gray house, turning the windows into shadowy mouths behind the skeleton trees. From beneath the nearest, a gaunt figure materialized, hardly more than a gray silhouette. Meech shaded his eyes against the moon's glare.

"Mea-cham." A whisper drifted through the partly opened window.

"Who's that?" Meech asked, half to himself.

The figure glided forward, raised a long thin object above its head. A leaf rake? With a start, Meech recognized Mrs. Foss.

"Mea-cham." She drew his name out in long syllables.

"Go away," Meech said through chattering teeth. "You're dead. I never have to rake your leaves again." He went back to bed to lie stiff and sleepless for the next hour. Just as he was beginning to think he'd had another dream, he heard the whisper again, much closer.

"Mea-cham."

Against his will, he turned his head to the window, to see her floating in the air outside, the moon shining through her face, out her eyes. She pointed the rake at him.

"No." Meech dove beneath the blankets. When he looked again, he saw only the face of the moon. He wiped his sweaty hands on his pajama top, breathed deeply until his heart stopped pounding, and tried to relax. What a night for dreams.

The mysterious silence had given way to normal night sounds—the grandfather clock ticked downstairs, his father snored, the house creaked. Meech stretched, pummeled his pillow into shape, and closed his eyes. But the image of Mrs. Foss stayed in his mind, stealing his sleep. After a long span of twisting and wrestling with the bedclothes, Meech rolled over and listened. Silence.

Slowly, he opened his eyes. The moon no longer shone through the window, but a dim light still filtered across his bookshelves and desk, across the oak-leaf wallpaper. Cold filled the room, a dank cold, heavy with the smell of decay.

"Mea-cham."

The whisper came from the murky corner nearest the door. Meech sat partway up, clutching the sheet under his chin with both hands.

He could not see her, but he knew she was there, lurking in the shadows. He could almost see two gleaming eyes, staring at him. His skin prickled with tiny needles of ice.

He cowered back under the blanket. Whimpering with fear, he curled into a tight ball. When his muscles began to sting with tension, he chanced another quick look. The shadowed corner was empty, but the numbing chill remained in the room, as if she'd left it to remind him of her. After a long while it receded, taking the horrible odor with it.

Sleep was now impossible. For the remaining hours of the night Meech tossed and sweated, reliving the night's encounters. He could think of nothing else. Only when the sky began to lighten did his terror diminish, to change to anger. How dare she try to scare him like that? He'd show her. What's more, he'd get back at her, even if she *was* dead. But how? Meech sat up, gazed out the window at the dawn, and thought. After a time, he began to smile. There was one way to get even. It would involve raking those leaves, but it would be worth it.

All day, Meech raked leaves and dragged them by the tarpful under the branches of the firs behind the empty house.

"I'll get you, you horrible old witch." He muttered constantly. "I'll get you." His hate and desire for revenge grew with every hour, every trip to the rapidly growing pile.

At dusk, he pulled the last load of leaves to the mound, but left them in the tarp. He rubbed his blistered palms, eased his back, and leaned on the rake. Looking down at it, he saw a crumpled piece of gray-green paper wedged between the tines. A five-dollar bill. He stared, unwilling to touch it, half wondering if the old lady had dropped it before she died, for him to find.

"You're not going to buy me off," he said, finally. "It's not your money I want this time." With his shoe he scraped the bill off and kicked it onto the leaf pile.

As the sun dropped, a wind sighed through the fir trees, and the piled leaves whispered in answer.

"Don't you go flying off," Meech told them under his breath. "I have far better plans for you."

He pulled the corners of the tarp together, hefted it over his shoulder, and lugged it in between two of

the firs. Before him lay the oldest part of the graveyard, many of its tombstones leaning at precarious
angles. As soon as darkness fell and he assured himself that all visitors had gone, he skirted the old
stones, dragging the tarp beyond the first two rows
to Mrs. Foss' grave. He knew where it was, because
his mom had made him go to the funeral. He threw
the tarp down, unfolded it, and grabbed a huge armload of leaves, crushing them against his chest. He
felt their dry tips against his neck and hands, smelled
their sweet, dead odor. For a moment he stood still,
savoring his vengeance. Then he flung them upon
the grave.

"You want more?" he shouted. "You just wait."

Back he went to the pile of leaves, packed more
into the tarp, wincing as crisp leaf edges poked into
his blisters. The pain fed his anger, gave him the
energy he needed to carry the tarp, to hurl even more
armloads of maple leaves on the grave. He felt hot
all over, his head and back ached, but he marched
back and forth until the grave was awash with leaves,
until they covered the new, straight-edged stone with
its inscription, "Elvira Foss, 1898–1988."

The last load, from the bottom of the heap by the
firs, left his hands earth covered, clammy, and reek-
ing of mold. Stepping back, he wiped them on his
jeans.

"There you are, Mrs. Foss. You can rake your own
leaves now." He threw the leaf rake into the pile and
walked away.

When he had almost reached the firs, he stopped

and listened. Something trailed him, whispering between the tombstones. He felt the hair on his arms
begin to rise until he realized his follower was nothing but the wind. It gusted between the firs, moaned
in the upper branches of the leafless maples. It sang
into the service porch when he opened the back
door. He thought the wind sang for him, celebrating
his triumph.

A stray leaf clung to his sweater. He picked it off,
dropped it on the back steps for the wind to play
with, and shut the door.

Meech went to bed early, sleeping soundly until
the midnight chimes of the grandfather clock woke
him. Moonlight streamed in the window, and the
awful silence was back. Without wanting to, he stood
up and moved to the window. The full moon hung
above the tips of the firs, which gyrated in the wind.
As he watched, a flock of birds flew up from behind
them, across the face of the moon, a flock which
broadened until it filled the sky. What kind of birds
would flock by night?

They were headed straight for him, and as they
drew closer, he recognized them. His stomach
shrank to a hard knot, his throat tightened. He forced
down a scream.

They weren't birds. They were leaves, flying toward him on the wailing wind. Coming closer and
closer. Meech slammed the window shut, but the
dark silence ate the sound. He leaped for his bed.
Black leaf shapes piled one on another against the

window until they blotted out the moonlight, buried his bedroom with smothering darkness. And then, cutting through the stillness, came raspy slitherings against the glass, like a host of spiders trying to get in. The window frame creaked. Just when he thought it wouldn't hold, the sounds ceased, the darkness withdrew.

Meech held his breath. The household drowned in silence. Carefully, he inched back out of bed, and crept to the corner of the window. Nothing clung to the cracks in the frame, and the moon showed him no sign of leaves when he risked raising the window and looking out. If it weren't for the awful quiet, he'd think everything was as usual. He waited, sitting on the edge of his bed, listening hard. Nothing. But no sooner had he crawled back under his blankets than he heard, on the edge of the silence, the back door click open. He must have forgotten to latch it. He had better get up and do it now, before the wind blew in.

When he had gone halfway down the hall, the rustling began downstairs. He paused at the top step and squinted into the dark below, heard scratching sounds coming nearer, coming up the stairs. Tamping down panic, Meech backed into his room and locked the door. He huddled on his bed, arms wrapped tight around his knees, trying to make himself believe he hadn't seen the masses of crackling leaves swarming toward him.

The wind sighed outside his door and a rattling followed, as if rivers of leaves poured into the hall.

"Mea-cham," came a whisper.

Something scuttled along the bottom of his door.

A leaf slid slowly beneath and stopped, rocking back and forth, its tips curled up like claws.

Jack Straw

by Midori Snyder

The first time I saw Jack Straw was in the winter. I was sick. Very sick. Mama had kept me home from school, just hoping the fever I'd caught would take care of itself. That week there was a blizzard, and the snow piled up in huge, white drifts beneath my window. The thermometer outside kept dropping, while the one in my mouth just went higher. Mama wasn't sure which way to go, keep me dry at home and hope for the best, or take me out in the damp cold and risk the long drive from our farm to the hospital. I heard her talking late one night to Daddy and Granny Frank. "Just wait a little longer," Daddy had said, "just wait a little longer." So they waited, one after another in my bedroom, sitting in the old rocking chair and watching for hopeful signs. Granny Frank's knitting needles clicked and clicked like a worried bug caught on the windowpane.

Funny thing about being sick. The worse off you are, the less you're able to tell folks. *I knew* I wasn't doing good at all. Beneath the blankets they'd piled on me for warmth, my bones rattled with the chills. I couldn't breathe too well either—each time I drew in air it felt sticky, and each time I let air out, it sort of oozed up my throat and wheezed. I couldn't tell Mama that nothing in the room looked the same. The petals on the wallpaper daisies were turning brown, and I could see them peeling off the wall and floating down to the floor. The hollow sounds of the wind against the pane made me see big white dogs, their hairy faces crowding my bed, steaming up the room with their breath.

Only thing that seemed to hold me firm in the bed was my quilt. Mama made it for me when I was little out of all the pieces left over in Granny Frank's rag-bag. It was beautiful, and I knew where each piece had come from. The blue polka dot was Aunt Anna's dress that she wore to meet Uncle George when he came back from the war. The red-and-white-striped bit was from Granny Frank's confirmation dress, and the green silk triangles were Great-Grandma Jenny's riding dress, made from imported fabric. There was a yellow-flowered calico that was Mama's summer dress when she was a teenager, and there was a square of white-and-pink apples that was mine when I was a baby. I liked to think about all those women in my family saving those bits and pieces of themselves, never wasting a thing if they could turn it to another purpose. After Mama had pieced it all together, Granny Frank sewed fancy stitches around each piece, setting each one off with its own frame of embroidery.

I was holding tight to my quilt, just praying that the blue polka dots would stop rolling off the fabric, when Jack Straw came up to the bed. I looked up feeling the cold draft and saw him step out of a mist into the moonlight that fell across the room.

He had his hands stuck in the pockets of a pair of old overalls, and a battered hat with a torn brim was pulled low over his face.

"Who are you?" I asked.

"Jack. Jack Straw," he answered, and I felt the chill creep over my spine at the dry sound.

He looked liked a scarecrow, old corn stalks tied together and dressed like a man. When he moved he rustled, and the mist sort of followed after him, rising off his hunched shoulders.

"I don't know you," I said weakly, struggling to sit up, and all the while pulling my quilt higher to my chin.

"Everyone knows me," he said, and pushed back his hat to show me his face.

Thin it was, with a nose that hooked down sharply trying to reach his chin. He smiled, and the creases in his cheeks folded with a scratchy sound.

He was right. Soon as I saw those white eyes, with shining black stones for a center, I knew him. Granny Frank told me once about old Jack Straw, shuffling through the fields on his way to harvest. But it wasn't crops he raked in, it was people. Right then I knew I was dying, even though my heart pounded like a bass drum and blood heated up my face like a furnace fire.

He pulled a hand from his pocket and reached out to me. Fingers of bundled sticks went to pluck the quilt from me, but I clutched it tighter, refusing to let go.

"I ain't going with you," I said angrily.

"No point in your refusing," he answered, and stepped closer to take a firmer hold of the quilt. The cold mist swirled toward me, and I felt its icy touch on my forehead.

"No!" I yelled, and then, "Mama!" I called for her where she was sitting in the chair, still sleeping. She didn't stir, and for an awful moment I feared Jack Straw had already taken me.

"Now wait here, Jack Straw," I said, yanking my quilt back from his spindly fingers. In my panicked thinking I had remembered something Granny Frank told me about Jack Straw. "I'll make you a bargain."

He frowned at me, and his eyes narrowed. Ever so slowly, he slipped his hand back into his pocket and stood, rocking on his heels. Thinking, I guessed.

"What sort of bargain?"

"I'll riddle you one, and if you can't guess, then I get to keep my life."

"Forever?" he asked with a sneer, and I noticed now that his teeth were sharp and jagged.

"No," I answered, shaking my head. "Just the usual span of time."

He laughed as if I'd said something really funny. "There ain't no season in which I can't harvest, ain't no span of time that's usual."

"Not for you maybe, but for me there is. I got things I want to do," I argued. "I still got a life I want to live."

Jack Straw sat on the bed with a whispery noise like the wind shaking the stooks in the field.

"All right," he said. "Give me your riddle."

All the while I had been trying to convince Jack Straw to bargain, I'd been desperately trying to think on a good riddle. I figured he'd probably already heard every one ever given out, so I knew it had to be a riddle that only I knew, that only I had cause to make happen right then. I stared down at that old quilt, Granny Frank's stitches like silver ribbons in the moonlight, and tried to think.

"Give me your riddle," he said again, and this time I heard the spreading coldness in his voice.

It came to me all of a moment, and in that same moment I felt the fear go out of me. I looked up from the quilt and stared straight into his dry, crackling face. "I'll riddle it to you," I started, just like Granny Frank did in the story, and I saw him straighten his back in expectation. "I died in pieces and was reborn whole. I followed the road over ridges and valleys but never moved."

I held my breath as I watched him figure the riddle. He didn't move, but stayed there black eyed and rigid. The cold mist was settling around the bed, and a drop of it trickled down the side of my face. But I couldn't move, couldn't take my eyes from him.

Then with a snarl he sprang up from my bed. The wind howled outside and rattled the panes as if to break them. Hands upraised over his head, Jack Straw called to the howling wind. The mist thickened in the room, and the white dogs were there beside him, snapping and baying. Hoarfrost cobwebbed across my quilt as Jack Straw shook his raggedy arms at me in fury. I screamed then, fearing he meant to take me, though he'd not given me my answer.

But the scream was scarce from my mouth when he disappeared, and it was Mama who reached out to take me, her arms sleep warm and soft.

"Hush now, hush," she whispered in my ear. "You're dreaming, Katie," she said. "You're dreaming. Mama's right here." She held me tight, and after a bit I felt my fear thaw and stopped shaking.

And even though I knew she was wrong, that I hadn't been dreaming, I let her lay me back on the pillows and tuck in the blankets around me again. She bent over and kissed me, one hand pushing back the wet hair from my forehead.

"My quilt," I whispered to her proudly, and saw her look of confusion.

"Your quilt's here, honey," she said to soothe me.

"No," I said. "That's the answer to the riddle."

"Sure it is," she murmured. She thought I was talking in my sleep, still dreaming. But it didn't matter. The truth was I was still alive because I had beaten Jack Straw.

Just before I fell back to sleep, I heard her talking in low whispers to Daddy. "She's gonna be fine," I heard her say. "Looks like the fever's breaking." Daddy mumbled something. Mama answered. "No, just dreaming, I guess. She's sleeping good now. I think the worst's over."

And in my bed, half asleep, I thought so, too.

But it wasn't. Somehow the worst had only begun.

I stayed in bed another five days and then went back to school. I had five days of lying in my bed to think over what had happened. Oh, I was happy to be alive, to be waking up each day and watching the sun shine through my windows, lighting up the white daisies on my wallpaper. Everything was just as it had been before I got sick. And that scared me. I had sent Jack Straw on his way. But I got to thinking that I was going to spend the rest of my life looking over my shoulder, waiting for him to sneak up on me. And the thought of that dry face, those long spindly arms reaching out to grab me when I wasn't looking, made my victory seem cold.

"Look at your face," Granny Frank said on the morning I got up to eat breakfast before going to school.

"What's the matter with it?" I asked.

"It's screwed tight. Grim as a soldier's. Where's that smile of yours, child?"

"It's there," I snapped, and then felt bad for being cross with her. "I just don't feel like smiling," I said more softly.

"Worried about school?"

"Uh-huh," I answered, because it was easier than telling her the truth.

"It'll be fine," she said, picking up her knitting. "You'll be caught up in no time."

But school wasn't fine. It was terrible. Things had changed while I was out sick. They had painted the halls a new white with a blue stripe down the middle to hide where everybody's hand sort of naturally drags and leaves a dirty smear. The posters on my classroom wall had all been changed, the map showed a new continent, and the desks had been rearranged. People had changed too. My best friend, Mary Beth, came up to me as soon I got into school and gave me a big hug. I didn't recognize her at first because she'd gone and cut off her beautiful long red braids and curled her hair. So instead of being happy to see her, I was mad.

"Why'd you cut your hair?" I yelled.

"Looks better this way," she said, tossing back the short curls. "More grown-up."

"What's so good about growing up?" I said angrily. "You just die anyway."

Mary Beth opened her mouth and then shut it again without saying anything. She waited a few moments, maybe to see if I'd come to my senses and say something nice. But I didn't, so she turned on her heel and left me standing there in that new-painted hallway.

Everything new made me feel scared, made me tremble. Change was an enemy that stole away my hard-won victory and left me open to the next coming of Jack Straw. I wanted time just to stop, for everything and everyone around me to stay safe in its place. But the world isn't like that, is it? It just keeps on going, and I knew that sooner or later Jack Straw would come around again to me. So every day when I left for school, I felt the fear draw tighter and tighter around me as I tried to shut my eyes and ears to the changes. Granny Frank was right in calling me a grim soldier, because I faced each new thing like a battle. Even my own riddle came back to haunt me, for like Granny Frank's stitches, I followed a road over hills and valleys, but never moved.

Whatever illness it was that took me came again and caught Daddy. I found him one day in the barn, just leaning his head against the old cow, too sick with fever to stand. His breathing was harsh, and his eyes burned a fiery red. I helped him to the house and into bed. For two weeks after school and at night, I stood guard over him, waiting lest Jack Straw come to take him. Daddy thrashed with fevered dreams, and his cries wrenched me from the rocking chair to my feet in terror. But the fever broke, and except for a terrible cough that lingered, he mended.

Mama got it next, and for a second time I stood my guard, certain that this time Jack Straw was playing with me. Punishing me for beating him. I sat next to her bed, put cool cloths on her head, and held her hand while she struggled with the fever. When Granny Frank tried to get me to leave and have a rest of my own, I refused. I was so scared that if I moved one foot from that room while Mama was sick, Jack Straw would come for sure and take her behind my back. The first thing Mama did when she felt the fever come down was order me to bed. Only then did I leave her side.

I hardly noticed when winter changed and became wet spring. I had spent so much time worrying and fretting about things out of my hands that I walked around as ragged and worn as Jack Straw himself. The face I saw in the mirror was haggard, my eyes dark gray with purple smudges beneath. My hair had lost its shine, and my mouth was a sour frown. No wonder my friends shied away from me at school, talking in whispers when I passed like some spook down the halls.

They couldn't know how heavy my burden felt, for with the spring Granny Frank took sick with the fever. And with each day that she got weaker and weaker, my burden grew until I felt I could no longer lift my head with the weight of so much dread. Granny Frank would smile at me, pat my hand, and tell me it was all right. "Everything's got a season," she would say. I didn't understand her then and thought she meant the coming spring. Then one night I heard her singing in a tiny, sweet voice a song about spooning in the moonlight. She seemed so happy I thought maybe she'd been spared after all. But when I come closer and touched her head, I knew it wasn't so. Her forehead was hot and dry. Her eyes stared out, not seeing me, but set on some happier memory. I took her hand and clutched it tight.

A cold draft swept through the room. Looking up, I saw Jack Straw standing in the corner, just as before, with his hat pulled down and his hands stuck in his pockets.

"No," I shouted at him. "You can't have her!"

He pushed back his hat, and his face was wrinkled with sadness. "You mean to keep this one from me, too?" he asked.

"Yes," I said.

"Is that what she wants, or what you want?"

"Makes no difference." I stamped my foot like a child.

"Ask her then," he said.

I turned to look down at Granny Frank and bit back a cry. She had stopped singing and was lying quietly, peaceful as a sleeper. By the light of a small lamp I saw suddenly how tiny and frail she had become in the last few days. And how old. Her skin had lost its color, growing pale and yellow like the husk of the corn dollies she used to make. Her white hair was tangled as dried corn silk.

"Do you still want to riddle me, Katie?" Jack Straw asked, his voice no louder than the rustle of leaves.

I didn't answer. There was nothing to say. I realized then that just as I couldn't stop things from changing in life, I couldn't keep Granny Frank from her appointed death. I bowed my head, eyes squeezed shut, and clung to Granny Frank's hand. She squeezed back once, her grip firm for a moment as if to give me strength. And then her hand went limp. I shuddered as the cold draft circled my shoulders. When the room grew warm again, I knew she was gone with Jack Straw. And then I cried, cried hard, grief breaking like a branch within me.

We buried Granny Frank on a beautiful spring morning. From cemetery hill I could see down into the pockets of fields newly plowed, the mist rising like steam from the earth. The air was soft and warm, full of promise, as crocus and daffodil buds swelled and burst open with color.

I was done crying, though I wore the sadness of

Granny Frank's death like a long-needed relief. I had been so long frozen that Granny Frank's passing took me like a field set to by the plow blade. I was wounded, cut open, and yet, in the furrow left by her death, I also felt released. I looked up across the open grave into which they lowered Granny Frank's casket and saw Jack Straw one more time. He was standing between the preacher, who was saying the words, and Mrs. Johnson, who jiggled her new baby to keep him from fussing. He didn't look so frightening to me anymore now that I knew him. He looked over and gave me a sad, weathered smile, like he was satisfied with what he had done and sorry at the pain it had caused me.

Then he tipped me his hat in farewell and started ambling off toward the fields. I watched him as he went, like a freed scarecrow with his long, lanky body of dried yellowed stalks. And just before the morning mist swallowed him, I caught a glimpse of faint shimmering green: the new rye grass resurrecting in the fields around him.

Juniper, Gentian, and Rosemary

by Pamela Dean

The Hardy family moved in next door on a very bright day in October. There was some discussion, long after, about whether there had ever been a Hardy family, except for Dominic; but at the time everybody thought there was. Juniper and Gentian and Rosemary crowded into the bay window of their dining room, which conveniently overlooked the narrow driveway up which the unfortunate moving crew was carrying a lot of heavy-looking dark-wood furniture. There were large mirrors with melted-looking gold frames, and no less than three grandfather clocks, and a huge number of boxes, all of which made the people carrying them grunt and sweat and from time to time swear very loudly.

Gentian heard two phrases she had never encountered before, not even among the senior boys who smoked during lunch hour. She made a quiet bet with herself concerning when Juniper would choose to bring them out.

"It's grandparents," said Rosemary in disgust. "That's all old grown-up stuff."

"Maybe they're just rich," said Juniper.

"They wouldn't be moving in next door to us if they were," said their mother from the table, where she was pretending to pay the bills. If she had really been paying them, she would be swearing in German and throwing her pen across the room.

"If they are grandparents," said Gentian, "they might plant a lot of rosebushes and give us cookies."

"I give you cookies," said Juniper, affronted.

"You burn them."

"I cook them. You should just eat the dough, you—"

"Mom," said Rosemary, "would our grandparents have done that if we had any?"

"Cookies, probably," said their mother. "Your grandmother could kill a plant faster than anybody I ever knew."

"What about Daddy's mother?"

"She had mathematical hedges and cakes like a geometry diagram," said their father, coming in from the kitchen with a cup of coffee. He had filled it too full. Gentian bet with herself that he would spill three sploshes on the polished floor and one on the newly shampooed carpet. He spilled two on the floor and missed the carpet by moving so fast he slopped coffee on the table instead. Gentian owed herself either a large box of chocolate (not to be shared with her sisters) or a copy of *Bulfinch's Mythology*, depending on how her allowance was holding out, whether the Martins needed a baby-sitter this weekend, and whether Jamie Barrows smiled at her in gym class again.

"Well, where *are* they?" said Rosemary, standing on Gentian's foot in an effort to see further. She was tiny and blond and very fetching, and although she professed that she hauled a footstool around with her, and hated having to do so, in fact she usually used somebody else to reach the high places.

"In the house directing the movers, stupid," said Juniper. She was the tall and statuesque and beautiful sister, and she got away with saying many awful things because she had red hair and people liked to joke about her temper.

"I didn't see them go in," said Gentian, "and there's no car." She was the middle sister in all possible ways, including having gotten the freckles that ought to have belonged to Junie and the miserable sensitive skin that was Rosie's proper birthright. She had brown hair and boring, symmetrical features. She made up for these deficiencies by being clever. In fact, she wasn't as quick on the uptake as Rosemary or as good at mathematics as Juniper, but she read a great deal more than they ever bothered with, and could come out with peculiar facts or common-sense observations, as the situation warranted. Most people thought this was funny, but her father always thanked her gravely.

"You don't see *everything*, Genny," said Juniper, "even if you are as nosy as—"

"There isn't a car," said Gentian.

"Maybe they came in the van," said Rosemary, thoughtlessly. Gentian could see the precise moment in which she realized that she had been stupid, and watched her forestall Juniper's scathing comment with a shrill giggle. "Maybe they're vampires and they came in their coffins," said Rosemary.

"Those wooden chests!" said Gentian, collaborating happily.

"Vampire grandparents," said Juniper, relenting. "Watch your kittens when their grandchildren come to visit."

They pressed their foreheads to the glass and watched for coffins. A swirl of wind drove a shower of yellow leaves from their maple, and when it had subsided they saw a boy climb out of the truck.

"There, Junie!" said Rosemary. "A vampire grandchild."

"Is he cute?" said their mother.

"His hair is black, his eyes are blue, his lips as red as wine," said their father, reflectively. "Or do his teeth brightly shine?"

"He's *got* black hair," said Juniper. "Oh, God, Mom, he's as tall as me."

"He's too old for you, then," said her mother.

"Why should his teeth shine?" said Gentian, turning around and addressing her father. If the boy was too old for Juniper, she might as well forget him; and anyway, he was probably like all the seniors.

"If he's a vampire," said her father.

On a dull day in November, the vampire grandmother came to the back door and asked to borrow a snake. Rosemary, who answered the door, was thrown into utter confusion by this request. Gentian, doing her homework at the kitchen table because they were reading Poe's stories and those scared her too silly to sit up in the attic by herself, looked up and saw a thin, gray-haired woman in blue clothes, squinting at the bewildered Rosemary.

"Is your drain clogged up?" asked Gentian.

"I thought you used a fish for that," said Rosemary.

"No, dummy, that's for electrical work. Let her in, Rosie."

The woman came in, blinking in the fluorescent light as if she didn't much care for it. "I'm Mrs. Hardy," she said. "We moved in next door."

"I'm Genny," said Gentian. She was embarrassed. Juniper had been pestering her parents to go over and welcome the new neighbors, but her father was not sociable and her mother had said she wasn't going to bother people who were busy moving in just because her daughters had an obsession about vampires. "This is Rosemary. Give her some coffee, Rosie, and I'll get Mom."

Mom, when gotten, managed to persuade Mrs. Hardy to sit down and drink her coffee, which was more than the dithering Rosemary had done. Gentian and Rosemary sat very quiet while the two women talked about the neighborhood and the dreadfulness of drains and the worse dreadfulness of plumbers. Gentian saw that the woman's fingers were of the usual length with regard to one another, and that her canine teeth were no more pointed than anybody else's. They didn't shine, either; she probably needed to go to the dentist.

Mrs. Hardy and Gentian's mother had begun to talk about their families. Mr. Hardy was, it appeared, hopeless with plumbing.

"What about your son?" said Gentian's mother.

The woman looked very startled, and then began to laugh weakly. "Him? Oh, no," she said. She seemed to realize that this response was lacking something, and added, looking at Gentian with her nondescript eyes, "I think he's about your age."

"He's tall for twelve," said Gentian's mother.

"I'm wrong, then," said Mrs. Hardy. "He's fourteen."

"He's tall for that, too," said Gentian. "Tell him to watch out for my big sister."

Mrs. Hardy looked dubiously at Rosemary, who was trying not to laugh; and Gentian's mother changed the subject.

On a bitter day in December the boy brought back the snake. Gentian was once more at the kitchen table, making Christmas lists and counting her money and cursing the purchase of *Bulfinch's Mythology*, which had given her a series of unpleasant dreams and set her back financially.

She opened the door, scowling, and in the blast of subzero air that came in, she hastily rearranged her expression. His hair was black, and his eyes were blue, and his lips were as red as wine, though that was probably from the cold. He was beautiful. He was taller than Junie, but Junie was out ice-skating with one of the smoking seniors.

He smiled at her. His teeth shone, but were no more pointed than anyone else's. "I'm Dominic Hardy," he said. "Here's your snake, and my mother sent some cookies."

"Come in; you'll freeze," said Gentian intelligently, and banged the door behind him so Rosie would hear and come help her out. Rosie was too young and shy to be a problem yet, and perhaps Dominic would think she was funny. "Give me your coat," said Gentian. "I was just going to make some fudge." She had never made it in her life, but she had hung around plaguing Junie when Junie made it. There were cookies and divinity and fruitcake already, but Juniper had made all those and Gentian would have to say so. "You could wait and take some back with you." You've come such a long way, she thought, and snickered at her own absurdity.

Dominic either had good manners or didn't want to go home. "Thank you," he said, and sat down.

He was not very conversational. He admitted to liking every band Gentian mentioned, and to watching every television show she asked about, and to reading Poe, and even to playing the recorder; but he would not discuss any of these things in detail, and he didn't ask her any questions in return. Gentian finally gave up on him and concentrated on the fudge, which was giving her difficulties.

She had burned her tongue for the sixth time, and the fudge still refused to form a ball in the cold water, when Junie came back. She banged the back door behind her, and shot the bolt, which Gentian always forgot to do. The sound made Dominic jump, which was some satisfaction. Juniper pulled off her green beret, shook out all her long red hair, and said, "What are you burning?"

"None of your business," said Gentian. "Say hello to Dominic."

Juniper didn't even blink. "Hello, Dominic," she said. "I'm Junie."

Dominic studied her for several seconds as if she were a kind of food he had never seen before, and then smiled at her, Gentian saw Junie melt, and made a bet with herself about how long it would be before they went out together. He was better than the smoking seniors, anyway; if Mom ever found out about *them* she was liable to ground all three girls until they were twenty.

Rosemary came slouching into the kitchen in Juniper's bathrobe, which she liked because it was too long for her and she could sweep the skirts around the floor, gathering cat hair and playing at being a princess. She stared at Dominic as if he were a food she knew and didn't like. He smiled at her, too. Gentian fully expected Rosemary to turn red and run away, which was her usual method of dealing with people who were nice to her. But Rosemary spoke to him. "You've got the broken chair," she said. "You need the cushion."

And she swept Juniper's bathrobe around and exited without tripping on it, to return bearing the fat gold-and-black-and-white Hmong pillow that they had given their mother for her birthday last year.

Gentian supposed that it had had to happen sometime. Rosie would probably appreciate somebody
who had no conversation; it would save her having
to make any. She could get pregnant and be the
family statistic.

A horrible smell of burnt sugar and chocolate
smote her nose, and as she recoiled from that she
felt herself recoiling also at the thoughts she had just
had. It was all right to think that way about Juniper;
Juniper was acting like an idiot and had been for a
year now. But Rosie was all right.

"Get away from that pan!" shouted Juniper.

Gentian got out of her way and yielded up the
wooden spoon cheerfully, and went to sit at the table
and watch Rosie be worshipful and Dominic see Juniper in a temper.

"I have a project I need help with," said Dominic,
impartially to both of them. Gentian stared; he had
actually volunteered a piece of information. She
wondered if Rosemary's attitude was responsible.
She tried to look encouraging, and Dominic explained further. "I want to build a time machine."

Rosemary looked stunned. Gentian said, "What
for?"

"Well," said Dominic, "I'll tell you if you'll tell
me, what is the maid without a tress?"

"Bald," said Rosemary.

Dominic grinned at her. "No," he said.

"Junie didn't have any hair until she was almost
three," said Gentian meanly.

Juniper, beating the fudge, ignored this feeble

thrust, but Dominic leaned back against the Hmong cushion and looked carefully at her. "Well, we'd better have Junie, then," he said.

Gentian, feeling conspired against, said, "Well, what do you want to build a time machine for?"

Dominic said, "What was the tower without a crest?"

"Topless," said Rosemary, and then giggled and turned red.

"Ilium had topless towers," said Juniper.

"They didn't finish the Tower of Babel," said Gentian.

Dominic leaned his elbows on the table and stared at her until she felt herself turning redder than Rosemary, and she hadn't even made a dirty remark. "We'll have you, too," said Dominic.

"You still haven't said why you want to—"

"Where is the road without any dust?"

"The Milky Way," said Rosemary, who loved riddles.

"We'll have Rosie, too," said Dominic.

"Why do you want to?" said Gentian.

"You think about those riddles," said Dominic, "and you'll know. Do you have a place here where we could build it?"

"The attic," said Juniper.

"That's *mine*," said Gentian.

"You don't need all that space."

"You could decide when we could use it, Genny," said Dominic. Gentian, who was calculating rather than sentimental in most of her friendships, felt a most peculiar shiver up her spine when he used her name. She was not altogether sure she liked it.

"Well, in that case," she said.

Their father was amused and their mother was wary. But once their father had made it clear to them that a time machine violated the laws of physics and they might as well build a perpetual-motion machine or try to make the philosphers' stone, he raised no objection; and once their mother had made it clear to them that there were always to be at least two girls up there with Dominic, she raised none either. She didn't like Dominic, once she had met him; she said it was unnatural for a fourteen-year-old boy to be that polite.

"And will trouble come of it?" asked Juniper.

"Not if I can help it," said their mother.

They began after New Year's, and nothing was as any of them had expected. Dominic was not polite to them, nor charming either; but he got what he wanted by seeming to be ready to be charming to one of them if she would side with him against the other two. They carried heaps of heavy, awkward objects up three flights of steps; they gave up ice-skating and birthday parties and being in the school play to work on the awful thing; they neglected their homework and their friends; they bruised their fingers with hammering and their egos with trying to please Dominic.

But there was no pleasing Dominic.

They had long ago looked up one another's names in their mother's various herbals, and discovered that Juniper was a diuretic ("Junie pisses people off!"), that Gentian was an emetic ("Genny makes people sick!"), and that Rosemary, although disappointingly to her sisters a sweet and wholesome plant that signified love and remembrance, also dilated the capillaries ("Rosie makes people's blood boil!"). As a test case for these attributes, Dominic would have made the authors of the herbals very proud. He got mad at Juniper about three times a day because she wouldn't do any work that might break a fingernail or drip solder on her T-shirt; he said that the faint scent of Gentian's lavender soap disgusted him, and continued to remark on it from time to time long after she had switched to Ivory; he tolerated Rosie very well for days on end but would suddenly shout at her for five minutes because she had asked him a Bennett Cerf riddle.

And yet he kept coming back. Their mother said he was probably lonely, although it was no more than he deserved; their father said Dominic couldn't resist looking at three beautiful girls and was probably hoping that next time they would keep their mouths shut; Juniper said he came for her chocolate-chip cookies; and Rosemary opined that he came because they had a VCR and would show him tapes of shows his parents wouldn't let him watch. Gentian did not have an opinion, or even a bet with herself. She had a kind of hope in the back of her head, but she did not bring it forward where she could think about it.

It sat there like an unlit candle, for when she needed a light of interest in her.

"He's a wimp," said Juniper, scowling. "He *snapped* at me for saying—"

"Don't say it, or somebody else will snap at you," said her mother.

"Well, honey," said her father, "they say the devil's a gentleman, you know."

His entire family gazed at him in a familiar bafflement. Gentian had often thought that if she could ever accurately define her father's "they," she would be able to have whatever she wanted, all the kingdoms of the world and the glory of them, with no devil at her back, gentleman or otherwise, to make the gift go sour, either. On the other hand, her father presumably could define his own "they," and he had not the kingdoms of the world, but a wife who read Goethe and a completely unruly and ungrateful gaggle of daughters.

"The trouble with Dom," said Rosemary, "is that he wants to have all the fun."

"Nine tenths of the law of chivalry," said their father, in a satisfied tone.

His daughters gazed in bafflement; but his wife sat up straight. "You don't like him any better than I do!"

"Liking has nothing to do with it," said their father, with the extreme blandness that meant you were trespassing on his private feelings. "Just making observations, that's all."

"Are you calling him a gentleman again?" said Gentian.

"Very good," said her father.

"Gentlemen don't ask riddles all the time," said Rosemary.

"Ask him why he asks them; riddle him that," said their father.

"He says because he can't remember the answers."

Their father sat up straight and looked delighted. Their mother said dryly, "Can't he look them up?"

"He says that's cheating," said Juniper.

"Told you he was a gentleman," said their father.

"If you mean he abides by a strict set of arbitrary rules of no use to him or anybody else, you're right," said their mother.

Juniper got fed up first. She had cut her finger on a piece of sheet metal the day before, and although Dominic had been unexpectedly gracious about the blood dripped on his nice clean chassis, Gentian suspected the finger was still hurting her. Also Juniper was used to being in charge, and to having her temper paid attention to and sometimes feared. Dominic only laughed at her. She quit, officially, in a storm of furious tears, on the first of April.

"There goes the water without any sand," said Dominic, in a pleased tone.

"You're a jerk," said Gentian. "Did you know that?"

"It's good for Junie to be thwarted," said Dominic.

"Yes, but not like this."

"Did you get those connections soldered?"

Rosemary quit on the last day of April. In the first place, she had gotten a hunk of hair caught in something sticky of Dominic's and had to have her hair cut a great deal shorter than was becoming to her. And in the second place, her best friend was giving a May Day party and she wanted to go. Dominic was put out, because if she did go, he and Gentian would not, according to the edict laid down by their mother, be able to work on the machine that day. "You're acting just like the maid without a tress," he said austerely.

"Junie?" said Rosemary, caught off-guard.

"A baby," said Gentian blandly.

Rosemary, having said, "I'm going, and I don't care," about ninety-five times, finally made a dignified exit, merely remarking to Gentian on her way out, "Genny, you're just as much a jerk as he is."

Gentian was beginning to suspect that this was true. But Dominic was still beautiful when he kept his mouth shut; he was the only boy whose undivided, however impolite, attention she had ever had; and the time machine was enormously convincing. It had a great many very real things in it, bits of computers and circuit boards and four abandoned desk chairs and Volumes II and IV of the *Child Ballads*.

"Will she tell your mother?" said Dominic.

"Not unless she's asked."

"And will you tell her?"

"Not unless I'm asked."

"And will she ask you?"

"I can probably forestall her," said Gentian, a little breathlessly. She was not accustomed to disobeying her mother; but whatever Dominic wanted, it wasn't what her mother was afraid he wanted. He wanted slave labor, in fact, and slavish encouragement, and the supply of cookies and brownies and cakes that Juniper still provided, although she wouldn't speak to him. And when Gentian had figured out why any of them had been willing to give him these things, then, she bet herself, she would know something.

Summer went by—peonies, roses, day lilies, rainy afternoons in the library, sunny mornings in the hammock, swimming, baby-sitting, writing poetry, reading mystery novels, all unnoticed or forgotten. Gentian crouched in the broiling attic with a Dominic who never sweated, and put things together at his direction. She apologized once for dripping perspiration on one of his keyboards, and he grinned at her and said, "That's salt without sand, too." Autumn blazed in like a concourse of peacocks and departed muttering in a swirl of sodden leaves. Gentian took apart three old transistor radios and one that had vacuum tubes in it, and reassembled them for Dominic, who asked her, "When has a forest no leaves?" and received her irritable "When it's a forest of evergreens" with amiable satisfaction.

On Halloween night her parents wouldn't let him

in. Juniper and Rosemary had gone trick-or-treating, and Gentian, alternately enraged and relieved, went to bed early. She dreamed uneasily of ribbon cable and capacitors and coils of copper and gutted video terminals, and was awakened suddenly by an ungodly thumping and a flash of blue light.

Flinging back the blankets, Gentian stalked through to the other attic room in her red-flannel nightgown, forming in her fuddled mind imprecations for the intruders. Junie and Rosie had probably come up here to put their costumes away, and stumbled over the time machine, which was by now the size of three swing sets.

It was Dominic. He smiled at her. "It's done," said he.

"How'd you get in here?"

He smiled again, and Gentian felt that shiver up her spine. He said, "You forgot to lock the kitchen door. Junie and Rosie aren't back yet."

"My parents will kill me."

"They won't know."

"You think they didn't hear that god-awful noise?"

"That was for you," said Dominic. "Now come here. Hold this. Thank you. Now plug that cable in and type 'Go.' "

Gentian did as she was told, and an enormous humming filled her senses. "There!" said Dominic, and he closed his warm hands over her cold wrists and kissed her on the mouth.

It was like the time some of Junie's smoking seniors had put vodka in Gentian's Seven-Up. She had liked it enormously, but had been quite sure that she shouldn't.

Dominic seemed to feel the same way; he pulled his mouth away suddenly and sat down hard on the floor. Gentian looked sideways at him, hoping to exchange some sympathetic glance, and saw that he was pale and sweaty, and swallowing hard. It was like the vodka. It didn't last.

"I do make you sick!" she cried. "Why did you do it, if you didn't like it?"

Dominic looked at her with great intentness, and suddenly smacked the palm of his hand into his forehead, as if he had just figured out the answer to a physics problem. "Juniper, Gentian, and Rosemary," he said. "Girls! How could I know it would be girls? Why, what a monstrous trick," said Dominic. "What could be worse than girls?"

"You!" shrieked Gentian. "You're worse than any girl I've ever known! You're *worse* than a vampire!"

Dominic stood up, which alarmed her, and then he smiled, which hurt her, because a smile, from anybody, was not going to be enough, anymore. "That's not my name," he said, "but we'll call it a fair answer. Good-bye." And he went over to the window, opened it, snapped the screen out, and stepped off the sill. Gentian lurched to her feet and flung herself across the room and stuck her head out the window. Right below her was the door she had forgotten to lock, with the light over it burning for Junie and Rosie. It shone brightly on an empty patch of sidewalk. She had heard nothing hit the ground.

She turned around and looked at the time machine. Very likely it *was* against the laws of physics. What Dominic had just done was against the laws of physics. But she remembered Junie's blood, and Rosie's hair, and her own sweat, and how very welcome they had been to Dominic. She looked at the ordinary ivory-colored light switch that he had set into a little metal box, to be the On switch for his time machine. Would it work? Would it take them to the fifteenth century, or the twenty-fifth? What good would that do him? *What had he wanted it for?* Because babies had no hair, and the Tower of Babel was never finished? Because there was no sand in tears and no leaves in an evergreen forest? Because she did not give his name but answered his question with himself? Who was he?

She didn't know. But she turned off the time machine's switch. She unplugged its eight plugs, and took from the wall sockets the adaptors that had made it possible to plug in so many. She pulled out all the computer cables and all the ribbon cables. Then she began ripping out wires by the handful, and finally she picked up the four keyboards one after the other and used them to smash the rest of it. Then she dried her face on her sleeve and stomped downstairs.

Her father was reading in the kitchen, and did not, of course, look up.

"Why did you name us what you named us?" said Gentian in a trembling voice.

"I thought you'd read those herbals," said her father, turning a page. "Juniper, Gentian, and Rosemary ward off witches, and evil spirits, and so on. Ghosties and ghoulies and long-legged beasties."

"And vampires?"

"Very probably."

"Dominic's not a vampire."

"Close enough," said her father. "He's sucked you girls dry enough, one way or another."

"Junie and Rose make him angry and I make him sick."

"That's what we hoped."

"But why," said Gentian, "did he want a time machine?"

Her father closed the book and looked at her. "Why does anybody want one? To do something over."

Gentian thought of the things she would do over. She said, "But something good or bad?"

"You think about all those riddles he asked you, and you'll know," said her father. "And when you think you do, you can come and tell me. Because if I'd been *sure* that boy was up to nothing good, I wouldn't have let him set up an alchemist's laboratory in my attic."

"What about the riddles?" said Gentian. "They weren't very good ones. And sometimes he acted like every question was a riddle, and no matter what kind of answer you gave him, he thought you were answering the riddle. He asked me what could be worse than girls, and I told him he could, and he said that was a fair answer."

Her father was looking delighted again. "The devil

is worse nor woman was," he said. "So he remembered his riddles at the end."

"He kissed me," said Gentian, who was not accustomed to confiding in her father and was rather surprised to find herself doing so.

"I'm not surprised," said her father.

"And he didn't like it."

"That's a compliment, sweetheart."

"I don't want," said Gentian, sticking to the one thing she was sure of, "to go through life making people sick."

"You won't make everybody sick. Just amnesic gentlemen with improbable ambitions."

"But what if I *like* amnesic gentlemen with improbable ambitions?" It was just like parents to give you a name that protected you from what you liked.

"Learn all the riddles you can, until your taste matures," said her father, dryly. "What have you done with his time machine?"

"Smashed it."

"It's probably just as well," said her father, but he looked wistful.

"If he hadn't kissed me," said Gentian.

"If kissing you could make him sick," said her father, "then I wouldn't care to trust him with a time machine."

Gentian, having heard as much as she cared to assimilate, wandered into the dining room and peered out the bay window. There was a blank darkness where the Hardy house should be, and beyond it the straight line of the next house's hedge stood up against the starry sky. She tried to remember what the Hardy house had looked like, and couldn't. She wondered—assuming the house had ever really been there at all—what Mrs. Hardy had needed that snake for.

About the Authors

BRUCE COVILLE is the popular author of such books as *The Monster's Ring* and *Sarah's Unicorn*. Before becoming a full-time writer, he was a teacher and part-time grave digger. Mr. Coville lives in Syracuse, New York, and has three children.

ANNE E. CROMPTON has written many stories and books for young readers, including the picture book *The Winter Wife* and the young-adult novel *The Sorcerer*. She is a mother and a grandmother and lives with her husband in a farmhouse in Chesterfield, Massachusetts.

KARA DALKEY, who lives in Minneapolis, is the author of three fantasy novels—*The Curse of Sagamore*, *Euryale*, and *The Nightingale*. She is a musician and an artist as well as a writer, and she lives with three "looney" cats.

PAMELA DEAN also lives in Minneapolis and has wanted to be a writer since the fifth grade. She has published five poems in obscure places, two fantasy novels—*The Secret Country* and *The Hidden Land*—and a number of short stories. Ms. Dean has a cat she is fond of and a husband, she says, she likes even better.

CHARLES de LINT was born in the Netherlands and now lives with his artist wife, MaryAnn, in Ottawa, Canada. Besides being a popular novelist (*Yarrow*, *Jack the Giant-Killer*, and *Wolf Moon* are a few of his fantasy books), he is a professional musician and plays the fiddle, bouzouki, guitar, and bodhran, which is an Irish goatskin drum.

MARTIN H. GREENBERG is an indefatigable anthologist who lives with his wife and new baby daughter in Green Bay, Wisconsin, where he is a college professor.

MELISSA MIA HALL is a widely published Texan whose short stories have appeared in fantasy and horror anthologies and magazines. She is also a book reviewer for the *Fort Worth Star-Telegram*, writes poetry, and has had photographs published.

LEIGH ANN HUSSEY, a young writer who lives with her husband in Berkeley, California, has had several short stories published in magazines and anthologies. A musician who plays over a dozen different instruments, she has had two tapes recorded as well.

DIANA WYNNE JONES is one of today's most popular fantasy novelists for young readers. Her many books—including the prize-winning *Archer's Goon*—are popular in both England and America. She lives in Bristol, England, with her husband in a house that sits against a cliffside.

ADDIE LACOE is a western Massachusetts writer who is, by profession, a genealogist. She runs her own small press, specializing in science fiction and fantasy. Ms. Lacoe and her husband have six children, two foster children, six grandchildren, and a dog.

AMY LAWSON, author of the fantasy novel for young readers *The Talking Bird & the Story Pouch*, lives with her husband and two young children in New Hampshire, where she also teaches drama to seventh and eighth graders.

JYMN MAGON, who lives in Los Angeles, has been with Walt Disney Studios for over twelve years, during which time he has produced over 100 children's records. In 1984 he joined with the Television Animation Group, writing and story editing for "Duck Tales" and "Gummi Bears." He lives with his wife, three children, and "four thousand bubble-gum cards."

WILLIAM SLEATOR is the well-known, award-winning author of such books for young readers as *House of Stairs* and *Interstellar Pig*. A world traveler, Sleator makes his home in Boston, Massachusetts.

SHERWOOD SMITH has written for Hollywood and has produced a number of young-adult paperbacks under the name of Robyn Tallis. This is her second published short story.

MIDORI SNYDER, who operates a small publishing company called Leaping Hart Press, is the author of several published fantasy novels, including *Soulstring* and *New Moon,* and a novella, "Demon," in an anthology. She is finishing her graduate work in African languages and literature. Ms. Snyder lives in Milwaukee with her husband and two children.

ELISABETH WATERS, who lives in Berkeley, California, with several other writers, one dog (part wolf), and two cats, is the author of almost a dozen published short stories.

MARY WHITTINGTON lives in Kirkland, Washington, where she is also a writing teacher and a music teacher specializing in recorders and other early instruments. She has two picture books coming out soon, and this is her second short story to be published.

JANE YOLEN, award-winning author of over 100 books including *Owl Moon, Piggins, Dragon's Blood,* and *The Devil's Arithmetic,* lives in Hatfield, Massachusetts, with her husband. She is the mother of three grown children.

MARY FRANCES ZAMBRENO, who teaches college in Chicago, has had several short stories published in anthologies. She is the fantasy and children's book reviewer for *American*

Fantasy magazine. This is her first published story for young readers.

MARK ZASLOVE is Story Editor/Producer for Walt Disney Studios with story credits on "Gummi Bears," "Duck Tales," and "Winnie-the-Pooh." He has a degree in astrophysics from the University of California at Berkeley, and is the author of a number of published short stories and a novel, *Travail*.